HIDDEN MAGIC

BOOK TWO OF THE ANCIENT COURT TRILOGY

AMY PATRICK

OXFORD SOUTH PRESS

Oxford South Press/August 2017
    Cover design by Cover Your Dreams

PROLOGUE

The room was dimly lit and very quiet—except for his slow and steady breathing. Closing the heavy wooden door quietly behind me, I let my eyes adjust and tried to regulate my own rapid breaths and heartbeat.

A low-burning fireplace cast flickering shadows on the stone walls of the bedchamber. Dark drapes were drawn closed over the floor-to-ceiling windows, making midday seem like midnight. Nerves prickling, ears attuned to the slightest sounds, I crossed the cavernous room, my shoes scuffing softly on the Aubusson rug as I approached the bed.

When I reached Nic, my lungs emptied in a wheeze, leaving me gasping. His face was covered in a kaleidoscope pattern of small cuts, the result of his struggle with Dr. Schmitt last night and all the broken glass. Dark circles underscored his eyes, and even in his sedated deep sleep, a furrow marked his tanned brow, making him look like he was trapped in a troubled dream.

I probably should have felt some satisfaction at seeing him there, helpless and hurt. After all, he had betrayed me. And all for *her*.

But my desire for revenge drained away as my eyes roamed his unconscious face and long, motionless body. It wasn't his fault. It was hers. It was all of them. *This* was what they did to us—made us weak—made us turn against each other. Dr. Schmitt was right. About everything.

And that was why I would help Dr. Schmitt enact his plan. We'd be rid of the troublesome and oh-so-prolific human race once and for all, and we'd finally be safe.

Just as I turned to go, Nic made a noise, a muffled cry, as if perhaps he were shouting down some threat within his dream. Or trying to warn someone. On instinct I reached for him but recoiled, withdrawing my hand before it made contact with his face.

My touch would not comfort him, would not heal his injuries. It would only make him sicker.

I spun and headed for the door, startling when it opened before I even touched it. Giant frozen fingers squeezed my heart as two people stepped inside. And then I let out the breath I'd swallowed.

"Mamma, Babbo—what are you doing here?"

"What are *you* doing in here, Alessia?" my mother asked, her stern tone matching the hard look in her eyes. She disapproved. *Well, what's new?*

"I… came to check on him. He *is* still my fiancé."

"That's not what we heard. We were told you'd lost *another* one," my father said.

My back stiffened, and my eyes blurred in a spontaneous wash of moisture. I blinked forcefully to keep it from spilling over. "No. The wedding is still on. As soon as he recovers. Nothing has changed."

Both of them studied me in silence. Finally, Mamma said, "Good. But you should probably keep your distance until he *is* fully recovered. You know with your…" She left off the rest of the sentence, but the familiar look of distaste on her face said it all.

"I know," I interrupted. "I didn't touch him."

"And you haven't told anyone?" Babbo asked, his voice ringing with anxiety.

"Of course not." I had to turn away and face the bed because the hot tears were back, rushing too quickly this time for me to contain them.

I had *never* told anyone about my secondary glamour. My musical glamour was obvious—it was the cornerstone of my career as a performer—but I had followed my parents' strict instructions my whole life and kept my *other* glamour a secret. No royal family wanted that particular "gift" in their gene pool. No one would want *me* if they found out. And that was the other reason I found it difficult to stay too angry with Nic.

He *did* know. His annoying glamour had outed me on the first occasion we'd met. He'd read my deepest desire—to be rid of this curse—which had made me furious. But he'd promised to tell no one, and he was nothing if not honorable. So other than him and my parents, only Dr. Schmitt knew the whole truth about me.

I made people sick. Literally.

It was most powerful with humans—I couldn't get close to them at all, unless I wanted them passing out or vomiting on my shoes. And though it was less severe with other Elves, the effect was still there. After enough time in close proximity to me I could see their faces contract and sour, and they inevitably excused themselves to "get some air" or "go to the toilet."

So I kept my distance. From everyone. It was fine. I was used to it. Even my own parents had avoided touching me as much as possible since birth and had taught me not to touch others. It wasn't that big of a deal. I didn't *need* physical contact anyway. I didn't get why other people—especially humans—were so touchy-feely.

Whether because I seemed cold and standoffish to them or because they had an innate sense of the danger I posed, people of every variety generally tended to avoid me. Only Dr. Schmitt had ever sought out my company. He actually *admired* my hidden glamour. He'd picked it up immediately after seeing me near one of the fan pod girls in his clinic and was even helping me learn to control it somewhat.

"It's there for a reason, Alessia," he'd assured me. "It's a defense mechanism, and a magnificent one. If only all our people had it—we wouldn't even need the Plague. You are a miracle. And you are uniquely qualified to help our race survive and conquer."

He would be expecting me soon, ready to continue our work. Thinking of his accepting smile, I was overcome with the urge to get out of this suffocating room and back to his clinic, the only place I felt truly wanted in this castle. Anywhere, in fact.

I swallowed the lump in my throat and swiped quickly at my wet cheeks before turning back to my parents. "You never told me what you're doing here."

My father smiled. "We came to see if it's true. If Nicolo really did come into contact with nymph blood. I never in all my days imagined something like that was actually possible."

"Well, he's alive, isn't he?" I snapped. "And his cuts are healing quickly. Dr. Schmitt said they'll probably vanish by the end of the day. There's not that much to see."

Mamma pushed past me, moving to Nic's bedside and turning on the lamp. Peering at him in wonder, she clasped her hands over her sternum. "It's remarkable. Just imagine what we could do with her blood."

"*He* won't like it," Babbo said, tossing his head toward Nic's sleeping form.

"He'll do what's best for his people—as we all do," Mamma said sharply. "And Dr. Schmitt says the nymph will be drained and long gone before the young prince ever wakes up."

Nic's legs twitched violently, causing both my parents to take a step back from the bed. "Let's hope so," My father said. "I'd hate to be on the wrong end of one of those kicks—he does it professionally after all—barbaric sport."

"We should go now." I was slightly unnerved by the sight of my parents looming over Nic's unconscious form. And by the paranoid thought he might be able to hear the conversation occurring around him. "We're disturbing his rest."

The three of us left the room together. I cast one last glance at Nic before pulling the door closed behind me. The next time I saw him, all this turmoil would be just a bad memory. Along with the girl who'd come between us, and all the people she knew and loved.

1

MACY

Now I had *two* ghosts following me.

Before, as I backpacked across Europe, I was trying—not very successfully—to outrun the memory of how I'd ruined my sister Lily's life and let my family down. Only spending time with Nic had made me feel there might still be some point to everything, made me feel like I could possibly do some *good* with my life still. He'd given me hope. He'd given me... love.

But now—well, now he was gone, and soon the entire human race would be gone if Nox and his friends couldn't figure out how to stop Dr. Schmitt and his Plague. I shivered. *Dr. Schmitt.*

Though it had been nearly ten months since my real-life nightmare, I rarely spent a night without seeing him and trying to escape his creepy dungeon clinic. I'd bolted awake early this morning in a cold sweat, my shouts of terror waking up my roommates at the youth hostel. No doubt they were *thrilled* to learn the gloomy Missouri girl with *sleep issues* was moving on today.

I looked up at the towering profiles of the skyscrapers all

7

around me as I trudged down the street toward the Port Authority bus terminal. The sidewalks swarmed with busy Manhattan-ites on their way to work, with tourists from every corner of the world staring wide-eyed at the famous city's colossal billboards and the enticing storefronts lining Times Square.

It had been a good place to get lost for a while. The fascinating array of people, the street performers, the odd jobs I'd been able to pick up, the cheap but good food options. It had all provided a much-needed distraction from my inner monologue of doom and depression, besides giving me another checkmark on my map of major U.S. points of interest.

The map was the only thing keeping me going. Nox's bond-mate had chased me down the driveway with it when I'd left their beachfront mansion in L.A. all those months ago. She'd pressed the folded paper into my hands, wishing me safe travels and good luck. As much as I would have liked to wave it away and dismiss her encouraging words, there was something in her eyes when I met them that told me she was no stranger to grief herself.

"Thanks," I'd mumbled. "Tell Nox I'll check in soon."

It was about time to do that again. For my parents' sanity, I contacted them every few weeks to let them know I was still alive and where I was traveling. Nox had asked me for the same courtesy, and I owed it to him to do at least that much. I also needed to check on Olly. She was home in England with her parents and safe, but it made me uncomfortable to know Dr. Schmitt and Alessia and who-knew-who-else in the Ancient Court knew exactly where to find her—if they ever wanted to do so.

The internet café was right where one of the girls at the hostel had said it would be. I ducked inside, ordered some breakfast, and chose an empty terminal. The place was crowded, overly warm, and scented with a blend of coffee and cooking grease, but it had a friendly, welcoming vibe.

Cafés like this one abounded in Europe but were pretty rare in the U.S. Of course, New York had at least one of *everything*, and it actually had quite a few places you could use a computer and get online—even some Burger Kings offered public computers. I needed to take advantage of the opportunity before boarding the bus to my next destination, which might or might not have a place like this where I could spend an hour or so sending emails and perusing the internet, catching up on news.

Logging on and opening my inbox, I found several emails from Mom, each of them filled with news about my family and friends back home. One had an attachment—a picture of Lily, dressed up and smiling widely in her wheelchair at her middle school's semi-formal dance. A rush of emotion flooded my chest and blocked my throat—a wistful blend of pride and guilt that was unavoidable anytime I thought about her.

As usual, Mom's chatty updates were laced with a subtle note of concern for her absentee daughter. As usual, I ignored it and focused my response on the positive. I told her about New York as well as my tours of Maine and Rhode Island, the last two places I'd visited before coming to the city. After informing her that New Orleans would be my next stop and promising to check in again soon, I emailed Nox.

When I'd left his house ten months ago, I'd gone straight to the bus station and taken a cross-country trip, working my way to the East Coast. He and his friends and bandmates had been great, but I'd needed to get as far away as possible from them all. A pack of hot Elven guys always hanging around was not exactly helping me move past what had happened with Nic. Nox, Anders, Rolf, and Matteus were living, breathing reminders of a painful past I had no choice but to get over.

He must have been up early and online or have his emails going to his phone because his reply came quickly.

Nox: Where are you?

Hmm. That was odd. He always began his communications with a friendly greeting or something silly to make me laugh. This one seemed abrupt and even... urgent? My pulse quickened, my fingers flying as I typed my response.

Macy: Heading to the bus station. Leaving New York for New Orleans today. What's up?

This time the reply took longer.

Nox: Just wondering. Everything going all right? Ready to leave that crappy East Coast weather and come back West where all the happy people live?

There was the silliness. I joked back with him.

Macy: I've met quite a few happy people here. And they'd be *happy* to beat your soft West Coast behind to prove it.

Nox: Okay then, let me rephrase. Are you ready to come back and be with your *friends*—who miss you?

This one gave me a twinge in my mid-section. I missed them, too. But I wasn't going back there. They were better off without me—I'd already ruined enough lives. And frankly, *I* was better alone. I kept myself so busy during the day, working and seeing the sights, I didn't have time to think about Nic, about the coming disaster.

It was only at night, when I had no control over my thoughts and emotions, that it all backed up on me. If there was a medication I could take that would prevent me from sleeping—or at least from dreaming—I'd gladly take it.

Macy: I can't. Lots of places still left to see. Thanks, though. I really do appreciate it.

Before closing the chat window I added, **Maybe in a few months. I *am* moving back in your direction, slowly but surely. Talk to you in a few weeks. Tell everyone hello from me.**

Nox: Take care. Don't be a stranger.

Okay then. Two down, one to go.

I checked the clock window in the bottom right corner of the computer screen. It was almost nine-thirty, which meant it was about two-thirty p.m. Olly's time in England. I hoped she was home from school.

Opening the video messaging app we'd been using, I pressed the invitation button. Then I put a smile on my face. As always when we chatted, I would keep things light and friendly, but not too personal. After a few minutes, Olly's video window popped up, and there she was, her face pink from the winter air, wearing her school uniform. She looked a little older than when we'd first met, but not much.

"Macy! Hi!" She beamed. "Where are you?"

"Hey there! I've been in New York City for the past few weeks. About to get back on the road. How are things? How are you? Still good?"

Though Olly had been released from the fan pod early and said she hadn't undergone anything too unusual during her exam with Dr. Schmitt—just a blood draw and some "vaccinations"—I was still nervous. Those of us who'd stayed in Nic's castle had been closer than any other humans to the source of the Plague virus Dr. Schmitt was creating. If Olly *did* start to show any telling symptoms, I'd promised to notify Nox immediately.

He'd heard nothing from overseas regarding a virus meant to wipe out all the humans, but he might not be on the short list for that kind of information. He'd made his pro-human position clear to the European leaders during his trips there. On my good days I hoped they'd been forced to drop the plan—maybe Nic had managed to kill Dr. Schmitt before dying himself? Nox said the creepy doctor hadn't been seen in a while either. Or maybe the Ancient Court was just reluctant to lose its source of servants and fan pod devotees, now that Nic was gone and along with him, their plan for replacing them with hybrid Elven-human slaves. I had no way of knowing, but surely, this many months later, Olly would show some symptoms if she *had* been infected? Her answer reassured me further.

"I feel great. I'm so jealous of you. I wish I was eighteen too and could travel like you do. I've always wanted to see New York my whole life."

I smiled. Her *whole life* had been just fourteen years. "You will. And it'll probably be even cooler by the time you make it here. I'm heading south. Where do you think I should go next?"

"Disney World!" The response was immediate and made me laugh out loud. Her enthusiastic suggestions always amused me, though this was one I wouldn't take. I had a limited budget, and I'd already visited the parks when I was a kid with my family. Going back there alone would be too sad. New Orleans was somewhere I'd never been, and it seemed like another great city to disappear in.

Before I could respond, Olly had another idea.

"Come and see me here—please, please, please. Mum and Nanna are so keen to meet you. You'll love the street art, and we can go shopping at Cabot Circus and get a ninety-nine from Mr. Whippy."

"What? What's a ninety-nine? Who's Mr. Whippy?"

"Mr. Whippy isn't a man—it's a kind of ice cream, silly. Oh, it's the best. A ninety-nine is a soft-serve cone that has a Cadbury Flake chocolate stuck in it. You *have* to try it. Please Macy. Come see me. We have an extra room now that my brother Wes has moved out, so you can stay as long as you like. I'd come see you, but I'm on total lockdown since I ran away. They only let me go to school and back."

Her plea was so sweet, so heartfelt, and her little pout was so cute. I hated to disappoint her. But I couldn't say "yes." I couldn't go back to Europe—not yet. Probably not ever.

Nic had made me promise to get out only hours before he'd died trying to save me and the other fan pod girls—and the rest of my race. England had been where I'd started my backpacking adventure before moving on to Belgium, Paris, and eventually Corsica, where I'd met Nic. If my nightly visions of him felt real *here*—four thousand miles and an ocean away—how much worse would the nightmares be on European soil? He was already like a ghost who followed me no matter where I went.

"I don't think so kiddo. I'm not sure I could handle being over there. Please try to understand."

"I do. But I still miss you."

My dead heart actually felt something—a painful squeeze. I missed her, too. That was the *other* reason I couldn't go. I cared about Olly. I wanted her to be happy and healthy. What I didn't want was to get any closer—I didn't want to grow to *love* her like I loved Lily and Mom and Dad. And she was so much like my little sister, so sweet and open and loving herself, I knew it would be inevitable if we spent any considerable time together. She already hero-worshipped me the way Lily used to. It was better for me—and for Olly—if we kept our friendship limited to just long-distance messaging and the occasional Skype chat. I just couldn't handle more than that.

"You, too," I said quickly, adding, "Maybe one of these days."

I was about to say good-bye when Olly's wispy, high voice piped up.

"Macy... there's something I've been meaning to say to

you. I know you're sad. And I know what happened to us over there was bad. What happened to Nic was really bad. But life is not *all* bad. Good can still happen. Mum always says life is filled with surprises. You never know what's around the corner."

Her mom was wrong about that. I *knew* what was around the corner. A world-ending plague. A race of arrogant evil Dark Elves in the Ancient Court whose attitude was, "If you can't rule them, kill them." And I was powerless to stop any of it.

Sometimes I wished I didn't even know about this incredible world-within-our-own. Then I could just carry on in ignorant bliss until the inevitable happened. Then I could believe, like sweet, innocent Olly did, that good *could* still happen.

As it was, the best I could do was keep moving, try to forget, and hope that the *worst* didn't happen. Somehow.

"Okay kiddo. Thanks. Talk to you soon."

I closed the window and logged off the computer, grabbing my pack and heading for the door. Moving on once again—alone. And I'd stay alone—except for my ghosts.

2

ANDERS

I could hear the screams even before the taxi stopped in front of the gate and the door opened. How many kids did Ian invite to this thing anyway?

"Oh wow," Kayla said as she got out of the cab's other door and stood, not moving away from the car but staring at my family's home in Brentwood. "This is some kinda house. It's like, freaking ginormous. Are your parents, like, movie stars or something?"

"Uh… yeah, well, kind of. My mom was an actress. She's retired. My dad's a musician." She turned and batted a big, brown, heavily made up eye at me. "Well, you coulda warned me you lived in a freaking mansion."

"I don't. My parents and my brother do. It was… a nice place to grow up," I said, chuckling quietly at the shock and awe, handing the cab driver several bills before taking her arm to lead her through the gate, down the long drive, and around the side of the "ginormous" house toward the backyard.

I hadn't bothered to "warn" Kayla because she wasn't exactly going to be a regular visitor to my family's home. She was here for one purpose—deflection. I'd already learned not to expose my lovebird parents to any serious Anders-should-settle-down candidates. Kayla and I had gone out once, and I'd never called again until now, when I needed something—some*one* rather—to help keep the conversation at home superficial. Kayla was a nice enough girl—there just wasn't anything there, which was totally fine. She was cute and friendly and not-too-smart—in other words, perfect.

The volume of the high-pitched screams and shouts and laughter tripled as we rounded the corner of the house, and all the kids came into view. They were dressed in swimsuits, jumping in and out of the pool, streaking across the yard to the bounce house, running in circles chasing each other. Mom had gone all-out with the decorations. The theme was Legos—Ian's obsession—and all the movies were represented in some way. There were life-sized sculptures that looked like they'd been airlifted here from Legoland. Maybe they had been.

Surveying the crowd of sweaty little bodies, I spotted the top of Ian's ultra-blond head. He was surrounded by a pack of boys. Armed with candy-colored water cannons, they seemed to be planning some sort of mischief regarding the group of girls sunbathing nearby on the deck.

"Yo—squirt," I shouted.

My mini-me brother's head popped up from the huddle, and he twisted one way then the other, searching. When he finally spotted me, his face split into a wide smile. His eyes brightened the way they always did when I came around, making my heart feel like the sun was shining directly on it. He ran toward me at top speed, crashing into me and wrapping his wiry arms around my waist.

"Anders! You made it."

"Of course. I wasn't going to miss my brochacho's eleventh birthday."

He reared back with a puzzled, but flattered, expression. "Hey—I'm only eight!"

"Are you sure?" I teased. "You look at *least* ten to me. How many inches did you grow since I saw you? It's only been three months."

"Two and a half," he said proudly. "I'm so glad you came. Mom said you might not make it in time because of, you know, airports and traffic and stuff."

"Nah. I told them the world's greatest eight-year-old pianist was having a party, and they all cleared the way for me." I made a plane out of my hand and sailed it at him, landing it on his head where I ruffled the fine, light hair. It was cut exactly like mine—short around the sides and back, a bit longer on top. "It was smooth sailing."

"Is that my present?" Ian asked, eyeing the large bag I held in the other hand.

I presented it to him. "All yours buddy."

He ripped the tissue paper out of it and lifted the box from inside. "Whoa! You got me the helicarrier? Awesome! Thank you, Anders. Thank you." Burying his face in my stomach, he hugged me again hard.

I patted his back. "You're welcome, squirt. Happy birthday."

Just noticing the girl beside me, Ian darted a shy glance at her then brought questioning eyes back to meet mine.

"Oh. This is my friend Kayla," I said. "She heard this was going to be an epic party and wanted to come along. You don't mind, do you?"

He cut a mischievous grin at her. "No. Not as long as she doesn't scream when the cool snake guy gets here from the zoo. I told the girls in my class they could come to my party but—No. Screaming."

"That's a reasonable request." Turning to my female companion, whose face had gone pale, I asked, "Kayla, do you think you can manage not to scream when the cool snake guy gets here?"

"Um... I don't know. I really, *really* don't like snakes." Her voice was shaky, the carefully crafted Valley-girl accent momentarily dislodged.

Ian's face scrunched and he gave me a *Really dude?* look. I gave him a what're-ya-gonna-do look in return.

You don't love *her, do you?* he asked me mind-to-mind, his mental tone highly disapproving.

Don't worry, I assured him. *She's just a friend. I am still single and loving it.*

Good, he said, nodding with satisfaction. *Whenever you DO get a bond-mate, make sure she likes cool snakes first.*

Good advice my man, good advice.

"Come and meet my friends." Ian spoke aloud this time and clutched my hand, tugging me across the yard. I laughed and followed. Kayla did *not* laugh, but she followed, too. I had a feeling I'd be calling a cab for my "date" before this party was through.

Ian introduced me to what felt like about two hundred kids, most of them his human classmates, though there were a few Elven friends as well. Afterward, I made my way through the throng to the patio, where my parents were setting up for lunch.

"Anders, honey, you made it," Mom declared in a delighted tone. She set down the colorful paper plates she was holding and crossed the patio to hug me. "You look wonderful. How was your flight?"

"Great. Fine. Our show was only in Denver, so it wasn't a long one. How are you holding up? This is some crazy scene."

She laughed. "Well, you know your father." She nodded toward the tall, ultra-fit man across the patio working the grill. "Nothing is too good for his boys."

She was being kind by adding the "s" to that last word. It

had been a while, but I remembered all my birthdays very well, and there certainly had never been a party like this for *any* of them, with a cast of thousands and a bouncy house *and* a visit from the zoo's snake guy.

"I think Dad's getting a little indulgent in his old age," she added with an eye-roll. "Ian doesn't even know about the dirt bike yet."

Though her words were scolding, the look she threw his way was filled with fondness. Dad could have carted the entire zoo over here and bought Ian a monster truck, and she wouldn't have complained. One, because she was crazy about my brother. And two, my dad could do no wrong in her eyes. They'd been married for fifty-four years, and they were not only bond-mates, they were soul mates.

My parents were a rarity in the Dark Court, married by choice rather than arrangement. A prolific songwriter, my father swore he'd heard a complete *symphony* the moment he met my mother. Luckily for them, their parents had been the Elven equivalent of hippies—believers in true love, freedom of choice, and Elven-human equality. Unlike many of their contemporaries, neither of them had ever kept a fan pod. Also unlike many of my friends' parents, they hadn't chosen a bond-mate for me by age eighteen. Instead they'd encouraged me to follow my heart.

So far, all it had led me to was music, but Mom was certain "that special someone" was just around the corner and advised me to keep an eye out. She took one look at Kayla, and I could tell Mom knew as well as I did that *this* one wasn't it.

"Hello," she said pleasantly. "I'm Patrice."

"Oh, sorry. Mom, this is Kayla. Kayla, my mom."

"Hello Mrs. J. It's super nice to meet you. You have a gorgeous home, and Anders told me you were a movie star?"

Mom blinked, apparently caught off guard. "Yes, I used to

act quite a bit. That was… a while ago. Now I'm a full-time mommy and party hostess extraordinaire," she joked.

"Oh yeah. It *is* a good party," Kayla said, missing the sarcasm altogether. "This is like every one of my parties growing up, all smashed together into one."

"Well, we're older parents," Mom explained. "Almost like grandparents, really. We might spoil him *just* a bit."

Kayla tilted her head to one side like a bewildered puppy, eying my tan, fit, unwrinkled mother. "You don't look old."

Realizing her slip, Mom laughed a tad too brightly and put a hand on Kayla's shoulder. "Aren't you sweet? Listen, would you mind helping me put out the rest of the plates? I suspect we're going to be attacked by a horde of ravenous beasts any minute now. Ian can't go more than a couple hours before declaring he's 'starving.' Anders, too." She winked at me and led Kayla away toward the table. "So, are you an aspiring actress?" I heard her ask my date in an effort to further distract her.

Kayla bought it—for full price. "Oh yes. I model now, but I love acting, and I really, really really want to be famous someday. Maybe you could…"

Her predictable words faded as I made my way over to the large built-in grill where Dad was removing some burgers to a large platter on the counter of the outdoor kitchen.

"Need any help?" I asked.

"Son." Dad glanced back over his shoulder with a smile. "I think I've got this part covered. Though you can pull the hot dogs out of the fridge for me there. Top shelf."

I turned and opened the refrigerator, lifting a monstrous package of hot dogs to the countertop and opening it.

Once the last burger was off the fire, Dad turned around to clap me firmly on the back and embrace me in a brief hug. "How are you? Just get into town?"

"Yep. Drove straight from the airport to Kayla's house and then here."

"Tired?"

"Not too bad. I slept on the plane some."

He did not ask me about our show. He never did. Instead, he asked if I'd gotten in any hiking while in Colorado.

"Actually, yes. I did Pike's Peak this time. It was only an hour and a half from Denver. Really nice. Perfect weather for it."

"That's great. I'm jealous. Wish I could have joined you, but I'm running up against a deadline on this current job—it's a movie score for J.J. I've only got a few weeks to turn it around."

"Awesome. J.J. always delivers." Hesitating first, I decided to go ahead and mention my own latest project. "I actually got tapped to do another one."

"Oh. Which picture?"

"It's a smaller one, but the script is brilliant, and there's good buzz about it. I've seen some of the dailies. Looks like it might have a chance at the awards this year."

"Okay, well have fun with it." His tone was less than enthusiastic, toeing the line of boredom. "Let me know if you need any help."

Though I fought it with everything in me, heat surged from my chest to my face. "Yeah. Thanks. Well, if you've got this covered, I think I'll go rescue Kayla from birthday party servitude."

"Sure. Make sure we catch up before you go. Glad you could make it, son."

I nodded tersely and turned away, striding toward the long confetti-strewn table. "Come inside with me," I muttered close to Kayla's ear. "I'll get you a drink."

"Oooh. Okay," she squealed happily. "I'll see you later, Mrs. J. Everything looks so cute."

Mom lifted a hand in a bemused wave and raised a single brow at me. *Stay on the first floor. No "tours" of the bedrooms.*

Mom. I flared my eyes at her, leading Kayla quickly toward the open French doors. Not quickly enough. I could still hear my mother's unsolicited advice.

I'm just saying—don't put yourself in a position that's too tempting. You're already six months past bonding age. I know it's not easy.

Can we please *not talk about this?* Now my face was hot for a different reason, though the air inside was cool.

I just don't want you to settle. Sometimes life gives you what you crave just before it gives you what you really need. It's a distraction. Don't fall for it.

Okay, Mom. Thanks. I'll... keep that in mind.

Kayla and I walked through the sunroom toward the kitchen—not toward the bedrooms—where I opened the refrigerator, took out a couple sodas and some bottled water and put them on the counter then went to get some glasses from a cabinet.

"Oh," she said, wearing a funny look. "When you said 'drink,' I thought you meant..."

It took me a minute. "Oh. No. I don't think it's a good idea to get smashed at my little brother's birthday party. I know there are sodas and water out there, too. I just thought it would be nice to get out of the heat and away from all the noise." *And my parents.*

"Yes, it is." She regarded me with far too much interest, sidling over to stand right next to me. "It's nice to be alone with you. I really didn't think you were ever going to call again."

Uh oh.

"I've been really busy, traveling a lot."

"It's okay. You're here now. So... where do you want to go

after this?" She dipped her chin and raised one brow suggestively.

I turned away, studiously filling the glasses with ice. "I might have to go home and get some work done—depending on how long this thing goes."

"Well, we *could* skip out early and go back to my place or something. I'm not in a real big hurry to see Mr. Snake or whoever."

I hesitated. "Maybe. We have to at least stay for cake and the Happy Birthday song."

"Oh, totally. No problem."

I had a problem. In my effort to save myself from parental grief, I'd inadvertently led this girl on. I'd thought she felt the same as I did about our extremely brief relationship—that it was strictly about fun, no emotions involved—that's why she'd been the one I called. Apparently there was more interest on her part than I'd counted on.

I heard the back door open and let in a cacophony of sound—chattering eight year olds and running wet feet slapping the tile floor. Apparently the party was moving indoors. I met Mom in the hallway. "What's going on?"

"Ian's going to play us his latest piece," she answered before being swept along in the tidal wave of diminutive bodies scurrying toward the great room.

That was where the baby grand lived—the piano Dad treasured like a third child and had used to teach his two actual children how to play. Of course, being a child prodigy, the *second* one had needed *far* less instruction than the first.

Kayla and I followed the group along the hallway toward the large room. She stopped in her tracks, her jaw dropping as she stared at the wall.

"Oh my God. Are these what I think they are?"

My bottom lip pulled up to disappear behind the top one.

I released a long here-we-go-again breath. "Yeah. They're Grammy awards."

The shiny gold phonograph trophies lined the corridor on glass shelves, each with its own tiny spotlight. A trip to my parents' house was sort of like visiting the Rock and Roll Hall of Fame, West Coast location.

"Wow. How many *are* there?"

A new voice entered the conversation. "Twenty-three. I'm nominated again this year. If I win, it'll make it an even two dozen."

Kayla turned, showing a whole new interest in my father. "That is amazing. Do I know your songs?"

"Well I don't know," he said with a wink. "Do you listen to the radio?"

She giggled, and he began listing the hit songs he'd written over the years. I left them to it and wandered into the living room where Ian had already slid onto the piano bench and lifted the keyboard cover.

At the urging of their parents and nannies, children took seats on the floor, sitting cross-legged in pairs or clumps, boys on one side of the room, girls on the other, naturally. I wondered if this was the first time his classmates had heard him play or if they'd had previous exposure to the brilliance that was my little brother. As he began to play, I got my answer.

Jaws dropped around the room. The parents seemed more impressed than the children, which made sense. They had more context, more experience, more ability to understand the significance of his talent. At age eight-and-one-day, my brother had more natural ability in his pinky finger than I had in my whole body—or would ever have. As much as I loved music, as much as I'd practiced over the years, as much as I'd hoped, wished, and prayed when I was young, I had not inherited my father's musical glamour. Ian had.

My eyes drifted in a search of Dad and found him standing at the back of the room beside Kayla, watching Ian play. Pride radiated from him like a golden aura. It lit his face, making him look more youthful, energetic, and alive than I'd seen him in years.

I turned away as a spiky weight settled on my chest and pushed through the surface, puncturing my lungs. If he'd ever looked at me like that—just once—my eternal life could have been cut short at any point, and I would have still felt complete.

As it was, I felt... less than that. I knew he loved me. No question. He'd always been kind, caring, protective. And I had idolized him in the way most young boys look up to their fathers. I'd wanted, more than anything, to be just like him. I'd sat and listened to him play the piano, guitar, whatever instrument he'd picked up, for hours, went into the studio to hear him record, gone to concerts where I'd nearly combusted with pride as crowds cheered him.

And I'd worked feverishly to emulate him. I'd played my own miniature instruments until my fingers ached and even bled at times. I'd trained myself with every available resource in the art of songwriting and performance. And yet...

None of it mattered.

I'd read music critics' glowing assessments of my abilities over the past couple of years since I'd been with The Hidden, and I'd heard my music teachers' praise. I knew there were millions of fans who appreciated what I'd created—some even called my songs life-changing. Hell, The Hidden was nominated for four Grammys this year. But compared to my father—compared to Ian—I was nothing.

Watching Ian's grubby fingers fly over the keys like an osprey gliding over the surface of a glassy pond, it was as if there was a direct plumbing line between my heart and my eyes. It squeezed, my eyes watered. I was proud of him. And I was pretty freaking jealous, too. Not in the way where you want to take away something someone else has, but in the way where you wish you could have a duplicate of what they've got. No, not even a duplicate—a fraction.

As he finished his song, Ian looked up, and his bright blue eyes met mine. His expression was expectant, his lips pursed in an almost-smile, his blond brows raised nearly to his hairline.

I lifted my hands in front of me and clapped, loudly and deliberately, and gave him a genuine smile. His face burst into sunshine at my approval. Only then did he break eye contact and look around the room. Other claps joined mine, and then the house filled with applause and exclamations of wonder and delight. When it all finally died down, Mom's voice came from the back hallway.

"Now it's time for *another* song."

She entered the room pushing a cart that held an enormous birthday cake, topped by eight lit candles. It was decorated to look like it had been made of a million Lego bricks and drew "oohs" and "ahs" from the kids in attendance. My mother sang the opening words of the birthday song. I joined in loudly, replacing the name Ian with "squirt" when the appropriate moment came. My brother, who'd left the piano and run toward the confectionary masterpiece as soon as he'd seen it, sucked in a noisy breath and blew out all the candles at the song's closing note.

The next twenty minutes were a feeding frenzy, after which Mom threw a panicked glance around her beautiful living room.

"All right—let's have all sticky sweet children out of the house and into the swimming pool!"

They stampeded toward the back door. Chuckling, I fell

into step behind the crowd. When we got outside, Kayla, apparently recovered from her Grammy-induced daze, pulled up beside me and leaned in, speaking in a low voice.

"Um... your mom said the snake guy is on his way, so could we uh..."

"Sure. We can go. Let me just say good-bye to my family."

Ian was already in the pool. Squatting at the edge of the deep end, I told him I had to go and wished him a happy birthday one more time.

"You're leaving? You're going to miss the snakes."

"I know. It's a bummer. But, you know..." *Girls*, I said to him in a grumpy mental tone I knew would elicit a smile.

"Okay, well, I'll see you soon. Thanks for my present again."

"You're welcome, buddy. I'll take you surfing next week. Hey, do you know where Dad went?"

"I think he went back into the kitchen for some more drinks."

"Okay. I'll go help him before we leave. Enjoy your party, squirt."

I turned to Kayla. "Be right back. Wait here."

Stepping back into the house, I found Dad pulling drinks out of the refrigerator and stacking them on the counter.

"Hey. We're getting ready to take off."

He pulled his head from the refrigerator and straightened. "So soon? I was hoping we'd get a chance to talk."

I stiffened. "If it's about Kayla, Mom's already—"

"No—it's not about the girl. I already know you're not interested in her. It's about your future."

"My future?"

"Yes, you know my manager had a stroke recently. His wife has let me know he's in no shape to return to work—he

27

probably never will. I don't have time to handle both the creative and business sides of my career. And I thought…"

His words drifted off, leaving me to fill in the blanks.

"You thought what?" And then it hit me. My fingers gripped the edge of the counter so hard they turned white. "You want *me* to manage *your* career?"

"You're old enough now. There's no one I trust more than you, and you're fully capable—"

"Capable?" I snapped. "Capable—of *managing*? *You?*" I had to stop and take a calming breath before continuing. "I appreciate the confidence, but what about *my* career? What about my music? You know I can't manage you and still write for the band, perform, and do my movie composition work."

He stared at me steadily. "I know. There isn't enough time for everything. I thought maybe you'd like to start doing something that you're…" Again he stopped without finishing his sentence.

"What? Say it. Go ahead and say it. Something I'm actually *good* at?"

"No. Something more… in line with your natural inclinations."

My inclination at the moment was to punch my father in the jaw. Of course I wouldn't. I'd never struck him in my life, and I had too much respect for him to start now. Besides, he was seventy-two years older than me, which meant he could flatten my ass if he wanted to. Unlike humans, Elves gained strength with age.

Instead of yelling in response, I lowered my voice to a calm, quiet recitation of facts. "I'm doing really well with my music. We have four Grammy nominations, you know. And there's a good chance the movie score I did last year will be seriously considered for Oscar nomination."

"But it is not your glamour gift, son."

"No—believe me I know. You never let me forget it. I'm

not like you, I'm not like Ian. But I do have talent. I work my ass off. And a lot of people *like* my music."

He held up his hands between us in a placating gesture. "That is not what I mean, son. Calm down. I only think of you when I say this—of your happiness. I want you to have the kind of fulfillment I have in my job—and in your personal life."

"I *am* fulfilled."

"Then why do you obsess over these awards—Grammys, Oscars?"

"Says the man with a hallway lined in golden statues."

"That's not why I do it. Those things come on their own. They are side effects of me doing what I was born to do. The music is part of me—I can't *not* do it."

"You don't have the market cornered on musical passion, you know. I love it, too."

"And the girls?"

"What about them?" I growled, though I already knew what he was getting at. I hadn't loved any of them. Not even close.

"Each time I see you or talk to you, you're with a different one. And none of them has any potential to be your—"

"Look—not everyone is like you and Mom. Not everyone finds that *legendary* love. Not everyone is even capable of loving like that."

I certainly wasn't. With all the girls I'd dated, if it hadn't happened by now, it wasn't happening. The only way *I'd* hear a symphony with a girl was if I took her to see the Philharmonic at the Hollywood Bowl.

"I don't even want it," I told him. "I have good friends, I have fun with the girls I see, and I'm in love with my music. That's all I need."

Taking in his unhappy expression and his loaded silence, I let out a sigh. "I'll… see you guys soon. I've got to get Kayla out of here before the snakes show up and I end up carrying her out."

Father nodded, his eyes sad and weary-looking. He'd never understand. He couldn't. He had it *all*.

My phone rang, and I pulled it from my pocket, checking the screen. Nox. I chuffed a laugh. *Another* guy who had it all. I'd have to call him back once I was alone. I swiped the screen to send the call to voicemail and told my father good-bye. Finding Mom, I gave her a hug and a quick cheek kiss along with a promise to visit soon on a less crazy day. Then I headed for the back deck to collect Kayla.

I was eager to get rid of her and get back to my condo and my keyboard and lose myself in the creative process. No matter what my father said, I was going to prove myself musically. If it took winning more Grammys and Oscars than any songwriter in history, that's what I'd do. And that meant no fooling around tonight. Hopefully Kayla wouldn't pout about being dropped off early at her own place.

"I really like your family," she said as we left the party together, walking toward the front of the house. "You're so cute with your little brother. I can tell you're going to be a great dad someday."

My eyes crept to the side to meet her dreamy look. Ugh. *Here we go again.* It was starting to seem inevitable. I was careful to go out with only girls who said they had no interest in a serious relationship. But somehow after a few dates, they all changed their minds and started talking about the future. That was usually my cue to move on, to find someone new who would hopefully be happy with just hooking up and having a good time.

"Um, yeah maybe," I mumbled. "I don't know. That's way, way, *way* off in the future—if it ever happens."

Kayla's expression clouded. She nodded and quickened her pace on the driveway, heading for the front gate. As she walked slightly ahead of me, I checked out her long, tanned legs along with the rest of her shapely build. She was without question, hot. I might not be capable of epic love, but I was a normal, healthy, eighteen-year-old male. I did feel *other* things. More and more often lately.

Maybe I should just go ahead and do it—pick one of them and get it over with.

Kayla was beautiful. She was nice and seemed to like my family. Maybe that was as good as it was ever going to get. What was the point of going through the same ridiculous motions over and over again when the result was always going to be the same?

I lengthened my stride and caught up to her, filled with a new determination. I was going to do it. *It* it. Tonight. I was going to invite her to come home with me, *not* stop myself this time at the very moment I *least* wanted to stop, and just be done with the whole dating and searching and waiting thing.

My mom would be sad when she found out I'd bonded with someone I didn't love, but she couldn't understand any more than my father could. While I thought it was awesome they'd experienced love at first sight leading to eternal happiness, not all of us were so lucky. I laughed at the irony of my own thought—considering my glamour, no one would call me unlucky. No one but me.

But I was *about* to get lucky—finally. At least in one sense of the word.

We reached the estate's iron gate, and I hit a button on the control box to open it. The residential street outside was quiet and traffic-less.

"Did you call us a cab already?" Kayla asked, turning to me with a quizzical look.

"No, but don't worry about it. One will come along."

"What?" She cocked her head, and her eyebrows pulled together like she suspected I was unbalanced.

"Don't worry about it." I reached out and took one of her hands, pulling her toward me. "Listen, I was thinking—"

The beep of my phone's text tone interrupted. I ignored it. "I was thinking you could—"

"Maybe you should get that," Kayla said as the tone sounded again, then again. "It's probably the cab driver. I bet he's lost. This neighborhood is a maze, and you can't see any of the houses with all these privacy walls."

"It's not…" I let out an irritated sigh and then a resigned one. How could I explain to her I hadn't called a cab, but that one would be coming along any minute anyway? I couldn't.

Pulling out my phone, I checked the screen. *Weird.* Nox had not only left a phone message, but now he was texting.

Nox: Not sure where you are but I need to talk to you. It's urgent.

Nox: Give me a call.

Nox: Actually swing by my place if you can. There's been a development with M and the AC. I've got a favor to ask you.

My heart pinged around inside my chest as I tapped out a quick response. **On my way.** Then I looked up at Kayla's expectant blue eyes.

"Is he close?" she asked.

"Yeah." I nodded, and a yellow cab rolled into view, starting to pass the drive. I hurried to the curb and flagged him down.

The driver rolled down the passenger window. "Somebody need a ride?"

"Yes, the lady does. Take her wherever she'd like to go." I handed the guy four twenties and told him to keep the change then opened the back door for Kayla.

She didn't immediately climb inside. "Wait—you're not coming with me?"

I gave her a tight-lipped smile. "Change of plans. That text was about work. I'll… call another ride for myself."

She nodded and slid into the back seat, wearing a look of displeasure and disappointment. "Take care. I'll see you soon," I said, closing the door and watching the cab pull away then disappear around a curve.

It wasn't true. I wouldn't see her soon. And I probably wouldn't be taking my brother surfing next week, either. I might not see any of them again for a while. Because there was only one favor I could think of that Nox would want regarding Macy and the Ancient Court. And he'd only ask *me* to do it if he was truly desperate.

3

MACY

G etting off the air-conditioned bus and stepping onto the streets of New Orleans was like walking straight from the refrigerator into an oven set on broil. I'd never been so hot in all my life, and that was saying something because central Missouri summers weren't exactly cool. Sweat was pooling under my backpack and literally rolling down my legs by the time I'd made it the nine blocks to Jackson Square.

The sights and sounds there helped me forget the heat somewhat. Jazz music drifted on the hot breeze. Musicians stood at each corner of the park square, playing their instruments and nodding their thanks whenever a passerby dropped coins or bills into a tip can or open instrument case. Sidewalk artists busily sketched and painted and chatted up the customers who'd agreed to stop and pose for an impromptu portrait.

A red neon sign in the window of a cafe advertised "Free Smells," which made me laugh. New Orleans was certainly a city of "smells." I'd passed a few rather unpleasant ones on my walk to the square, but here, the scent of strong chicory coffee combined with the aromas of food, both sweet and savory, made my mouth water. All of it was underscored by the ever-present odor of alcoholic beverages.

The crowd around me was a blend of vacationing families, hand-holding couples, and raucous groups of young twenty-somethings, already wearing beads and silly hats and walking around with open bottles of their beverages of choice, though it wasn't even dark yet, only seven-thirty. Loud, colorful, and full of energy, this was the New Orleans I'd heard about, read about, and always wanted to see.

I crossed the park toward St. Louis cathedral, an old and imposing triple-spired structure that overlooked the square and provided a calming contrast to the circus atmosphere surrounding it. The French Quarter reminded me somewhat of Europe, which was good—and bad. It was beautiful, but as I stepped into the cathedral's deep shadow, I nearly reeled from a surge of despair and a sudden, intense longing for Nic. Even here, five thousand miles away and ten months after his death, he was still with me somehow.

Stop it Macy. You've got to move on.

Closing my eyes, I breathed deeply and regrouped. At least it was cooler here—maybe fifteen degrees cooler than it had been in the direct sun. I leaned against one of the pediments, resting and checking the paper map I'd bought at the bus station, getting my bearings before making the hike to the youth hostel I'd pinpointed during my internet cafe session back in New York.

The people-watching here was spectacular. It seemed no group had been left out. Preppy college kids, artsy bohemians, moms in workout gear pushing strollers, white-haired senior citizens holding tour maps, the tattooed, pierced, and dreadlocked free spirits, nicely dressed people dining in the open-air restaurants and sidewalk cafes that bordered the square, a few homeless people. All mingled together in close proximity, here to either entertain or to be entertained.

It was a good place—a place I could stay for a while. I knew no one in the city. No one knew me. I'd see the sights, pass some time, find some temporary work to earn more traveling money, and then move on to the next place, taking my U.S. map and my brand new checkmark with me.

Pushing away from the column, I squatted to lift my heavy backpack from the sidewalk, preparing to set off in search of the hostel. Hopefully it was air-conditioned and there was an available shower. Thank God I *didn't* know anyone around here. I was a sweaty mess, and the all-day bus trip had left me no opportunity for freshening up.

Hefting the bag and standing in one move, I took a step out into the end-of-day sun but stopped abruptly. Blinded by its low angle, I'd collided with another pedestrian who was no doubt trying to get *out* of its harsh rays.

"Sorry," I mumbled, barely glancing at the tall guy whose chest I'd just face-planted into. It was a nice chest, and very nice-smelling. I scooted to the side, embarrassed and eager to escape, re-adjusted my bag, and kept moving.

"Macy?"

The guy's voice, somewhat familiar sounding, caused me to spin back to face him. The prototypical California boy stared back at me—tall, tan, and blond, with sky blue eyes and the kind of dazzling white smile that made you forget your name for a minute. His hair was clipped short, and there was just a trace of light blond scruff on his handsome Elven face.

"Anders? Oh my God—what are you doing here?" My mind swirled from the shock of seeing him again.

The ultra-blue eyes widened at the sight of me. The wrinkly, sweaty, dirty-haired makeup-free sight of me. *Great.* I looked horrendous. But then, it didn't really matter, did it? I lunged forward and hugged him, astonished by how good it was to see a familiar face for a change.

He laughed and wrapped his arms around me, squeezing me tightly before sliding his hands to my biceps and setting me back a bit so he could look at me. "Wow. How are you? Where have you been? Don't tell me you walked all the way here from California?"

"No. I've taken a few bus trips in between hiking. What are you doing in New Orleans? Is the band playing in town?"

Suddenly I was very excited to see *all* of them again. The realization washed over me—I'd been *lonely*. Seeing Anders after all this time was like a jump start to a stalled engine. My heart whirred in my chest, feeling joyful and awake.

"No. It's just me. We're on a break from touring. Nox has some 'official business' to tend to in L.A., and the rest of us are doing some writing, getting ready to go back into the studio. I've got a side project I'm working on, too."

"That is awesome. So your side project is here? Dabbling in jazz now?" I teased.

"Oh, I've always loved jazz, but really, I could work on it anywhere. I'm just here to gather some inspiration." He pulled at the front of his t-shirt. "And apparently some perspiration. Man, this place is hot."

"You're not kidding." I fanned myself. "I was just about to head to my place and shower."

"Yeah, I need to find a hotel pretty soon, too. Which one are you staying in?"

"It's not a hotel. It's a youth hostel. Much more affordable."

"Is that safe?"

I snorted. "Well, since I've been living in them for almost the past two years now, I'd say yes."

He nodded but squinted, not exactly appearing convinced. "Listen, I'm starved. Want to grab a bite to eat with me? I was thinking of hitting up Cafe Du Monde—check out the famous beignets and cafe au lait, you know?"

Now that he mentioned it, my stomach let out a long, low growl. The delicious coffee-and-sugar smell I'd detected earlier was without a doubt coming from the other side of the square, where the iconic New Orleans landmark, Cafe Du Monde, stood sending out its siren scents and drawing a steady stream of tourists and locals alike to its green-and-white awnings twenty-four hours a day. It *was* one of the first places I'd wanted to visit in the city.

Prompted by one more growl, this one even longer and louder, I said, "Sure, why not?"

By the time we'd trekked across the square, I found out why not. The line to get into the place was incredible. I groaned.

"It'll take hours to get a seat. Want to just go over there?" I asked, pointing at another shop across the block, which had no line at all. "That place says it has donuts and coffee, too."

"First of all, they aren't donuts—they're beignets. *Big* difference. Secondly, that is *not* Cafe du Monde. Let's just get in line. I bet it'll clear out quickly."

"I don't know. It's sweltering," I whined, eying the long line stretching far down the steamy sidewalk.

Anders grinned and steered me toward the end of it. "Trust me, will you?"

We'd been standing there all of two minutes when someone started shouting a few feet away. "It's Taylor Swift! Taylor Swift is signing autographs and taking pictures with people right over there on the other side of the square."

People in the line around us started straining to see the scene across the block, chattering with excitement.

"She's giving away free samples of her new album," the town crier added.

Now the people in the Cafe du Monde line started *leaving*

the line, heading for the gathering crowd on the other side of the square. As people left the queue, Anders and I moved forward until there were only two couples left ahead of us.

I looked up at him in wonder. "Wow. That is *so* weird." But then I looked across at the mass of bodies on the opposite side of the square with a twinge of longing. Only the top of the tall, blonde singer's head was visible.

"You want to meet her, too, don't you?" Anders asked, showing remarkable perception.

I peeked up at him. "I *do* like her. But the line is gone, and I know you want your beignets... maybe you could get a table and I could—"

"Hold on a sec."

The host indicated for us to follow him, and Anders did not hesitate, taking my elbow and steering me toward the shaded outdoor table the host indicated. Once the guy left, Anders smiled at me from across the small, round table.

"How about this? Beignets and coffee now—Taylor later."

"What?"

Grinning, he pulled his phone from his pocket and scrolled down to a number, then tapped the screen and lifted the phone to his ear.

"Hey! How the hell are ya? Great. Listen, dude, would Taylor have a few minutes later tonight to say hello? Yeah, of course to me, but I just saw her in L.A. There's a friend of mine here in New Orleans who'd love to meet her. Yeah? Great, that's awesome. Sure, nine o'clock would be perfect. Great, see you then."

He set the phone down on the table and looked up at me, a wicked smile decorating his lips and crinkling the corners of his eyes.

"What just happened?" I asked when I'd managed to pick my jaw up off the table.

"Beignets and coffee now. Taylor later. Like I said." He

shrugged as if it was no big deal. As if he hadn't just picked up the phone and dialed Taylor Swift's manager or boyfriend or whomever he'd just spoken to in a best-buddy tone and arranged a private meeting with one of the world's biggest musical stars. Then it occurred to me—maybe *he* was her boyfriend.

"Are you... *dating* her?"

He winked. "Not anymore. Actually, we were just friends." He lowered his voice and leaned closer before adding, "I only date human girls."

I gasped. "*She's...*" But actually it made perfect sense.

A waitress came to our table, and we placed our orders. Less than ten minutes had passed since we'd first gotten into the line. The whopping line that had all but disappeared as soon as we got into it. Now we were seated, and food was on its way.

"So... you were right about the line clearing quickly," I said, suspicious now. "Did you know she was going to be here or something?"

"Nope."

"Did you sway them all to leave?"

"Nope." Then, looking sheepish, he admitted, "But I knew the line would move fast."

"How? Have you been here before? Are there, like, a thousand tables at this place?"

He shook his head, looking up at the hazy sky overhead. "No. I just... don't wait in many lines. It happens all the time. It's just my thing, I guess."

"Your glamour, you mean."

His eyes flickered back to mine. "Uh, yeah. That's right. I'm not used to discussing it around humans. I keep forgetting you know everything already."

"Well, not everything, but some things. I know about glamour. So, what is yours *exactly*—the ability to clear a room at will?"

He laughed. "No. Though sometimes when I start telling jokes..." His expression sobered a bit. "It's luck. I have exceptionally good luck." This was followed by a soft laugh that was somehow devoid of humor.

"That must come in handy," I said with caution, sensing there was more to the story than he was letting on.

"Yeah. It's not bad. Especially when I'm as starved as I am right now." His eyes lifted to the plates of food being delivered by our waitress.

"Platter," was the more accurate word when it came to his plate. Where I'd ordered three beignets—two for now, one to save for later—Anders had gotten an even dozen. Flaky and square-shaped, each was sprinkled with powdered sugar and emitted a steamy sweetness that begged me to dig in. I might not have one left over after all.

"You are never going to eat all of those," I told him as he picked up the first one and took a bite.

Anders chewed and swallowed then offered me a sugar-coated smile. "Challenge accepted."

So, I'd been wrong. Again. Anders had a way of disproving my doubts that was almost uncanny. It was certainly irritating. I hated being wrong.

Both of our plates sitting empty before us, we enjoyed our coffee refills and leaned back in our chairs. I lifted my face to the breeze that had begun to blow in off the nearby water, relaxed and replete and starting to get very excited about the rest of my evening. I'd have to beg Anders to take a couple of pictures of me with Taylor and email them to me, since I didn't have a phone. I cracked my eyes to see him studying me with a half-smile on his face.

"I have to hand it to you," I drawled. "It was a good suggestion, coming here."

"Well, you picked the city—I just picked the meal. You can't find *this* in Manhattan, huh?" he said.

My full-belly languor dissolved immediately. I sat up straight and pinned him with a glare.

"How did you know I just left New York?"

"You mentioned it," he said, but the rush of color to his cheeks supported my suspicion.

"No. I didn't. Nox told you, didn't he?" The suspicion morphed into a certainty, and the sugar hurtling through my veins caramelized as my blood began to boil. "He *sent* you here."

Anders held up his hands in a calm-down gesture. "I didn't lie to you, Macy. I *am* working on a side project and looking for inspiration."

"But you said you could do it anywhere. How did you 'happen' to choose New Orleans?"

He hesitated a long time and took a deep breath before answering. "Nox sent me here."

I stood abruptly, the metal chair scraping loudly on the patio behind me. "I *knew* I should have shut down that email account." Digging some money out of my pocket, I threw it on the table. "Good luck on your project."

I started to stomp off, but Anders leapt from his chair and captured my arm. "Hold on. Don't leave. Why are you so angry?"

"Oh, let's see… maybe it's because I don't like being tracked and stalked like some sort of tagged safari animal."

"It's not stalking. We're *trying* to protect you."

"I don't need protecting. And I don't need a babysitter. I've been traveling on my own just fine since long before I met Nox—or you."

I tried pulling my arm away but Anders held fast. "Macy."

His tone was quieter now, more urgent. "Things have changed."

"What do you mean?"

"Nox got some information that agents from the Ancient Court were in New York. They got close to you before you slipped away."

I stilled completely, my skin going cold and goose bumps rising as he continued.

"They've been searching for you for some time, and he's been keeping tabs on them. But you've been moving so often and leaving no real trail. This is the first time they've ever been reported in the same location at the same time as you. He's worried. He never liked you traveling on your own, but now it's not negotiable."

"Not negotiable? What does that mean?"

"What it sounds like. It isn't up to you anymore."

I stared at him, finding it hard to believe my ears. "That's ridiculous. It's *my* life. And frankly, it's not worth all that much to me anymore. They might be doing me a favor by putting me out of my misery."

Anders looked stricken. "Don't say that. Your life is very valuable. You're young. You have a future ahead of you. Besides, I don't think they want to kill you. It's more likely they're planning to capture you and take you back to the Ancient Court. That cannot happen—for your sake, and for ours. You've been on the inside of the American Dark Court. You know things. That's the only reason we can come up with that the Ancient Court is so determined to find you and bring you back. And that's why it's *our* responsibility to protect you."

"Oh—and you drew the short straw, I guess."

His color deepened. "No. I... I was the logical choice because I have the time to do it. Like I said, I can work on my project anywhere. It's... not a problem."

"It *is* a problem—for *me*. The whole point of my traveling is so I have *freedom*. Having an overgrown beach bum tailing my every move isn't exactly freedom."

I saw that my insult had hit its mark. Anders' face contracted into a slight frown, and his eyes clouded. But instead of satisfaction, I felt a flicker of regret. He didn't have a choice in the matter. Nox was his king. He was following orders. Instead of returning my cruelty tit-for-tat, he answered me in a very calm, very kind voice.

"You don't want freedom, Macy. You want to run away. You're trying to escape your own thoughts and feelings. I get it. But eventually you're going to have to stop running and deal with reality. You could let someone help you, you know."

My temper flared again.

"Who? You? Yeah, that's rich. Talk about trying to escape reality—look at you. You're what, six months, a year past Elven bonding age? And you're with a different girl every week, no matter where you are in the world. What's the old sailing term—a girl in every port?" I huffed. "If I didn't know you were Elven, I would assume you'd fathered twenty illegitimate babies by now."

He let out a short, sharp laugh, clearly shocked by my outburst. "Yeah, that's all the world needs—a bunch of little untalented hacks running around." He took a step toward me. "We're talking about you—not me. We could spend days dissecting *my* issues, but that's not the concern here. Your safety is. Now, are you going to cooperate and let me do my job, or are you going to make it hard on me and get me in trouble with my boss?"

I snorted. "He's not your boss—he's your best friend. You and Nox are like brothers."

"Maybe so, but he's still my king, and I have orders. I'm going to protect you whether you like it or not."

I sagged, wiped out from a combination of the heat and the futility of the situation. "Are you *sure* they're after me? Are you sure it's necessary for *you* to stay with me?" My tone expressed my misery with crystal clarity.

Anders chuckled. "Well, now, don't flatter me too much. I might get a big head."

"No, I mean, it's nothing personal—well, it kind of is. I don't know if I can handle seeing you on a daily basis."

He smirked. "Even if I shower and shave?"

I rolled my eyes, his silliness making me feel only slightly less miserable. "You look… amazing just as you are—and you know it."

"Amazing, huh? I think my head *is* getting bigger."

"Yes, amazing. Tall and tanned and built and… perfect. All of you are. That's why I left. It's why I haven't been back to visit. It's just… you remind me of Nic. I can't… bear to think of him, and when I'm with you and the other guys, I can't help it."

His smile faltered, his stance deflating a bit. "Oh. I see. So, we all look the same to you, then?"

"No. Of course not. You have to know what I mean. Don't you?"

"Yeah. I get it," he said, his tone flat now. "But it doesn't change the fact that you're in danger. I mean, the guys who tracked you to New York could be here right now. They might have found a way to pick up your digital trail and read your emails and see your online ticket purchases, or hack your social media accounts or something. You're going to have to go dark on all of those, by the way. And by that I mean no more logging on—not even one time—either that or delete them altogether. And no more emails—to your parents, to Nox. Nobody. Basically, you and electronics are no longer friends."

I fell back a few steps in shock. It was starting to hit me

that this "danger" Anders had mentioned was a real thing, not just some vague idea or unfounded worry. I *had* mentioned to Nox, my mom, and Olly that New Orleans was my next destination. It creeped me all the way out to think of someone back in the Ancient Court reading the things I'd written, the things my friends and family had written to me.

"In that case, I... shouldn't stay here. I should go back to the bus station and leave. Tonight."

He nodded. "Trains are a lot faster. But we'll wait till morning." He pulled two Amtrak tickets from his back pocket and held them out to me.

I reached out and took them. My hand was shaking. "Memphis? Why there?"

He shrugged. "It's unpredictable. And these tickets were available on short notice. Nox suspects they're watching the airports, plus it's impossible to get a plane ticket without going online and inputting your name—one that *matches* your I.D. Trains are much more relaxed about everything."

"Well, okay then. I guess I'll see you at the train station at..." I peeked back at the print-out. "Eight tomorrow morning."

The squinty-eyed look of regret returned. "Yeah, about that. You can't sleep at the youth hostel tonight."

"I told you they're perfectly safe. I've been sleeping in them for months and months with no problems."

"That *is* the problem. You've established a pattern. If the Ancient Court's agents *are* in the city, it's the first place they'll look for you. You've got to change things up, do the opposite of what you've been doing."

"I see. So, you've apparently thought this all out. What, pray tell, is the opposite of staying at the youth hostel?"

He grinned. "Staying at the Windsor Court."

4

ANDERS

I couldn't believe it. She was actually agreeing to it. Standing there in that alley I was sure I'd never get Macy to come to the hotel willingly and would have to resort to using Sway to get the job done. I think it was my point that *other* people could be endangered if she didn't agree that finally convinced her.

"What about the other kids at the hostel? There could be a struggle, and anyone else in the room could be hurt or even killed."

She blew out an irritated breath. "Fine. Fine. Let's go to the Windsor Court. I hope you made a *lot* of money on your latest album because I'm going to order lobster from room service for dinner *and* breakfast."

I laughed. "Fine. Whatever you want. You *should* have a little luxury after the way you've been living for the past year."

"Hey—I *like* the way I've been living. I'm going five-star only under duress, and as soon as all this is over, I'm going back to my life."

"What about the life you had before? You know, gymnastics and stuff. Don't you ever miss it?"

That caused her to pause. "Sometimes. But that's history. It's not something I… can do anymore."

"You still look like you're in good shape to me."

"Eyes straight ahead, mister. I am not one of your groupies, who you can charm with a few pretty words and that sparkly smile of yours."

I turned and flashed her an over the shoulder grin. "You like my smile, huh? 'Tall, tanned, built'—*and* a sparkly smile. My head's getting bigger all the time."

"Shut up. You are completely obnoxious."

"And 'perfect'—don't forget that one. Obnoxious and 'perfect.'" I laughed and skipped out of the way as she took an irritated swipe at me.

I managed to get adjoining rooms for us, and as we reached our side-by-side doorways, she slid her key card and opened her door, obviously planning to go inside without another word.

"Meet you here at eight-forty-five?" I asked.

"I told you—I'm getting room service. It's probably too dangerous to go out into the city tonight anyway, right?"

"No. I mean, yes—we *should* eat in. I was talking about meeting Taylor. She's staying in this hotel as well. We can go to her suite and meet her—if you'd still like to."

For the first time since she'd discovered we didn't meet by happenstance, Macy's expression looked something other than irritated. She didn't speak for a full minute. Finally, she lifted her eyes to meet mine. Green. They were a beautiful green. I'd always thought they were pretty, but in this moment, they were spectacular, like those Fourth of July fireworks that burn with colored flames.

"Yes. I would like to—if it's still okay."

"Of course. First Taylor. Then lobster with lobster sauce, lobster cocktail, and lobster soufflé for dessert."

She cracked a reluctant smile and gave me a little shove toward my own door. "See you at eight-forty-five."

Late that night, we stood in nearly the same place after not only meeting Taylor but hanging out for several hours in her suite. Macy had looked like a doll standing next to the statuesque singer-songwriter, but they'd gotten along famously. Taylor was great that way—her fans were her friends. I considered her a role model for all Elven celebrities.

Macy still wore a happy expression. That was rare for her these days, and it made *me* happy, to have been able to give her something she truly enjoyed and appreciated.

"You know," I said on a whim. "You *are* going to be happy again someday—all the time. You won't have to run away. You'll never forget… him, but you'll be able to move forward and have a normal life. You can't let what happened be the end of your life. You're still living, and there's a lot of good things out there waiting for you."

She looked at me for a long moment, her blissful expression replaced by a serious one. I wasn't sure if she was going to thank me, or punch me, or what.

"Maybe you're right. Maybe there are a lot of good things ahead, but I'm about as likely to move on and let go of my past as *you* are to give up all your inter-continental 'band bunnies,' fall madly in love, and settle down with a permanent bond-mate."

I raised a brow, duly chastened. "Touché."

She had me there. I'd never fallen in love and doubted I ever would. I just wasn't made that way apparently. There was an awkward moment where I wasn't sure what to say next.

"Well, I'll see you in the morning. Try to get some rest.

And keep the door between our rooms *open*. Don't worry about a thing—I'm here to protect you."

"The only thing I'm worried about is you *snoring* and keeping me awake all night." She smirked. "If that happens, the door is *closing*."

Just as I turned to go to my room, she said, "Anders."

I spun around so fast it made me dizzy. "Yeah?"

"Why did you agree to do this? It's got to be an incredible inconvenience, and despite what you said about orders, I know Nox. He wouldn't force you."

Her question stunned me into silence for a moment. She was right. Nox wasn't forcing me. So why *was* I doing this?

I shrugged and laughed off her sincere question. "I figured you could use some *good* luck on your side for a change."

She shook her head, not buying it. "Be serious. The truth."

The truthful answer was, *I don't know.* The one I gave her was, "My side project. It's a movie score. It's a romantic comedy, a road trip film. So you see, this arrangement is perfect."

She frowned in confusion. "What do you mean?"

"Well, I might not know jack about love, but I *can* travel. Inspiration. You know?"

Slowly, she nodded, backing away from the doorway. "Right. Well, thanks for being here. Goodnight."

"Goodnight Macy. Sleep well. Tomorrow is the first day of the rest of your life, you know."

5

NIC

T*wo months later*

DEAR MACY,

There's so much I want to say to you, I don't even know where to start. I guess I'll start with I'm sorry. I'm sorry I haven't been there for you. I'm sorry it's been a year since you've heard from me. I'm sorry that I don't even know where you are, what you're doing, who you're with. Believe me, if I'd had any control over it, you would have been with me.

I'm sorry if you've been sad. Nox told me that you—that everyone—believed I was dead. Maybe you still believe it. I don't know how you feel about that. If your feelings for me were anything like mine for you, it was devastating news. I honestly don't think I could live without you, which means you're stronger than I am—which I already knew.

I am on my way to you, my heart filled with hope, and every part of my body burning with the need to touch you, to hold you again. I don't know where I'll find you. I don't know what will have changed. It's been a year for you. For me, it seems like we were together only days ago. I don't know if you are still mine to touch and hold. I do know this, though—I am yours. Nothing will change that. Ever. The inside of a traditional Elven wedding band reads: My eternity belongs to you.

It's true.

I have so much to tell you, Macy. Wonderful things. Terrible things. But the thing I'll say to you first—and every day that I'm allowed to be in your presence until the sun no longer rises and sets is this—I love you. With all my heart. Always.

I SAT FOR A MOMENT, pen in hand, and contemplated signing the letter. Sighing, I clicked the pen closed and put it in my sport coat pocket then folded the letter into quarters and put that in my pocket as well, staring absentmindedly at the palm trees and new-looking buildings whizzing past outside my limo window.

There was no point in signing the letter. The only way Macy would ever see it was if I put it in her hand myself. I had no idea where to send it. Nox had told me over the phone that she was constantly on the move and no longer using any form of online communication. The only clue he had as to her whereabouts was a message he'd gotten from a friend of his—one of his bandmates. The rest he insisted on telling me when I got to his house in Malibu.

I leaned forward, addressing the cab driver through the small opening in the clear plexiglass partition. "How much longer?"

"Are we there yet?" He chuckled at his joke. "Another half

hour. I can tell from your accent you're not from around here. Welcome to L.A. traffic."

Groaning, I sat back in my seat, fidgeting impatiently. A full hour later, the car stopped in front of a grand seaside mansion. I paid the man, got out, and stretched. I was exhausted, but also exhilarated. Finally, I was here. Maybe not in the same state, but I was in the same country as Macy, and soon I'd find her.

A vine-covered gate opened on one side of the house, and Nox bounded through it, smiling widely.

"You made it. How was the trip?"

"Too long but not so bad. U.S. Customs moved quickly. Where can we talk?"

He laughed. "Okay, so no small talk. Just as well. Come on —let's go around back to the deck. My cook has prepared some food for us, and we can eat outside while we catch up."

I followed him through the gate and toward the pristine beach, breathing in the fresh ocean air and feeling revived, eager to share the information I had for him and even more eager to find out what he knew about Macy.

"So, I know you've got some questions," Nox said as he took a seat and indicated for me to take a chair at the table. "But first, I've gotta know—what happened to you, man? Where have you been for the past year? Why has no one seen you?"

Macy had already warned him about Dr. Schmitt's attempted creation of a hybrid human-Elven slave race and why the slaves were "needed," the Plague that lay in wait for the human race. I filled him in on the details of my battle with Dr. Schmitt in the clinic, how he'd sedated me and kept me in a coma for the past year to keep me out of his way, how he had intended to make my sleep a permanent one.

Nox leaned back in his chair and let out a long, whistling breath. "Wow. Evil bastard. I can't believe he had the balls to try to murder you. Thank God you're alive. So… how are we going to stop him?"

"Him, you don't have to worry about. He is dead. My father killed him just as he was about to murder me. That experience turned Papà around—he is no longer in favor of unleashing the Plague. But he is alone in the Ancient Court. The others are still on board. And Alessia—my former fiancée—she is now spearheading the plan. The threat is still very real."

"*Former* fiancée. So I guess you called it off officially. Isn't that her second…"

"Broken betrothal? Yes. And it might have been the final straw for her sanity. I couldn't help it, though."

Nox nodded. "I get it. You fell in love. With Macy."

"Yes, but there's more to it. We are… I am bonded to her."

His eyebrows shot up. "Oh. Wow." He considered it for a minute then shook his head. "That changes things. I guess we don't even have to talk about that thing I mentioned on the phone then about the other…"

I leaned forward in my chair, my pulse tapping out an emergency warning message. "What? The other what?"

He smiled. "Never mind. I was obviously wrong."

As I continued to bore a hole through him with my eyes, he explained. "It's just… a couple months ago I got reports that some Ancient Court agents were in the country and had caught up to Macy. I sent someone after her, to protect her, you know? The two of them have been lying low, traveling together—for her safety. And well… based on some things he said last time we talked, I thought they might be making a connection."

He hastened to add. "Obviously, I misread the situation. I had no idea you were bonded to each other."

I inhaled deeply then let it out, working to stay calm.

"Well, that's not exactly accurate. I am bonded to her. She is not bonded to me."

He narrowed his eyes. "You mean because she's human, and they can be with more than one person in a lifetime?"

"No." I paused, trying to decide if I could trust him with this information about Macy. Considering what I'd already seen of his character and his willingness to come to the defense of humans, I determined it was safe to fill him in on Macy's true nature. "She's not... human. She *can* be with more than one mate in a lifetime though—many, many more actually—at least based on what I've read about... nymphs."

He sat up straight, and his shocked hand gesture nearly knocked over his glass of ice water. "Did you say 'nymphs?' I thought they were—"

I nodded. "Yes. So did we all. But it's true. And now she is being hunted for her blood—by my people."

Again Nox released a long breath of consternation. "Whoa. Now I understand. I was wracking my brain trying to figure out what they'd want with a little human gymnast. I thought maybe they were doing a sweep of all their former fan pod members to, you know, tie up loose ends and keep them quiet or something. Or perhaps they'd figured out how she escaped the castle and wanted to question her about me and the inner workings of the Dark Court here."

"No, I only wish they wanted to question her. They— Alessia in particular—want to use her, to experiment on her." *To hurt her.* "I'm not sure how much you know about nymph lore, but they were highly valued for the healing power of their blood—and for their fertility."

He nodded. "We studied it a little as kids—in history. Weren't they also hunted by witches?"

"Yes. For the same reasons. Their blood was the core ingredient in many healing potions and spells. She's not in danger from *that* population, but she certainly is from my former friends in the Ancient Court. I *have* to find her before they do. Even if I wasn't in love with her, it would be my duty to protect her from capture and the torture they have planned for her. Where did your friend say they were?"

"The last I heard, they were in Houston, Texas. The GPS has them downtown somewhere."

"Excellent." I stood. "That's where I'll go then. How long will it take to fly there?"

"About five and a half hours, maybe a bit less."

"I'll get the first flight out. May I use your computer to purchase a plane ticket?"

Nox did a double-take. "You've just flown for thirteen hours straight, not to mention a two-hour limo ride in L.A. traffic. Don't you want to at least stay the night and rest a bit?"

"I'll sleep on the plane. I need to get to her."

He nodded. "Okay. How about this—I've got a couple of planes at my disposal. Why don't you shower and take a nap or something. I'll call my pilot and see how quickly he can get one of them ready to fly." He gestured to the table. "And bring your plate—you've got to eat something."

I took him up on the suggestion, grateful to have found this unexpected ally when I needed one most. I'd been told all my life how uncouth and radical the American Dark Court was, but Nox seemed like not only a good leader but a good person.

He led me to a guest suite that featured an attached bathroom and a small sitting area with a table.

"There are plenty of towels in the bathroom, fresh sheets on the bed. You relax. I'll let you know when we have a flight plan."

"Thank you, my friend."

"No problem. I'll leave you to it. Call if you need

anything." He went to the door but before stepping through it he turned back to me. "Nic?"

I set my plate of food down on the small table. "Yes?"

"I'm not sure what you're going to find when you, you know, catch up to them. I want you to know... well, my friend Anders... he's a good guy, and he's been through some hard stuff, too. Don't be too rough on him."

I read his meaning clearly. What he meant was don't beat the *merda* out of my friend if you find out she's fallen in love with him.

I nodded, answering him mind-to-mind so he would have no doubt of my sincerity—lying was impossible when communicating in the ancient Elven way. *I understand. I'm grateful to him—to you—for keeping her safe. Truly.*

"Okay. And one more thing... don't ever doubt that she *did* love you. I don't think I've ever seen anyone grieve like that in my entire life—I certainly never want to see it again. It's just... no one could keep that up forever. It would kill them."

I nodded again, this time unable to say anything but a quiet, "Thank you."

I went back to my dinner, forcefully pushing from my mind the disturbing images Nox's subtle warning had produced. I knew Macy had loved me once. And what I'd written in that letter stood, whether she still felt that way or not. I loved *her*. Her happiness and safety were my only concerns.

If she *had* moved on and—the thought made me gasp for breath—fallen in love with someone else... I would spend the rest of my life as her silent guardian, protecting her from every threat, without ever letting her know I was there.

6

MACY

I was breathless, having danced for the past hour to every song the old corner jukebox played. Anders beamed at me, looking as cool and unruffled as he had when we first arrived at the dungeon-dark, crowded dive bar in Neartown Houston's hip Montrose neighborhood.

"You never told me you were such a great dancer," I said, leaning against him in happy exhaustion and laughing. By now I was comfortable enough around him to not care whether *I* was a good dancer or not. I was having fun. For the first time in a long time, there were no "ghosts" hovering around me.

"You never asked," he quipped. "And you never told *me* you knew the words to every country song ever written." Pushing my hair back from my damp temples he asked, "Ready for a break?"

I nodded, and we made our way to a scarred wooden table near one of the black-painted, graffiti-covered walls. It was one of those long high-top tables you share with anyone and everyone who happens to come along, and we squeezed onto a bench together in the only available space.

"Want another drink?" Anders asked as a cocktail waitress moved in our direction.

"Water please. I'm so thirsty."

"I bet. You've gotten a pretty good workout." He flagged the waitress down and ordered our drinks.

As we waited, I looked around at the photos, and bits of paper, stolen street signs, and bumper stickers stuck to the walls and ceiling, the purple twinkle lights strewn around haphazardly, the heated pool tournament going on at two nearby billiards tables. Hundreds of liquor bottles lined the wall behind the bar, and several pairs of rather large undergarments hung from the rafters above—there must have been quite a story behind *that.*

"You know, this was a good idea—coming here." I leaned toward Anders to bump my shoulder against his arm. "When I first saw this place from the outside, I thought you were nuts."

"Haven't you learned to trust me by now? You said you'd never been to a dive bar before, and this is *the* dive bar. It's a Houston institution." He grinned. "Plus... you've been *begging* me to play for you." He nodded toward a keyboard set up on a small stage in preparation for the night's live musical act.

"I don't know about 'begging.' Oh, okay... I *do* want to hear you play."

"What should I play for you? You want some Luke Bryan or Blake Shelton... or maybe some old-school Willie?"

"I want to hear one of your songs. What about the movie theme you're working on?"

He glanced around. "I'm not sure this is a road-trip-love-story crowd."

"Who cares? Nobody's listening. And if they are, they're probably too drunk to care. And I'll bet you every person in here has fallen in love at least once—except for you, of course," I added in a teasing note.

He gave me a protracted stare, and then he finally moved, backing off the bench and heading for the dark stage. When I didn't immediately follow, he stopped and turned back to me, giving me the come-along gesture.

I followed him up onto the small stage, feeling conspicuous, though when I looked back over the bar crowd, no one was looking at us.

"Are we going to get in trouble?" I asked.

Anders gave me the universal expression for *Oh please* and took a seat on the stool in front of the keyboard, switched it on, and let his hands hover above the keys for a moment. I shifted until I was standing at the front of the large instrument, leaning on it slightly with my forearms, brimming with anticipation.

He started playing. The music didn't just reach my ears. I felt it reverberating through the keyboard into my arms and throughout my body, resonating in my chest where it competed with my heartbeat for dominance.

It was beautiful—the melody and the sight of his hands moving deftly from one end of the instrument to the other, his fingers flying in the dark. The sound was so full and complex, it seemed like more than one person was playing. Anders' skill as a musician was undeniable, but what really got to me was the song itself.

It was pure emotion translated into musical notes, alternately amusing and uplifting and then lilting and melancholy, tugging at every last one of my heartstrings. And I thought those had been snapped long ago. The incredible thing was he'd *made* this harmonic creation—from his own heart and mind. How did that work? How could someone create something out of nothing like that? Especially something as remarkable and affecting as this? It seemed like magic.

But of course, he *was* magical—he was Elven—and this

was no doubt his secondary glamour. Though if you asked me, it could have been his primary one.

As the song ended and I opened my eyes, I realized the rowdy late-night crowd had gone quiet, every bit as mesmerized by Anders' talent as I was. The applause began then grew and grew until it was a roar punctuated by clinking bottles and appreciative yells of praise and calls for more.

Anders didn't look at any of them. He looked at me, his eyes leery, his face surprisingly vulnerable.

"Anders," I breathed, nearly too overwhelmed to speak. "I…"

Before I could get my thoughts out, people started rushing the stage—mostly female people.

"It's the keyboard player from The Hidden," one woman exclaimed loudly. This caused more seats to empty until the dance floor in front of the stage was filled with bar patrons screaming, "Anders!" and reaching out to touch him and grasp at his clothing.

He stood from the stool and raised one hand, yelling, "Thank you. Thanks very much," to be heard above the clamor. With his other hand, he gripped mine and started pulling me toward the backstage door.

Together we ducked through it, he slid a lock into place, and we darted down a short passageway to the kitchen, through its heated clattering busyness and out into an alley beside the bar. Then we looked at each other and laughed.

"Wow. That was…" I shook my head, unable to come up with adequate words to describe what I'd seen.

He widened his eyes and blew out a breath. "Yeah. That's what it's like—only I'm not usually so close to the audience. And we have security guards at our shows."

"Yeah—I can see why."

"We should get out of here in case any of them gets the bright idea to come outside."

I nodded my agreement and accompanied him toward the sidewalk. Our hotel was only a few blocks away, and we'd walked here earlier, enjoying the colorful, thriving neighborhood. It was much quieter now, though certainly not deserted. Trying my best to keep up with his impossibly long-legged stride, I realized our hands were still linked. Filled with embarrassment, I tugged mine away, which earned me a speculative side glance from Anders.

He didn't mention it, though. Instead he asked, "So... what did you think of my song?"

His gaze went back to the sidewalk ahead as he waited for my reply.

"Oh. I thought it was..." I paused, searching for the right words to describe the experience of listening to his music. Because it *was* an experience, complete with sights and sounds and *feels*. It was different from anything I'd ever encountered before.

"You didn't like it," he said, sounding no less than crestfallen. As if my opinion truly mattered after the overwhelming approval he'd gotten back there from the crowd.

"No—I mean yes, I *did* like it. I liked it so much I'm having a hard time coming up with a way to express how much I liked it."

"You don't have to say that," he muttered.

I stopped in place on the sidewalk. After another step or two Anders realized it and stopped as well. He turned back to me with a quizzical glance. I closed the gap between us and came to stand directly in front of him, making sure he was looking right at me before I spoke.

"Anders. I *loved* it. It... *affected* me. I don't know how to describe it, but your song... the way you played... it did things to me."

One corner of his mouth quirked, and his eyes went to the side as if he wanted to smile but wasn't quite ready to let himself.

"You are... gifted," I went on. "You have a beautiful, incredible gift. Before, when I've encountered glamours, I've had mixed feelings about them, about whether they're a good thing or a bad thing. But yours—I know it can't be anything *but* a good thing because of the way it made me feel."

His face, which had been softening and reddening with emotion, now creased with displeasure. "I don't have musical glamour."

"You don't? Are you sure?" I was truly confused.

He huffed a laugh devoid of humor. "Yeah. I'm sure. As far as music goes, I might as well be a human."

I couldn't help but laugh at his derisive tone. "Oh that would be the worst thing in the world, wouldn't it? I'd hate to be a mere human—oh wait..." I grinned up at him, watching him realize how insulting his statement had been to present company, as in *me*.

He let out a reluctant laugh. "I'm sorry. That's not how I meant it. Well, okay maybe it *was* how I meant it, but now I'm sorry I said it. *Some* humans are okay."

"Lame apology accepted," I said with a pert nod. "You know, it's hard for me to believe you don't have musical glamour, but if you say so, I guess I do. And that leaves me to conclude... you don't *need* it. You are an incredible songwriter and musician all on your own—no magic tricks required."

For several long moments, Anders stood there looking at me, frozen, not saying a word. Sounds of traffic and the incessant tapping of suicidal moths dive-bombing the nearby street light filled the silence.

And then he leaned down. I thought he was planning to hug me, and I leaned forward to return the hug, but as his face got close to mine and he didn't turn his head, I realized what was really happening. He meant to kiss me.

My heart leapt up to block my airway. *What do I do? Stop him? Let him?* At the last second, just as his lips brushed the side of mine, I averted my face and pressed it into his chest, pretending I hadn't realized his intent. My arms squeezed him briefly, then I let go, backing away with a smile and a cheery tone.

"It's getting pretty late, isn't it? I had no idea how long we stayed at the bar, and we'd better rest up if we're spending the day at the rodeo tomorrow. That's why we're here, after all." I turned one way then the other on the sidewalk, momentarily disoriented by the night's surprising turn.

Anders didn't immediately respond but stood looking at me, his head bobbing slightly, as if he was giving himself a little talk.

"Yeah. I guess you're right," he finally said, motioning for me to come along as he started down the sidewalk again.

I was hoping that was the end of it. Anders had shocked me, and I wasn't quite sure what to make of it. I needed time to process.

We'd become friends over the past two months of traveling together, having every meal together, living in close quarters—often sleeping in the same room for the sake of security and economy—completely cut off from everyone else in my life. It was impossible not to like him—he was... likable. Adorable, really. And no matter what he'd said about working on his music, I knew he was making a sacrifice to be here with me.

Since he'd joined me on the road, I had begun to change, to heal. His consistent presence and never-ending optimism had done what I thought was the impossible—

pulled me out of my grief-stricken depression and reignited my interest in living again. I would always be grateful to him... but I wasn't sure about my other feelings toward him.

Apparently he was wondering about the same thing because after a minute of walking together in silence, he said, "I've been wanting to talk to you about something."

My pulse thudded in my neck and ears. "Oh?"

"Yeah. I've had a great time with you these past couple of months. We get along great, and I'm really comfortable with you. I think of you as one of my closest friends now. What would you think about... a relationship upgrade?"

Oh boy. Here we go. "Yes. We *are* friends, but Anders—"

He lifted a hand to the side, out in front of me. "Hear me out, okay? I've given this some thought. I've spent time with a lot of girls, but I've never been this close to any of them before. You and I have fun together, we get each other's humor. Neither of us snores. I think you're about the cutest girl I've ever seen, and I don't think you *hate* the way I look. In fact, if I remember correctly, you once even used the word, 'amazing.'" He lifted a brow and smirked.

"Yes, but—"

He ignored my attempt to interrupt and forged ahead. "In my book, this..." He gestured between us with one hand. "Is just about as good as it gets. Add bonding to that, and I think we could be really happy together."

I choked on the thin night air. *"Bonding?"*

"Yeah. From what I hear, it's a lot of fun. And it seems like the natural next step—especially to an Elven guy who's half a year past the usual age."

"But... if we were to..." I could hardly say the word. "... bond, then you would never be able to be with anyone else... in that way. Nic told me it was a one-partner-for-a-lifetime kind of deal.

"That's true. There's one of me and one of you. Why not us?"

"Well…"

I searched my shell-shocked brain cells for some logical reasoning. On one hand, I was flattered. This was a big deal for him. It meant no more band-bunnies. He'd always seemed to enjoy that aspect of celebrity *quite* a bit—even more than the other guys in the band. He must have been sincere about how much he liked me. And maybe he was right—maybe a close friendship with a nice guy like Anders *was* as good as it was going to get for me. I would never love anyone again—at least not the way I loved Nic. Maybe after we'd spent a few years together, I'd grow to love Anders in some lesser, un-epic way. But something about that just seemed… wrong.

"What if we do this, 'upgrade' our relationship as you said, and then you meet someone and you're instantly blown away by her? What if you fall madly in love with another girl, and you've already bonded yourself to me?"

He released an impatient sigh. "I promise you—*that* is not going to happen."

"How do you know?"

"Because it never has. I've certainly dated enough girls by now. If it was going to happen, it would have. Not everybody has the capacity for mind-bending, soul-scorching love."

I had my doubts about that, but he seemed so certain. I supposed he knew himself better than anyone did, and I should trust his word.

"What about the eternity thing? I'm not immortal. You are. What's going to happen when my life is done, and you're left alone with the mark? Forever."

"At least I'll have had a damn good time for a few decades." He laughed. "No, seriously. It doesn't matter. The fun of the whole bonding thing probably wears off after a while anyway. And it's not like all this virginity is doing me any good right now." He stopped and grabbed my hand to pull me to face him.

"I think it's a brilliant plan," he said. "It makes perfect sense. It gives both of us what we need. If I'm never going to fall in love, and you're never going to fall in love again, we might as well *not* fall in love with each other—right?"

In a way, it *did* make sense. But it was all happening too fast. I needed a good night's sleep and time to think.

"I… don't know." I wrinkled my nose in an apologetic gesture.

"Yes, you do, Macy. If you'd open that steel trap of a heart a teensy crack, you'd see—it's the best thing for both of us."

Anders gave me an intense, soul-penetrating look, and for a moment I got a flicker of butterfly wings in my chest, a glimpse of a potential future for us as bond-mates. The prospect left me a little dizzy.

He's swaying *me—the cheater.*

I took in a deep head-clearing breath and let it go while he watched and waited.

"It's a very, *very* nice offer, and you make a compelling case."

His eyebrows drew together, his lips pressing into a thin line, as if he was bracing for a strike to the face.

"But?"

"Is it okay if I take some time to think? I'd prefer to make a decision when I'm not under the influence of your Sway." I raised a significant brow at him.

He frowned. "I'm not swaying you."

I huffed a disbelieving laugh. "Really? Well then, not only are you just fine without musical glamour, you don't need Sway, either."

His lips curled in a rascally grin. "See, when you say things like that, I feel like I really *could* fall in love with you."

I rolled my eyes. "Yeah, well don't *strain* yourself. I don't want you to pull a muscle or something."

We resumed our walk, our hotel coming into sight a block away. I glanced over at Anders periodically, and every time, he was smiling to himself, as if re-living a happy memory.

Finally I could stand it no longer.

"What?" I asked. "Why are you grinning like that?"

"I'm happy," he explained, his tone matter-of-fact. "Because you're going to say yes."

"You don't know that," I argued, though in a good-natured tone. "Unless there's a future-predicting glamour you forgot to tell me about in there somewhere."

"No. I can't predict the future." He paused for so long, I thought that was all he was going to say, but then he added quietly, "But I *am* the luckiest guy I know."

7

NIC

D ear Macy,
     I'm on my way to you. Again. Still. Only now I don't know what I'll find when I reach you. And I don't know what I'll do when I get there. I may see you yet never speak to you again, if that's what's best for you. My heart aches when I think about it. I'd love nothing better than to put this letter, and the last one, into your tiny perfect hands and kiss you until neither of us can breathe. But I don't know if you'd let me. I don't know if you'd even want them—or me— anymore. Maybe you'd tear up my words or throw them away without even reading them.

All I know is that I have to say these things to you one way or another, and if I never get the chance to say them in person, at least I've gotten them out this way.

I don't know why all of this has happened to us. I don't know why you came into my life when you did. But I have to believe it all meant something. I can't go on if I don't believe that. All I have at this point is hope—hope that at least a small part of you remembers what we had and still longs for it, hope that somewhere in your heart there is still some love for me. Because mine belongs to you completely and always will.

I FINISHED the letter as the wheels touched down on the tarmac at Sugarland Regional Airport. Chuckling to myself at its pathetic sappiness, I folded it carefully and tucked it into my pocket, right next to the first love letter I'd penned to her.

A black Audi Q7 waited near the private airport facility's main hangar, and as I neared it, an Elven woman emerged from the front driver's side and approached me.

"Mr. Buonoccorsi? I'm Jodi. I'll be happy to take you wherever you'd like to go. Do you have a hotel in town already or would you like for me to make a call?"

Once again, Nox had apparently come through, arranging a ride for me at the airport.

"Oh. Um, I'm not sure how long I'll be here."

"Well, I imagine you're in town for the rodeo, right? You'll want to stay at least a few days to see everything."

"The rodeo? No. I… don't know anything about it." Her presumption made me wonder, though. If this "rodeo" was a big deal here in Houston, maybe that was where Macy would be. Her impulsive nature would draw her to the center of excitement, wherever that was.

"Is that a popular attraction here?" I asked Jodi.

She laughed, apparently amused by my ignorance. "You could say that. About two and a half million people attend it every spring. It's a two-week event that includes not only championship rodeo events every day but a giant fair and concerts by top musicians each night—many of our people perform there each year. Attendees come from all around— you should definitely check it out while you're here."

"Yes. I will. Take me there."

"What? Now? You don't want to go to your hotel first?"

"No. The rodeo is where I need to be."

I couldn't explain it, but I felt certain of that. I'd heard some bond-mates speaking as if they had a sixth sense about their partners, where they were, what they were thinking. Most of the time, though, they stayed so close together it wouldn't have been used for the purpose of tracking one another.

She grinned. "Okay then—let's rodeo."

When we reached NRG park $ in downtown Houston, I took in the enormous stadium, the other huge outbuildings, and the parking lot around them filled with carnival rides, food stands, and masses of people. I felt a mix of excitement and dismay. Excitement because if Macy was still in this city, this was definitely where she'd be. Dismay because I wasn't quite sure how I'd find her in this sea of humanity. The event grounds seemed as big as the whole island of Corsica to me.

Jodi dropped me off as close to the stadium entrance as she could get—which wasn't very close actually—promising to take my luggage to a suitable hotel and check me in, so I'd be sure to have a room later tonight.

"You're going to be thankful for a soft bed," she informed me. "Rodeo Houston is a bit overwhelming."

"Yes, I can see that."

I thanked her—hoping I would not be alone in that bed but sharing it with Macy. But I was getting ahead of myself. First I had to find her, and that would be no easy trick. If only nymphs used mind-to-mind communication the way Elves did. At least I didn't think they had that capacity. Not knowing any other nymphs or even that she was one, it wasn't likely Macy would be aware of that ability even if she did have it. It was something we'd have to figure out together once we *were* together again. I had to believe that would happen—until it was proven otherwise.

I maneuvered down a crowded walk lined with food and souvenir stands, my nose bombarded by the smells of frying dough and roasting meat, popcorn, and something sweet—taffy? Or maybe candy apples. A small girl passed me, burying her face in a large fluff of pink-and-blue spun sugar. Cotton Candy. That's what the sweet smell was.

The air was filled with music, dinging carnival games, the metallic swish and clatter of amusement park rides, and the excited squealing—and not-so-excited wailing—of children. Above my head a sky ride carried rodeo fans from one end of the vast complex to the other. I made a mental note to check that out later as a possible surveillance tool. But my goal for now was the immense stadium itself. It was straight ahead, looming over the outside festivities like a watchful parent at a playground.

As I neared it, a woman sashayed into my path, holding a platter in one hand and lifting a small bit of cooked meat on a toothpick toward me with the other. She was human, very pretty with deeply tanned skin, dark hair and eyes, and a chest that didn't look entirely… natural.

I couldn't help but notice that last part because it was amply displayed in a tiny tank top with the words "Slow Hand BBQ—Get Some While It's HOT," stretched across the front.

"How 'bout some barbecue, cowboy?" she said, running her eyes up and down my obviously non-western attire. At least I thought it was my clothes she was checking out.

I shook my head, impatient to get to the main arena. "No thank you. I'm not hungry. I'll get some later." I tried to walk past her, but the woman shifted her position to stand right in front of me. Naturally, I stopped so as not to mow her down.

She jutted out one denim-clad hip and pulled a slip of paper from one pocket—which was remarkable considering the tight fit of the skimpy cutoff shorts. "You're not going to get *this* later. It's a ticket to the World's championship barbecue contest *and* a private tent pass."

At my blank look, she continued, a bit less confident now. "You know—a tent pass? You're obviously not from around here, but these things are like gold. You can't even *buy* barbecue from the contest entrants—you have to be invited." Her lipstick grin was wide and lascivious. "And *you*—are invited."

I shook my head in bafflement. What did she want from me? I'd already said no thank you. And I'd never tasted barbecue in my life—it wasn't a common thing where I lived.

"I… appreciate it, but I'm not even sure I like what you're offering."

At this, she reached forward and brazenly tucked the ticket into my front waistband, letting her fingertips linger just inside below my navel as she pulled herself close to me. "Why don't you come do a taste test and find out?" she purred close to my ear.

Ah. Now I got it.

I'd like to have said all sexual urges had left my body once I'd become chemically bonded to Macy. That would have been nice. But it wasn't true. They were still there. In fact, the desire to bond was even stronger than before. But it had Macy's name, fingerprint, and DNA pattern all over it.

I had no desire for this woman or any other beside Macy. I hadn't even noticed her obvious flirting at first. Maybe that was what being bonded was—you weren't just *unable* to bond with another partner—you didn't even want to.

Manacling the woman's wrist, I removed her fingers from my waistband. "I said, 'no.' Now if you'll excuse me, I have to find my girlfriend."

I stepped around her and resumed my mission, not looking back.

"You have no idea what you're missing, Mr. Italian

Stallion. My Boston butt is legendary," she called after me, a bitter edge to her flirty tone.

I shook my head, not bothering to answer. She was wrong. I did know what I was missing—Macy. And I wasn't going to let anything interfere with finding her now that we were finally in the same city together. Perhaps within the same square mile. The thought gave me goosebumps.

Stepping into the main building, I was caught off guard by the incredible crowd noise. The huge arena was packed with people watching some kind of horse-riding exhibition. As I made my way to an empty seat, a loud crack sounded, and a gate at one end of the long dirt-floored arena opened.

A horse shot out of the opening, jumping and kicking as soon as he got clear of his confinement. On his back, a man clad in jeans and chaps and a tan leather vest that matched his cowboy hat clung to a rope and undulated with one hand in the air, his body whipping and snapping as the dappled brown-and-white horse spun and bucked.

It was violent and exciting. I'd never seen anything like it. My only impressions of what took place at a rodeo had come from movies and television. If they had anything like it in France or Italy, I'd never been there. Then again, it wasn't exactly my scene.

Was it Macy's? She was so American, and this seemed like such an American event, from the way people dressed to the types of foods I'd seen them eating. Fried Twinkies and pizza on a stick, for instance. My eyes searched the impossibly large crowd. She could be in this very building, and I'd have no chance of spotting her. I supposed I could walk out into the center of the arena and hope she spotted me. Of course I'd likely end up on the receiving end of those thrashing hooves or at least in handcuffs. No, there had to be a better way.

I ducked back out of the building into the steamy parking

lot. The sun was setting, but the air was not much cooler than it had been when the plane landed. Pulling out my phone, I dialed Nox.

He answered after one ring. "Hey—you in Houston? Jodi meet you at the airport?"

"Yes. I'm at the rodeo now. I was wondering... have you been able to reach your friend? I think I'm going to need a little help to find them—that or a miracle." The crowd milling about outside seemed even larger than the one inside the stadium.

"No, I'm sorry. I've called, but he seems to have his ringer off or something. Texted too. I tracked his phone—they're definitely still in downtown Houston. I'll try texting again—stress that it's urgent for him to get back to me. Do you want me to tell Anders about you and let him tell Macy... or did you want to do that yourself?"

I thought about it for a moment. "No. I want to tell her—I want her to see me so she knows it's real. But if you could pinpoint their exact location for me, it would be very helpful."

"I'll do my best. Good luck."

"Thank you." I slid the phone back into my pocket and scowled at the constant stream of bodies passing my location.

What were the odds I'd *happen* to see her? Not good. About as good as the odds of Anders eagerly responding to Nox's questions about his location if he was aware of my return—*and* if he'd fallen in love with my bond-mate. I couldn't count on that avenue of discovery.

In the meantime, I knew only one thing to do—start walking and hope that somehow the bond-mate sixth sense was real and our hearts would lead us back to each other.

8

MACY

My heart had been aching all day. I knew I was fine physically, but that old hollow pain had returned to my chest. Even as Anders and I watched the bull riding contest and the barrel racing and cuddled the baby pigs and goats at the livestock birthing center, the ghosts were back in full-haunt mode. I kept turning to glance over my shoulder, sensing a presence, feeling like I was being watched.

Maybe it was the fact I was considering letting *go* of Nic's ghost and accepting Anders' offer. The thought made me feel guilty. No, guilty wasn't the right word. It made me feel… rebellious, as if my illogical heart was rebelling against my brain's very logical line of thinking. Something inside of me still clung to Nic's memory, stubbornly refusing to release its choking grip.

Now, strolling around the Midway, I forced a smile when Anders asked how I'd liked the giant Ferris wheel.

"It was great," I said. "Way better than that octopus thing. I didn't think I'd live through that one."

"I thought you were a thrill seeker."

I sniffed a laugh. "Used to be. Not anymore. These days I play it safe."

Anders rolled his lips inward as his eyes narrowed to a speculative squinch. "Are you okay? You seem... I don't know... you seem different today."

I shook my head and smiled again. "I'm fine. Maybe I'm tired."

He nodded and glanced off into the distance. Then his gaze came back to mine and he grinned widely, catching my hand in his. "I know exactly what you need—come on."

Not waiting for my agreement, he set off in a brisk stride, pulling me with him. I had to nearly skip to keep up. "Where are we going?"

"You'll see."

"Wait, Anders, really. I am tired. I don't think I can walk much farther tonight. Maybe we should get the shuttle—"

In one swift move, Anders lifted me and swung me onto his back piggy-back style and wrapped his hands around my thighs, holding me securely in place as he kept moving at breakneck speed.

"Oh my God—what are you doing?" My hands scrabbled to grip his shirt, his shoulders—wow, he had amazing shoulders—so I didn't fall off and land on my butt in the parking lot.

He threw a grin back in my direction. "The show's about to start."

"The show?"

I peered over his head to the NRG stadium ahead.

"Yeah—the concert."

I'd read there were several musical acts each evening of the rodeo, but the headliners performed on the big stage in the stadium.

"Anders—people lined up for that a couple hours ago. We'll never get a seat," I argued.

He laughed. "You let me worry about that."

Inside the massive building the seats did look to be filled from field level to nosebleeds. I squinted up toward the sixth level, searching for any openings. But Anders didn't head for the stairs. He strolled right out onto the dirt, toward the stage and the season pass holder chairs set up in front of it. All of those were filled as well. It was only minutes from show time.

Supremely self-conscious, I squirmed to get down. Anders released me, stopping only a second for my feet to make contact with the dusty arena floor before resuming his determined stride.

"What are you *doing*?" I hissed as he strolled past the rows of pricey VIP seating and right up to the stage, which had just gone dark in preparation for the beginning of the concert. An announcer's voice came over the PA system.

"Ladies and gentlemen…"

Anders only smiled and gave me a quick wink. "You'll see."

Reaching the stage, he motioned for a roadie in black jeans and a black t-shirt to come over. The guy leaned down, listened to whatever it was Anders said close to his ear, then nodded and disappeared backstage. Within a minute he reappeared, holding two folding chairs, which he carried off-stage and set up in *front* of the front row. Then he shook Anders' hand and ran off backstage again.

I stood beside our out-of-thin air concert seats, gaping at Anders. Suddenly, blindingly bright lights illuminated the stage, and a loud guitar riff boomed from the speakers.

"How did you do that? Did you pay off that roadie?" I yelled over the opening notes of the first song.

He grinned. "Nope. It's a professional courtesy. Plus, I know this guy—he's a friend." His hand lifted toward the stage, where I finally trained my eyes.

A very tall, very well-built singer swaggered out into the lights, playing the guitar slung over his hip, and my breath rushed from my lungs in a whoosh. "Oh *wow*. Derrick McGinn."

Derrick was one of the hottest country stars around, with a few Grammys to his name and regular TV appearances. He played to sold-out crowds all over the country, and his songs seemed to be on the radio every time I tuned in to a country station. His voice was great, but I suspected his incredible good looks had as much, if not more, to do with Derrick's chart-topping success.

I turned to Anders again. "He's one of you." It wasn't a question because I already knew the answer. Now that I realized Elves existed in our world and often in the public eye, it was so obvious. Anders nodded and raised his hands in front of him, clapping in appreciation for his friend.

Judging from the crowd's reaction, if fan pods still existed in America, this guy would have had a busy one. I enjoyed the show as well, settling in and relaxing as it went on, my heart lightening song-by-song. How could I *not* feel better? It was full immersion this close to the lights and music. About twenty minutes into the show, I was nearly in a trance of happiness and well-being. Then Derrick began singing a familiar tune, a love ballad, one of my favorites.

I reached up to Anders neck and pulled him down to my level so he could hear me. "I love this song," I gushed.

Realizing my lips had grazed his ear, I jerked back abruptly, but Anders shifted and caught me against the front of his body. He hesitated only a second, his gaze penetrating mine, then he slid his hands around my jaw—and kissed me.

Whoa

I hadn't been expecting it. Hadn't even been thinking about it. But now that it was happening, I wasn't stopping it, either. It felt... nice... his hands on me, his lips moving gently over mine. *He* felt nice, and he smelled really, really good. It had been so long since I'd been kissed and held and—

A wild, internal panic enveloped me as my mind went back to the last time I'd kissed someone. Nic. That kiss had been born of true love and desperate hope. It had happened the night I'd lost him forever. I pulled away, staring up at Anders with wide eyes.

His lids opened languidly, as if he was emerging from a pleasant dream. As they roved over my face, the blue eyes were warm and appreciative and… happy.

I make him happy.

That thought gave me some satisfaction. Anders had been so good to me these past couple of months. He'd been patient and kind and self-sacrificing. He'd been a steady, cheerful presence just when I'd needed exactly that. He always knew how to pull me out of a blue mood. And he'd asked for nothing in return. Until last night.

That conversation came back to me in full detail. He'd suggested taking our friendship to the next level—upgrading —and *bonding*. Was it really such a crazy idea? Was a little affection too much to ask for in this life—especially when love was no longer an option?

Physically, kissing him had been good. Emotionally, mentally, it had been nothing like what I'd shared with Nic. But then, nothing ever could be. That ship had sailed, caught on fire, and sunk to the bottom of the ocean.

Who knew—maybe the mental part would come sometime later? Finally, I let myself smile back at him. I nodded, haltingly at first and then with more conviction.

"Okay."

His brows quirked. "Okay?"

I nodded again. "Okay. Let's… upgrade."

Finally getting my meaning, Anders gave me a huge,

ecstatic smile. He lifted me off my feet as he kissed me again, harder and deeper this time.

From the stage I heard an amused voice speaking into the mic and broadcasting throughout the arena. "Well, it *is* a love song. Guess it worked, didn't it?"

I broke the kiss to see Derrick laughing and looking at me and Anders. Then my eyes traveled to one of the big screens overhanging the stage. They faced out in a large circle, so that spectators from every angle had a great view. And there in the center of each one of them was my blushing face close to Anders' smiling one.

"Looks like we're on kiss-cam," he said.

"Oh my gosh." I ducked and covered my eyes, mortified.

"Glad you could make it tonight, buddy," Derrick said to Anders with a friendly wink and a long-distance fist-bump in the air before he began the next song.

I sat down in my chair for the first time tonight. My legs felt shaky, and my breathing was uncertain. Was it excitement over my decision? Fear? I couldn't be sure.

Anders leaned down to speak into my ear. "You want to go?"

I looked up and nodded. Anders took my hand and ducked, walking hunched over until we cleared the crowd seated on the arena floor. We walked in the darkness toward the arena exit, and Anders pulled his phone from his pocket.

"I'll check the shuttle schedule—see when the next one's leaving," he said. But then he stopped walking.

"What is it?" I asked.

Staring at his phone, he said, "Nox has called several times. And there's a text."

"What does it say? Everything okay?"

"Yeah. I'm sure it's fine." He didn't sound as convinced as his words indicated. "It's just… in his text he said it was urgent. I'll call him when we get outside where it's quieter."

Picking up the pace, we resumed our path to the main exit. Suddenly, without warning, Anders yanked me close to him and changed directions, ducking to the side and nearly flattening me against the base of one of the stadium seating risers.

"What—what's going on?" I stammered.

"Shhhh." He hissed into my ear. Lifting his head he surveyed the area then whispered, "Come on. Follow me and stay close to the wall."

My pulse pounding in my temples, I obeyed, staying right behind him as he crept along the base of the risers then ducked into an opening—it looked like one of the chutes the bulls and bucking broncos came out of during the riding events. I wasn't sure what was happening, but Anders was not joking, so I tried my best to match his breath-stealing pace and didn't ask questions.

We moved down the dark corridor, which came out into a wide space that seemed to be a holding area for the animals. Rows of horse stalls lined the aisle where Anders led, moving us steadily away from the main arena area.

Most of the stalls were occupied and bore nameplates— Whiskey Fire, Kinky Boots, Uncle Rio. Some of the horses were sleeping. Others munched quietly on hay. As we passed, several of them lifted their heads to investigate. One of them, a gigantic black horse whose name plate read El Diablo, stamped a powerful hoof and snorted at the late-night intrusion.

"Sorry," I whispered, unable to help myself. To Anders I said, "I don't think this is the way out."

"There are lots of ways out," Anders replied and kept moving.

Finally we reached a back exit. Anders pushed open one of the heavy metal doors and peeked outside, checking one direction then the other. He glanced back at me, his face tense with determination and readiness.

"When we clear the building, we're going to run until we're back in the carnival crowd. We'll make our way to the edge of the grounds. There's an apartment complex on the perimeter. I saw it on our way in. We'll go there and call a cab."

"Not the shuttle?"

"No. They might be checking those. Oh—wait a minute." He looked down at the phone in his hand, scowling at it as if it had sprouted teeth and bitten him.

Dropping my hand, he ran over to the stall housing the monstrous black horse and deposited his phone inside, alarming the already-agitated animal and causing it to rear and stomp. He gave one tight nod then jogged back to me. "Okay—let's go."

Before I had time to think about it or argue, Anders had pulled me from the building and we were running hand-in-hand for the crowded midway. We slowed our pace once we were camouflaged by the thick crowd again but kept moving steadily toward the rodeo grounds exit gate. Reaching it, we exited and ran across the street then ducked in between the buildings of the apartment complex, staying in the shadows.

Only then did Anders allow us to stop. He propped one forearm on the brick surface of the building and leaned over, breathing heavily. I sank to the warm concrete beside him, trying to catch my own breath.

I looked up at his sweat-soaked face. It was hot out, but we'd been in lots of hot places, and I'd never seen him perspire before—he'd only been joking about it in New Orleans. This was no joke. *Oh God.* What was happening?

"Anders—what's going on? What did you see?"

He let out a growl that turned into a near-roar. I jumped and scooted back from him, shocked at his outburst.

"I am so *stupid*," he said, adding a few swear words in a self-loathing tone.

"What? Why? What happened?"

He shook his head and kicked the wall. "I can't *believe* I did that. I got so carried away—being at the concert with you, getting to kiss you finally—and you telling me what you did about upgrading. I can't believe I put you at risk like that."

"Like what?"

"The big screen," he said in a guttural voice. "Your face was up there for everyone to see. I got careless. We haven't seen anyone all this time, going city to city. I let my guard down and got careless, and they *saw* you. I had *one* job, and I screwed it up."

"Who saw me? The agents from the Ancient Court? How do you know?"

"When we were back there, heading for the exit, I saw them—two of them. I recognized them from the castle on Corsica. They were walking toward the stage—if we'd been in the lights, they would have seen us. They must have been in the arena. They must have seen us on the screens."

"But how did they know we were at the rodeo? I haven't been on social media at all. I haven't emailed anyone or called anyone. We make day-to-day decisions about where to go. How could they have found me?"

He stared at me, a stoic look of regret on his face.

"They found you by finding *me*. They must have figured out I'm traveling with you and tracked us using my phone."

"Oh." I nodded in understanding. "That's why you left your phone in the safekeeping of El Diablo back there."

He snorted. "Yeah—good luck to the guy trying to retrieve that thing. May he carry the hoof prints on his face forever." He left the wall and started pacing. "That must have been what Nox was calling and texting about—to tell me they were onto us and right here in the city with us. They must have used GPS tracking to figure out our exact location." He shuddered. "That was close. My heart nearly stopped when I spotted them."

I blew out a breath. "Oh, Anders. Now you're in danger, too."

"No—that's not what I mean. I don't care about me. I just —when I saw them and thought they might have seen us—I wasn't sure if I'd be able to take them both out on my own, you know? Maybe you need more protection than I can give you. I'm no soldier. And I was careless."

He looked so distraught, beating himself up over a lapse in judgment, a momentary loss of control. I got to my feet and closed the distance between us, wrapping my arms around his middle. He was trembling. *Oh my.* That did something to my heart.

"It's okay. I'm okay. No soldier could have done a better job than you because no one cares as much as you do. You've been an amazing friend and a great protector. And neither of us will be careless anymore. Now we know they're after us *both*. So we'll both be more careful. We'll look after each other. And there's no more phone, so there's no way for them to track us now. We can disappear, and this time, they won't find us."

He nodded, relaxing by slow increments, wrapping his arms around me and resting his chin on the top of my head. "Okay," he breathed, sounding drained. "But I don't think we can take trains or buses anymore. They'll double down on watching those after losing us tonight. Definitely no airplanes. I can't use my credit card anymore, either—we're operating on a cash-only basis from here on out."

"I don't have too much left. What should we do —hitchhike?"

"For God's sake no. We'll buy a car. I've still got some

cash. We'll find a payphone, call a cab, and go to some shady dealer who doesn't require any I.D. I don't want there to be any record left behind."

"Okay," I nodded. "That sounds like a good plan. Where should we go when we get a car?"

Now Anders pulled back a bit so I could see his face clearly. He gave me a small grin, a mischievous light entering his eyes. "I think we should go somewhere my glamour can actually do us some good. And where we can replenish the cash supply."

"Okay..." I said, my tone of voice leading. "And where's that?"

"Where else?" He grinned. "Vegas, baby. Vegas."

9

NIC

I stood outside the stadium, scanning the crowd leaving the concert. I'd covered the entire rodeo grounds several times over, but I wasn't ready to give up yet. She was here somewhere—I felt it. I hadn't been able to get into the music venue because the show had already started, so now I was perched atop a souvenir truck, watching and waiting. It was late, but there were plenty of artificial lights to see by. There were so many people, though. Too many people.

I was at the point of desperation. Standing up and bellowing "Macy" over and over was starting to seem like a solid plan. And that's when I saw them.

Moving in unison, the towering Elven hunters emerged from the concert venue. They also scanned the crowd, their heads shifting side-to-side. *Damn it!* How had they found her? Had they followed *me* here? The thought made my blood run cold. I wanted to protect Macy, not endanger her further.

Whatever they were doing here, these guys were going down. They obviously hadn't captured her yet. I wasn't simply going to leave them be and give them any more opportunity to do that. Waiting until the men passed, I dropped quietly from the roof of the truck and followed them.

They moved through the carnival and the wine garden, surveying all the humans in their path and every once in a while looking at each other, communicating mind-to-mind, coordinating their hunt.

My blood simmered as I followed a few yards behind. Alessia was going to pay for this—having my bond-mate stalked and hunted as if she were an animal, some prize to hang on the wall to prove her own prowess and superiority.

As we reached Rodeo Plaza, the crowd thinned out. The food vendors were shutting down for the night, and rodeo fans were making their way toward the nearby tram stop. It was time to make my move.

We were near the NRG Center. Earlier in the day I'd discovered that's where the cattle were housed, displayed, judged, and auctioned as part of the livestock show. Something I'd seen there during my search earlier today gave me an idea of how to best deal with these two.

Slipping between two of the food trucks, I ran ahead of the agents and toward the building. I noted with satisfaction the doors were still open as the last of the cattle owners were packing up and leaving for the night. I waited until the hunters had nearly pulled even with my location then purposely stepped out onto the sidewalk in front of them.

Feigning shock, I stopped then rotated and ran, yelling, "Macy, run! They're right behind us."

Naturally they chased me. I sprinted into the building. One of the cowboys leaving the place called out, "Hey— they're turning off the lights buddy." Then, "Whoa—where's the fire?" as my two pursuers burst past him.

Taking advantage of my natural speed and agility, I stayed a few steps ahead of the men as they chased me into one of the building's conference halls and down the aisles of metal-gated animal pens. The overhead lights clicked off row by row, turning our chase into a dim obstacle course, illuminated only by the emergency lights spaced intermittently on the outer walls.

It didn't matter. I knew where I was going, and if they continued to follow, Macy's hunters were going to end up somewhere they definitely did *not* want to be.

Eschewing the aisles, I leapt over a metal railing into a pen full of drowsing cows, then over another one into an adjoining pen where a champion steer rested alone. I'd seen this guy several hours ago, winning a ribbon. His name was Peaches. He was docile and clearly accustomed to being handled by humans.

His neighbor housed a couple pens over—was not. I couldn't help but notice "Big Boy" today as I wandered the aisles of the place. A monstrous reddish-brown bull, he was two thousand pounds of muscle and bad temper. He had furious eyes and black-tipped horns that must have been thirty inches long each. He'd stomped and snorted any time someone had dared to come within five feet of his enclosure.

I stopped one pen away and waited for my pursuers to catch up. For guys who'd grown up on a European island estate, they were doing an admirable job of jumping fences and maneuvering around farm animals.

When they were just behind me, I climbed the extra-high fence and dropped into Big Boy's pen—right onto his sleeping back—using it as a sort of stepping stone to vault over the fence on the other side and safely out of the pen again.

Before I trampled on his spine, the tremendous beast had been sleeping. Now he was awake. Very awake. And that was unfortunate for the hunters who'd followed me right into the devil's den. As they landed in the dark pen, Big Boy bolted to his feet, which were now pawing the hay and bedding underneath him in preparation for his attack.

Both men let out cries of alarm and started scrambling up the fence. The fence where I waited at the top to block their exit.

"Ah ah ah—I don't think so gentlemen," I said.

"Let us out," one of the men cried in Italian.

My reply was calm and unhurried. "Certainly. As soon as you tell me how you caught up with Macy. Were you following me?"

"No," the man yelped, scrambling to the side as Big Boy charged and struck the fence directly beneath his feet. His hands were jarred loose by the impact, and he grappled frantically to re-secure them. "Please let us out, your highness—we'll explain. Don't let the beast kill us."

The other man offered a frantic, explanation. "She was spotted with one of the American musicians—the blond one —a few days ago. We started tracking him, since her digital signals all went dark. Now *please* let us out."

Another bone-jarring strike against the fence shook his hands loose of the rail, and he started to fall backward. I darted a hand out, snagging his shirtfront and hauling him back toward me.

"All right," I said. "One more question—and then I'll let you leave and go *home*, not in pursuit of Macy—or you'll wish you *had* been left alone in a pen with an angry bull. Where is she now?"

"You are not with them?" the first guy said in obvious disbelief. "The musician's phone GPS signal ends here. And we saw her face—up on a large video monitor at the concert."

The concert. I knew it. I had felt her presence there.

"As far as we know, she is still here on the rodeo grounds," the second hunter said.

He seemed to be telling the truth, and I definitely

wouldn't get any more out of them if they were stomped and/or gored to death. Besides, Big Boy was so worked up now I was concerned he might actually break the gate of his pen open. We'd all three be running for our lives if that happened.

"Okay, come on out." I backed away from the top of the fence and dropped to the dirt floor outside the pen.

The white-faced men clambered to the top and over, dropping to the dirt beside me. I seized each of them by the shoulder. They were both trembling.

"I was serious about what I said. You will stop following Macy and go back to Italy."

"We cannot go back without the girl. Alessia told us our lives are forfeit if we fail. I do not want an innocent to come to harm, but I don't want to die either."

"I feel the same. I was only following orders," the other one agreed. "The princess gave us no choice."

I considered the information for a moment, frowning in disappointment and once again feeling guilty for my part in Alessia's extreme transformation. If I'd honored our agreement and fulfilled my role as her betrothed, she would likely never have fallen in with Dr. Schmitt and become so influenced by him. And she certainly wouldn't harbor such a deep hatred of the human race. I had done what I felt I had to do, but my actions had affected her deeply. There was no denying it.

"Then go to France," I told the men. "I'll contact my father and request that he set you up with a place and position. You'll be safe under his jurisdiction. He is no longer cooperating with the Ancient Court's plan to capture Macy. But if he does not hear from you soon and see your faces within two days in his court—I will put out a hit on you with a bounty so rich, you won't live one more day past that."

"Yes, your highness. I will go straight there."

"As will I. Thank you for your mercy, highness. We will be good servants of the French court." The man drew in a breath as if he wanted to say more, but hesitated.

"Yes?"

"In light of your mercy toward us, I feel I should tell you —we are not the only ones who were sent to the States to search for the girl. There are at least two other teams here, though I don't know where they are operating, exactly."

A shudder passed through me. "I see. Thank you for telling me."

At my nod of consent, the men turned and fled—hopefully right to a street where they could catch a cab or bus to the airport. More slowly, I walked to the exit of the building, contemplating my next move. If Anders still had his phone with him, Nox could contact him and pinpoint their location, warn him that potentially several more teams of hunters were after them.

I hadn't wanted Nox to explain to Anders what was going on—partially because I wanted to tell Macy myself that I was alive—partly because I feared that if her companion did know I'd survived, he *might* withhold that information from her in order to keep her for himself. I didn't know him or what he was capable of, and her company *was* very compelling. But at this point, I didn't see what other choice I had. I knew Nox would tell me the truth about where his friend was, and I'd be able to get to her—and at least find out if it was too late.

Once outside the building, I dialed him. He answered immediately.

"Nic. Did you find her?"

"No. But I know she was here. Alessia's henchmen saw her on a video screen. I'm not sure where to look now. Do you have any idea? Have you heard from Anders?"

"No. I'm sorry. I called several times, and I sent an urgent text. I didn't get any response. At first I thought maybe something had happened to them, but it seems he's ditched his phone. When I called it just a short while ago, a man with a thick Texas accent answered it and told me his horse had stomped it and broken the screen. He was surprised when it still rang. Maybe Anders spotted Alessia's men," Nox suggested.

"Yeah." Or maybe he'd spotted *me* and decided to let the trail go completely cold—even as far as his own king was concerned.

"Maybe they're still around there?" Nox suggested.

I surveyed the nearly empty park, the darkened carnival rides and booths. "I don't think so. Whatever happened, I'm sure they'll be moving on now. I'm afraid I'll have to start the search from scratch."

"Oh man, I'm so sorry. I wish I could be more help. I'll definitely let you know if I hear from either of them."

"I know you will. Thank you, my friend."

I dialed Jodi and asked her to pick me up and take me to my hotel. I was dead on my feet at this point, and in this exhausted state, I couldn't even begin to imagine my next step. The trail hadn't just gone cold—it was buried in deep-packed ice.

I shuffled toward the pickup location we'd arranged, nodding and waving to the security guard who informed me NRG Park was closing for the night. I couldn't seem to catch a break. When I thought of how close I'd been to her tonight —my hand went to my chest and rubbed, trying to ease the sharp throbbing there. In all my life, I'd never felt more alone.

My phone rang again. Was Jodi already here? She must have been very close by to have made such good time to the park gate. Oh—the screen did not display her number, but Estelle's. *My sister.* Why was she calling at this time? It was just after six in the morning in Paris, and she was by no means an early riser.

"*Bonjour, ma soeur chere.* What has you up so early?" I said as I lifted the phone to my ear.

"It is not early, *mon frere*. It's quite late, in fact."

I couldn't believe how good it was to hear her voice, and it sounded so crisp and clear for an overseas connection. "Wait—where are you?"

"In America. I just landed. I've come to help you."

ANDERS

I was shocked we hadn't been pulled over on suspicion of drug-dealing.

The late-nineties model Lincoln Continental I'd purchased from a lot in one of Houston's less savory neighborhoods—the only one I could find open at eleven at night—had dark-tinted windows and a low-slung chassis. The "custom" paint job was a shade too bright, and the rims had enough bling on them to impress a whole roomful of rappers.

But the cushiony old land yacht had done its job and was actually quite comfortable on the twenty-two hour jaunt from Houston to Las Vegas. Still, I was exhausted.

We'd made the drive straight, and except for a bit of dozing while Macy took a driving shift, I hadn't slept since night before last at the hotel in Houston. By this point, I felt like I'd been on the losing end of a college bar fight. Macy looked absolutely worn out as well. During this final stretch, she'd fought to stay awake in order to help *me* stay awake.

As we cruised down the Strip, I glanced over at her mussed hair and puffy eyes. "Almost there."

She yawned. "Okay. Good. Which one should we stay in?"

There were so many choices. Any of them would do, really. They all had beds, blackout curtains, and on the main floor, plenty of slot machines and card games. "It doesn't matter to me. You choose."

"How about that one? It's pretty. And it's close," she said, pointing to a grand high-rise with a lighted tower and an ornate bridge.

"The Venetian? Nice taste. Sure—we can go there."

I'd been to the city several times for gigs, but I'd never stayed at the Venetian resort. I knew it had been designed and decorated to make guests feel like they were in Venice, right down to a replica of the Grand Canal complete with gondola rides.

I took the next right then followed the signs for valet parking, already chuckling in anticipation of climbing out of the rolling pimp-palace and handing over the key to one of the high-end establishment's uniformed valets.

Declining help from a bellman, I took both our bags from the trunk and carried them inside to the registration desk. Macy stumbled along beside me, looking as if she might drop any minute. Poor thing. She'd been through so much.

"Hang in there," I whispered as a friendly-faced woman clad in all black motioned us toward the counter.

"Welcome to the Venetian. Do you have a reservation?"

"Uh… no," I said. "But we'll take anything you've got."

She grinned. "We're really busy tonight, but we've got a Chairman Suite available at only twenty-five-thousand per night."

I nearly choked. Maybe tomorrow we'd be able to afford that—after I'd had a crack at the tables—but right now we'd need to live a bit more like interns than chairmen.

"Um… got anything a little…"

She laughed. "Just kidding. Actually, we are pretty booked

up, but I can put you in a Prima suite with premium bedding, twenty-four hour room service, available in-room massage, and a city view for four hundred," she enticed.

"Two beds?" I asked.

"I'm sorry sir. It's a king. I don't have anything with queens open right now—except for the Presidential and Chairman Suites, and… well, I've already given you the rate on that. I could call some of the other hotels and check for you."

"It doesn't matter," Macy spoke up, her voice sounding like she'd gargled gravel. "We'll take it. Just get the key."

She turned and wobbled toward a lobby chair, flopping into it to wait.

The clerk chuckled. "Looks like your girlfriend's had a rough day."

"You have no idea," I said, smiling secretly at her label of Macy as "my girlfriend." She was only the first of many who would know her by that title. I planned to introduce her to my parents when we returned to California in a few days for the Grammy awards. I had no doubt that this time, Mom would approve.

I gave the woman a fake name, paid for two nights in cash, and collected our room keys.

When I got the room door open, Macy trudged straight to the bed, kicked off her shoes, and fell into it, not even bothering to pull back the covers. It *did* look pretty comfortable. Thank God it was a king and not a queen. Though she wouldn't take up much room, my size made it uncomfortable for me to sleep in anything smaller than a king bed—even alone.

Taking a minute to brush my teeth and wash my face first, I joined Macy in the sleeping area, eager for bed myself. The air conditioning was set at a pretty chilly level, and I touched the skin on her bare arm lightly. It felt cold.

Going to adjust the thermostat first, I pulled back the soft, white comforter and sheet on my side of the bed then lifted Macy—who did not stir at all—and placed her there. She felt like a feather in my hands. I chuckled—much lighter *without* the keyboard case I'd used to smuggle her out of the castle on Corsica. Then I pulled the covers up to her chin and went to the other side of the bed to slide under the sheet myself.

For a few minutes I lay there, unable to sleep despite my exhaustion. This was strange. Of all the nights I'd spent with her these past two months, this was the first time we'd shared a bed. Of course all we'd do tonight was sleep. But what about tomorrow? And the next day? She'd said "yes" to my proposal to upgrade.

The thought filled me with anticipation—and apprehension. Was it really the right thing to do? There were no do-overs for me.

I rolled to my side and watched her sleeping face. She looked young and innocent and sweet. And really, really pretty. She'd gotten prettier to me each day since I met her. Maybe it was because I liked her insides so much, it made her outsides all the more attractive. Or maybe it was that I'd never slowed down enough in my frenetic dating life to ever focus on just one girl and get to know her inside and out.

Yes. It was the right thing to do. I wasn't going to find a girl I liked more than Macy. I wouldn't find anyone more attractive, kinder and more fun to be with. This was as good as it got, and I was going to lock down this gift of fate before it slipped away.

Much more relaxed now, *I* slipped away, allowing myself to fall into a deep, dreamless sleep. I could wait until tomorrow for my dreams to come true.

I woke before Macy did the next morning and crept quietly from the room to pick up some breakfast for us—as well as some supplies. While I was out, I'd tried calling Nox collect from a pay phone and gotten no answer. Later on, I'd have to find a place that sold GoPhones or something.

When I returned, Macy sat up abruptly in the bed, looking around in confusion before realizing where we were. Once she did, she stretched her arms above her head and let her head fall back into the plush pillows, smiling.

"I feel a thousand times better. How about you?"

"Maybe not a thousand—but a few hundred times for sure."

Dropping the pharmacy bag onto the bedside table, I leaned over and deposited one of the two food boxes onto Macy's lap. "Breakfast in bed, my lady."

"Oooh, fancy," she said with a cute giggle. She lifted the lid and peeked underneath at the sausage and cheese bagel sandwiches. "Mmmm. This smells so good. I feel like I haven't eaten in…" She craned her neck at the digital clock nearby. "Oh, that's why. I *haven't* eaten in fifteen hours. Wow. I can't believe I slept this late."

"You were tired. I haven't been up that long either."

She glanced up at me, her bedhead hair floating adorably around her face. "But *you* took a shower. I must look a mess."

"You're fine," I said as she slid from the bed and padded across the room to the bathroom mirror.

When she reached it she let out a shriek. "Oh my God. What a liar you are."

She charged back into the room, snapping up her backpack and retreating to the bathroom with it in tow. "I'm taking a shower, and I don't plan to re-emerge until every drop of the hot water is gone, so I hope you're not in a hurry."

"Well, you might want to leave at least a little hot water. We're going to need it for what comes *after* the shower."

Her carefree expression dropped, and her arm holding the backpack slackened, causing it to slide to the ground at the end of her fingertips. Her eyes were wide.

"What comes after the shower?" she asked in a strangled voice.

I gave a side-nod to the bag on the table. "Go look inside."

Leaving her backpack where it lay, Macy approached the pharmacy bag hesitantly, as if it might contain live reptiles or something. I grinned to myself, waiting for her to open it.

When she did, she laughed out loud, a happy, relieved sound. Reaching into the bag she pulled out its contents. "Hair dye? And bleach?" She looked at me with an incredulous stare.

"Yep. We're trading places. I'm about to be tall, dark, and dangerously handsome. And you—are going platinum, baby."

Now she frowned. "Do you really think it's necessary to alter our appearances?"

I nodded. "I do. The Dark Court agents have obviously seen photos of you—otherwise they wouldn't have recognized you up on the Jumbotron screens at the concert. And if they were tracking my phone—they know what I look like too. If not, all they'd have to do is check Instagram."

"And Tumblr, and Pinterest, and Facebook, and wherever else lovesick groupies post their fandom worship," she said, rolling her eyes. "There is going to be wailing and gnashing of teeth over the loss of those beautiful blonde locks, you know."

I couldn't suppress a grin. "No need to wail. When this is over, I'll cut off the dark hair and grow the blond back for you."

She threw the box of hair color across the room at me. "I didn't mean *me*, idiot."

An hour later, newly brunette and not too sure how I felt about that, I ran my hands through Macy's hair, washing the remaining shampoo from it. Leaning over the tub, she covered her eyes with her hands.

"How does it look? Am I Marilyn Monroe yet?"

"Hotter," I said to the back of her wet head. "Much hotter. Okay, let me grab the towel. Hold on—stay there so you don't soak your shirt."

Wrapping her head in terry cloth, I helped her to stand straight and guided her to the sink. "Ready for the moment of truth?"

We stood side-by-side, both staring into the large mirror. She nodded, looking petrified. Honestly, so was I. I'd never bleached anyone's hair before. I was half-convinced I'd pull off the towel and most of her hair would stay in it.

Please, please don't let her be bald.

She'd still look cute with a buzz cut, no doubt, but she'd be *so* pissed at me. There would be no bonding for the guy who'd scalped her.

Slowly she pulled the damp towel from her head and revealed wet, platinum blonde, and entirely intact (thank God) hair.

"Wow," she breathed. "It's... really different."

"Yeah." I scrubbed my hand through my inky dark locks. "Me, too. That's the idea, though, right? I bet yours is gonna look awesome. I can't wait to see it when it's dry. Look out Gwen Stefani."

She gave me a doubtful, but grateful grin. "Okay then, get out of here and let me do my thing. What should I dress for?"

"We're hitting the casinos, of course. I can't afford all this hot, blonde arm candy unless I win big."

She snapped me with the wet towel. "You are impossible. Go watch TV. I'll be ready in about half an hour."

Forty-five minutes later she emerged from the bathroom

wearing makeup, a short black skirt, a red halter-style top, high heels, and looking hotter than I'd ever thought someone could with nearly white hair.

I rose from the edge of the bed where I'd been sitting watching Sports Center. "Wow. You look smokin'."

"Really? I bought the outfit in New York City." She lifted a hand to touch the side of her hair, which was now curled and hanging over her shoulders. "You don't think it looks trashy like this?"

"Well… maybe a *little*—" I laughed at her offended jaw-drop. "I'm kidding. You look great. *Really* great. You're going to be the perfect distraction while I'm collecting every other guy's money down there at the roulette and blackjack tables."

"So you've been here before?"

"Vegas? Yes, but only in and out for shows—never to gamble—which is a good thing. I've gone to casinos in Lake Tahoe and Reno—overseas, too." I gave her a sheepish grin. "They don't tend to like me very much, and I got the distinct impression I was not *welcome* to return. But Vegas…" I spread my arms out to either side. "… is wide open. Come on, let's go."

We decided to start at a casino at the other end of the strip and work our way back, partly so we could check out the spectacular themed decor and partly because we wanted to end the day at our own hotel. It was also a good idea to spread out my winnings so I didn't draw unwanted attention from the pit bosses and upper management types. They got suspicious when your luck was "too good."

"Just so you know," I said to Macy as we trekked down the sunny sidewalk, "I use Sway to get the casinos to overlook the underage gambling thing, but I don't cheat. My play is all completely legit. So, you don't have to worry about us getting arrested or kicked out or something."

"I wasn't worried about that." She slid me a quick side

glance. "Isn't it *kind of* cheating though, since you're using your glamour? It's such an advantage."

"I don't think of it like that. I'm just using my natural, inborn abilities. People who are good at reading body language have an advantage in poker games. They use it, and no one can complain. Card counting is an advantage. It's not illegal or cheating, but it definitely benefits those who've got the kind of brain power to do it. And casinos hate it because it helps players win—the exact opposite of what they want."

I gestured around us, upward to the shiny high-rise towers and around at the beautifully landscaped casino hotel entrances. "All of *this* did not get built because casinos were *losing* money. Most people lose. A few—if they're really smart —or really lucky—win."

She returned my grin, clearly amused at my rationale and lack of guilt. "I see. So you're just shakin' what your momma gave ya, huh?" She punctuated her question with a sassy booty-shake that surprised me and made my eyes pop in appreciation.

I waggled my brows. "You'd better stop *that* or we're turning this thing around and heading back to the hotel room early."

Now her eyes went wide. "Anders!" She stuttered for a moment. "I can't believe you said that."

I shrugged. My response was unrepentant. "You never know. If my luck holds up, maybe I'll find out tonight why everybody says 'what happens in Vegas stays in Vegas.'"

Blushing deeply now, Macy increased her pace so she was walking ahead of me. Her voice came rapid fire over her shoulder. "Let's just win some money, okay? We've still got a ways to go before I'm ready to hand over any *other* prizes."

I laughed out loud, letting my eyes drift down the back of her cute little body. "I'll take that as a definite maybe."

NIC

Well, this is Vegas, all right. The ringing, dinging, and repetitive electronic music of slot machines met my ears as soon as I entered the passenger pickup area of McCarran International Airport.

Nox had readily agreed to let me take his private plane here from Houston, but Estelle was flying commercial from New York. I'd taken a cab over from the private air field to meet her here. We hadn't seen each other in over a year, since before my coma, and as soon as she spotted me, she let out a happy squeal and started running, throwing herself at me.

I hugged her tightly in return. When she pulled back, she grabbed a handful of my beard.

"Oh my God, this is *so* weird. Why didn't you shave it? You look much more handsome without it. No one can recognize you like this."

"I don't care. The only person I want to recognize me is Macy."

"Well your bond-mate will probably hate it, too."

I reached up to run a hand across it. "You think so?" For the first time since I'd awakened from sedation, I felt an urge to remove the facial hair. I didn't want Macy to be repulsed by the sight of me.

She shrugged. "I don't know. Some women like it. I'm into the clean cut Nordic look myself. Maybe nymphs are into hairy men. Who knows?"

"Could you keep your voice down?" I hissed.

People were already staring—they always stared at Estelle everywhere she went simply because she was stunning and tall. I didn't want her drawing any extra attention because of her loud-pitched conversation. Who knew where the Ancient Court agents were at this very moment?

Estelle had given me some very alarming information when we'd spoken on the phone two days ago—one of Alessia's henchmen had tracing glamour. He was uniquely able to follow and find anyone. Apparently, he hadn't been one of the men I'd encountered in Houston but part of another team of hunters.

The good news was Estelle had a pretty dangerous glamour of her own. It was like truth serum. Once applied, it was irresistible, and it worked on humans and Elves alike. I'd always hated it as a child growing up with her, but I certainly appreciated it in this instance.

She told me she'd recruited a source within Alessia's inner circle—one of her personal bodyguards. At first Estelle had used her glamour to question him—he'd spilled every detail he knew. After that, it was a simple matter of blackmail. He'd told her so much already he knew he was screwed if he didn't keep on providing any and all information Estelle requested. One phone call from her to Alessia, and he'd be executed for treason.

Last night he'd told her the Ancient Court agents had tracked Macy and Anders to Las Vegas— that was why we'd both booked emergency flights here today.

"Okay, so my source said the two Ancient Court hunters

checked into the Venetian resort. I'm betting that's where we'll find Macy and Anders," she said.

As soon as she collected her things, we set off in search of either the hunters or Macy, whichever we came across first. Spotting the Elves among the casino crowd would be easy, and hopefully they'd lead us to Macy. If they hadn't found her already. Shaving would have to wait.

We took a cab to the hotel, which looked like an architect's tribute to Venice. The inside as well was remarkable, strongly resembling an Italian Renaissance Palace with its marble-columned grand lobby and domed vault ceilings with hand-painted frescoes.

My heart quickened, thrumming with hope. Had Macy chosen this hotel? Had she picked it because it reminded her of our time together in Italy?

We followed a bellman across an Italian marble floor that was a replica of the one in the church of Santa Maria del Rosario and-set in a three dimensional, multi-colored pattern. At the reception desk, I was immediately greeted by a clerk whose name tag identified her as Nadia. "Welcome to the Venetian. How may I help you today?"

"Hello. I'd like to speak to one of your guests—a friend of mine. The name is Anders Jensen. Could you call his room please?"

"Certainly, sir. One moment please." She tapped a few keys on her computer keyboard.

"I'm sorry sir. There is no guest here by that name," she said. "Are you sure you have the right hotel? Could he be staying at our sister property, the Palazzo?"

God I hope not. "I'm pretty sure he's here at the Venetian." Would they have used Macy's name? "Check under Macy Moreno please."

Nadia did as I asked with the same results. "I'm so sorry. Will you and the lady be needing a room tonight?" She eyed the impressive collection of Vuitton luggage resting near Estelle's feet. "We have some lovely suites on the upper floors."

"No, we—" I stopped mid-sentence. If I did manage to find Macy today, we'd need a room for the night. At the very least, Estelle needed a place to store her bags. "Yes. I'll take one."

"Very good. The presidential suite offers two bedrooms, formal dining room, a personal fitness area with steam room and cedar wood sauna, a media room, three fireplaces, a fully stocked cocktail bar, baby grand piano, and twenty-four-hour butler service. The Chairman Suite offers all this plus a waterfall feature at the entrance and jetted hot tubs with plasma TV and a fabulous view of the Strip. It's also 2700 square feet larger than the presidential suite. Would you like to hear about the nightly rates?"

I shook my head and waved a hand abstractedly. "It doesn't matter. One of those will be fine."

The clerk's eyes brightened, and she smiled. "Very good sir. And how will you be paying?"

I handed her my credit card and went to speak with Estelle as she processed it. "Are you sure the report said they were seen here—at this hotel?"

"Yes. That's what the guard said."

I frowned. "Then they've gotten smarter about this and are traveling under assumed names. Which is good, I suppose. At least there's a chance the hunters don't know which room they're in."

"What if they've gone out? They could be spotted. They may not know they're being hunted."

"I know. They could be anywhere. I'm not sure what to do."

"How about this… you can stay here and keep watch. I'll go up and change into some shorts and trainers then I'll go out and look. I'll check to make sure they're not registered at the Palazzo next door. I can also call my source again and see if any further reports have come in."

I nodded, pacing now. "Okay, that sounds like a good plan."

"Mr. Buonoccorsi? I have your keys and your card for you sir," Nadia called out. When I returned to the desk, she eyed me with renewed interest. "You aren't... Nicolo Buonoccorsi, the soccer player, are you?"

I gave her a tight smile. I did *not* have time for this. "Yes, I am."

"Oh wow! I thought it was you, but..." She pointed at her own face and made a circle around her chin and jaw with one finger then whispered, "We're not really supposed to say anything. Oh, my brother is going to be so thrilled I met you. He was your biggest fan—so broken up over your early retirement."

"Yes, well... injuries, you know." I started backing away from the desk. "Thank you."

"Oh." She held up a piece of paper. "Would you mind signing this before you go?" She looked around, presumably checking for a supervisor and finding none in the area. "We're not supposed to bother the celebrity guests, but my brother *really* loves you, and he's going through a hard time right now with his divorce, and..."

I returned to the desk, taking the pen from her hand. "Of course. No problem."

After I'd autographed the paper, she said, "Thank you so much. Have a good stay. Let us know if there's anything you and your girlfriend need."

"Sister," I corrected. "My sister."

Now her eyelids did that flaring thing again. "Oh. Well, please let me know if there's any way *I* can help. My name is Nadia, and I'll be here until ten tonight, when I get off work."

She paused to let that sink in. "And we do have an Italian-speaker on staff, if that would be helpful to you. In fact, we had a couple of Italian men in here just a short while ago, asking for information, and Lorenzo helped them out."

I had already started to turn away, but I spun back to face the clerk. "Italian men, you say? This morning?"

She quirked her head at my sudden interest. "Um, yes. Were they teammates of yours or something? Now that I think of it they *were* really big and ripped."

I gestured to my sister. "Estelle. Would you come here a moment?" When she'd joined me at the desk, I said, "Nadia, would you go and get the Italian interpreter for us? My sister would like some recommendations on restaurants and shopping, and her English is not good."

"Um… sure. Okay. I'll be right back."

Nadia clicked away and disappeared through a doorway into an office, I presumed.

"What's going on?" Estelle asked. "Why did you lie about my English?"

"Sorry. I think there's someone here who spoke with the hunters a short time ago. Maybe you could find out what they asked him? Or maybe where they were headed next."

"Yes. Good idea."

Within minutes, Nadia was back. "He'll be right here. Want me to ask the bellman to take your things on up?"

"Yes, thank you. And thank you for calling the interpreter for us. You have been most helpful."

She beamed. "Happy to. And if you need someone to maybe show you around later tonight, I get off at ten," she reminded me.

I gave her a gentle smile. "I'm afraid we have plans for tonight already. Thank you again for your assistance."

She nodded, accepting her dismissal and retreated behind the desk, calling forth the next guest.

A few minutes later, a man in a nicely tailored suit and cheap, but well-polished shoes approached us. "Mr. and Ms. Buonoccorsi? I am Lorenzo. How may I be of service?"

Now it was Estelle's turn. She began speaking to him in perfect Italian, not asking about dining and shopping recommendations but about the men he'd spoken to earlier.

"The Italians you spoke to today… what did they want?"

His face showed visible resistance at her direct questioning about other hotel guests, but like everyone under my sister's glamour, he answered honestly. "They asked about two guests who they believed had checked in last night—Americans—a young man and woman. They described her as very short and brunette and him as tall and blond. I told them we do not disclose information about our guests."

"And *are* they staying here? The Americans?" Estelle demanded.

Again, the man visibly balked, but he answered. His face broke out in a sheen of sweat as if he was trying to hold in the words but found himself unable to keep them from coming out.

"I checked and did not find any record of either name they gave me. We host many famous guests, though, who wish to preserve their anonymity and privacy and use pseudonyms. Are you with the police or something?"

"No, but we are trying to protect the American couple. Did the Italians ask you about any other locations, give you any indication where they'd be searching next?"

He shook his head. "No, they said very little. Only asked questions. Like you."

Estelle turned to look at me. "I think that's all he knows." When I nodded my agreement, she turned back to the interpreter, her words laced with Sway. "If the Italians return, you will not mention this conversation. And if you do happen to see an American couple fitting that description, you will call our room and notify us. You will *not* inform the Italians."

"I understand," he said. And then, as if she'd been physically holding him and suddenly released him, he stumbled back a few steps.

Turning on her supermodel smile, Estelle said, "Thank you for your help, Lorenzo. I am looking forward to taking your suggestions and getting the most out of our Las Vegas visit."

She watched him walk away before turning to me. "What now? I guess we at least know the hunters are here, so my source's information is accurate."

"Yes. And *they* wouldn't be here unless Macy and Anders were. So, I think we stick to the original plan. I find myself a nice, out of the way spot here near the elevator banks so I can see who's coming and going. If Macy is out in the city somewhere, I'll see her when she returns. And if they're still here, I'll see them when they leave. They're bound to leave the room at some point, right?"

I could read the thoughts on my twin's face as clearly as if she'd said them aloud or spoken them directly to my brain. Estelle herself had just referred to Macy and Anders as a "couple." After spending the past two months together, it was entirely possible my betrothed and her "bodyguard" would *stay* holed up together in their luxury hotel room, ordering room service and watching movies, and enjoying other amenities I didn't even want to think about.

A sick feeling spread from my chest to my stomach. Heaving a hopeless sigh, I said, "I don't know what else to do."

Estelle touched my arm. "No. I think it is a good plan. No one can come or go from the guest room floors without passing through this area. I'm sure they will show up eventually. I will go change into better walking shoes and then I'll search around the Strip. I have the picture of Macy you sent me from your phone. And of course, there are plenty of photographs of Anders' beautiful face online. That's probably the one I'll show around the Strip. If anyone's seen *him*, they'll be likely to remember it."

Something in her tone caught my attention and lifted my spirits. "Clean-cut Nordic types, huh?" I teased. "Better watch out for that guy—I hear he's a real playboy."

"Shut up, Nicolo," she ordered, her cheeks going bright pink. "I eat playboys for breakfast."

"You're blushing though. Estelle's got a crush on a band boy," I teased in that sing-song tone reserved for brothers tormenting their sisters.

She narrowed her eyes into a flinty stare that threatened bodily harm. "Don't you need to find a spot for your stakeout?"

Still laughing, I handed her a key card and went off to find a comfortable seat from which to survey the elevator banks and wait out my prey.

Twenty minutes later, I watched as Estelle emerged from an elevator, dressed in comfortable walking clothes, and headed for the casino's front exits. Then the monotonous wait began. Over the next several hours, I scanned every male-female pair of unequal height who came and went, studying their faces.

Of course I'd recognize Macy from the back, the side, any angle without even seeing her face. I knew her walk, the way her hair moved around her shoulders. Hell, I'd recognize her without seeing her at all just from the sound of her voice and her laugh. As I'd lain helpless in a forced deep sleep during the past year, every detail about her and the time we'd spent together had become etched into my brain. Maybe it was the bond-mate thing, maybe it was the fact that I was in love with her.

I watched until my eyes burned and my belly growled with hunger, not even daring to look down at my phone for fear of missing her. None of the short-and-tall couples I spotted were the right one. I fought to control my thoughts, which wandered upstairs to the guest rooms, where Macy might be at this very moment stretched out on a plush-top mattress beside my replacement.

No. Stop. Don't go there. Think about something else.

I wondered how Estelle was doing. Just as I was about to risk a quick text to check her progress, I *did* see something of interest. Not Macy and Anders—the two Italian hunters.

Walking through the Venetian lobby, they looked strong and dangerous and very European. They weren't men I recognized from the castle—these must have been from Alessia's own household in Rome. Still, I knew they were the men looking for Macy. For one thing, they cornered Lorenzo in the lobby near the concierge desk. In obedience to Estelle's Sway, he shook his head, looking agitated, and held his palms up to the sides in the universal gesture for I-don't-know. *Good boy.*

Second, I knew Elves when I saw them, and what were the odds of a pair of predatory-looking Ancient Court members just happening to be here at this time if they weren't the ones who hunted her? I needed to make sure, and once I *was* sure, I needed to take them out of commission so they couldn't pursue her any further.

I went ahead and texted Estelle, instructing her to meet me as soon as possible back at the Venetian. Then, walking directly toward the men, I waited for them to notice me. They did, both reacting simultaneously.

Once eye contact was established, I broke into a run and

raced from the lobby area out onto the casino floor, hoping they'd follow the same way the hunters in Houston had pursued me into the cattle building. People don't usually run without a good reason. It was clear to these fellows I wasn't taking my daily exercise. So naturally they assumed I'd already caught up with Macy and was running *to* her location or running to avoid their questioning. Either way, they were right behind me, which was exactly where I wanted them.

Finally, nearing a security officer, I stopped and turned around to face them. When one of them drew close enough, I threw a punch then grabbed his shirtfront, holding him in place. Naturally, the scuffle caught the attention of the officer. He charged toward us, speaking into his walkie on the way, calling for backup.

"What's going on here?" the human officer demanded as he reached us.

"Thank God you're here, officer. I need help. These men attacked my sister today. I want them arrested."

The officer looked confused, and the two Elven agents looked even more perplexed.

"I saw you throw the first punch," the officer said, sounding suspicious of my story.

"They were chasing me," I explained. "I was a witness to the assault."

Now both men began protesting loudly in broken English. The security officer looked from them to me and back again, clearly unsure of what they were saying—or what to believe. Several other uniformed officers ran up and looked to him, expecting an explanation.

"Let's go to the security office," I suggested. "I will call my sister, and she can come and tell you what happened. You will see. These men are criminals." I spat in their direction. "Perverts! Attacking an innocent woman. And at a nice place like this. I would think for the money we're spending on the

Chairman Suite we could expect some safety and peace of mind on the property. You are lucky I don't kill you with my bare hands."

The officers, apparently convinced by my mention of the high-roller suite, if not my theatrics, sprang into action, taking the Ancient Court agents into custody and roughly zip-tying their hands behind them. Together, as if in some comical parade, we all weaved among the casino's bright and noisy gambling machines and to the security office. Once there, I dialed Estelle.

"I'm here," she said, sounding breathless. "At the front entrance. Where are you?"

"I am in the security office. Walk straight to the back of the casino floor and take a right. You'll see the sign over the door." Giving her a preview of our cover story, I added. "I found the men who assaulted you. They were still in the casino today, believe it or not. You will have your justice."

There. Now when she showed up, she'd be able to fake an appropriate reaction.

The "suspects" were placed in two hard chairs against the wall while the rest of us waited for Estelle to arrive. In the meantime, the original officer took a statement from me. A few minutes later, the security office door opened and Estelle came in, wide-eyed.

"Nic—they got the guys who tried to hurt me?" she wailed. "Where are they?" Then she turned and searched the office. When she spotted the large, obviously Elven men sitting against the wall wearing baleful expressions, she let out a sound of distress and rushed over to me for comfort. "Oh my God. It *is* them."

Good brother that I was, I wrapped my arms around her for comfort. "It's okay. They can't hurt you anymore. These brave officers have them in custody."

"Ma'am." One brave officer, who was clearly gobsmacked by Estelle's beauty, approached her, holding a clipboard. "Would you mind describing to me the nature of the offense these two scumbags committed against you?"

Her big brown eyes glistened with unspent tears as she sniffled and nodded bravely.

I had no idea you were such an actress, I told her mind-to-mind. *You were walking back from the swimming pool, and they attacked you in the corridor from the pool to the guest elevators.*

"I was walking back from the pool," she said. "I still had on my bikini, but with a little cover-up, you know?" She drew her hands over her chest in demonstration.

Every man in the room, except for me and her alleged attackers, stared at Estelle, following every word and no doubt picturing her in that bikini and "little" cover up.

"They jumped out at me and tried to drag me into a doorway. If Nic hadn't come along behind me, I don't know what would have happened. I thought I was safe here at this beautiful hotel, but now I'm not sure."

Oh, she was laying it on thick, and they were lapping it up like whipped cream.

"You are, miss. We'll be on watch day and night to make sure you don't experience any further problems—and these guys—they're going to be prosecuted to the extent of the law. The owner of the hotel will make sure of that."

"Oh thank you," she said with a delicate sob, offering hugs to the men, who were nearly slobbering at this point and elbowing each other to take their turns at a hug from the distraught supermodel. "I feel so much better now."

"Now wait a minute," one of the Elven henchmen spoke up in heavily-accented English. "We did not do what this girl said."

"We did nothing to her," the other man chimed in. "We are not even here for her."

Estelle whirled toward him, clearly sensing an opening.

Walking across the room, she came to a stop right in front of the accused pair. Uh oh.

I worked to suppress a grin. *Sorry boys—you're about to go down.*

"And why *did* you come here?" she demanded.

"To capture a different girl—a small one," the man answered, helpless against her truth serum glamour.

The officers in the room tensed noticeably. One of them moved his hand to the weapon strapped to his side. Another one let out a sound very close to a growl. I had no doubt they all interpreted the man's forced confession to mean he was here seeking a child to kidnap when he mentioned a "small girl."

"And what did you plan to *do* with this small girl?" Estelle asked, a very close approximation of horror on her face. She really was quite an actress.

"Capture her and take her back to Italy," the guy said matter-of-factly, though his eyes were wild with the effort to control his self-incriminating tongue. "Put her in the dungeon to be drained of her blood."

Aaaand our work here is done. These guys wouldn't be bothering Macy anymore.

After Estelle had accepted the comfort and protection vows of every last security officer, we made our way back toward the guest room elevators.

"Laying it on a bit thick, weren't you, sis?"

"Did you want them neutralized, or didn't you?"

I laughed. "I don't think they'll be just neutralized. They may be *neutered* by the time your badge-wearing fan club is finished with them."

She turned to me, her face now serious. "So, the threat to Macy is reduced—that's two more hunters out of commission. What's the next step? I had no luck today showing the picture around. No one I spoke to has seen them —at any of the places on the Strip."

"Maybe they're lying low," I said. *Hopefully not too closely together.* "I'll go back to what I've been doing all day— watching the elevators. If they're still here, I'll spot them eventually."

"Okay," she said. "I may go up and take a nap. That way I can relieve you later and let you get some sleep."

"Sounds good," I said to make her happy.

I had no intention of dozing in our suite. I was tired, but sleep wasn't worth missing my chance to see Macy tonight. Of course, I'd been *away* from my surveillance post near the elevators for close to two hours by now, dealing with the hunters. She might have passed by during the time I was gone. That thought made my chest hurt.

It was also possible she and Anders had already checked out and left the hotel for a new destination, but I didn't think so. My bond-mate sense told me she was still here— somewhere. Hopefully it wasn't all in my mind. As I settled back onto my bench in front of the elevator bank, I prayed it *was* real—and that it would be enough.

MACY

One hour earlier

It was bath time. Youth hostels typically offered showers but no bathtubs. It surprised me how much I'd missed that creature comfort during the past year and a half, and since I'd started traveling with Anders and staying in hotel rooms, I'd become a little obsessive about having a daily bath.

Now, after a full day of traipsing around after him, watching him win obscene amounts of chips at casino after casino, I was wiped out and ready for a relaxing soak. He, on the other hand, wasn't nearly ready to stop.

"You go on up," he'd said when we returned to the Venetian. "I've got a streak going. I'm going to hit the casino here for a bit. If I can win enough tonight, we'll be set for a long time. You should order some room service," he suggested. "I'll bet it's killer here."

Hot and dead on my feet, I nodded my agreement. "Good luck. I'll order something for you, too."

"Yeah, thanks. Get me some sushi," he said. "It'll keep in the room fridge."

"Okay. If I'm asleep when you get back, wake me up and tell me how it went."

"You bet." He flashed me a smile and headed toward the lights and cacophony of sounds that was the gaming area.

I walked to the elevator bank and pushed the call button, standing and glancing around at the posh surroundings. What was Anders paying for this place? I hoped he won a *lot* of money tonight to cover it.

At my insistence, we'd stayed at mostly moderately-priced hotels after that night in New Orleans. Last night when we'd arrived here, I'd been too tired to protest, but we'd have to cut back on spending for a while to make up for this splurge. Who knew how long we'd be staying on the road together?

Since learning of the Ancient Court's pursuit, I hadn't been able to take on any odd jobs, and I felt funny letting Anders support me. My debt tab to him was getting pretty long at this point.

As the elevator doors opened, I got the strangest feeling. Instead of getting into the car, I backtracked and wheeled around, looking behind me and scanning in all directions. There was no one else around. Not too many people headed back to their rooms this early in Las Vegas, I guessed. But I'd had the distinct sensation of… a presence.

Though both Anders and I were always on the lookout for possible Ancient Court agents, this sensation wasn't a *bad* one, exactly. It was more like… a melancholy *yearning* sort of thing. My eyes searched the area one more time, looking for some clue as to why I felt this way.

There was nothing, just a few other guests stepping onto or out of elevators, a small circular lobby area outside the elevator banks with a snack and newspaper stand, and an empty bench.

Taking a deep breath and letting it out again, I shook my

head at myself and turned back to the elevator doors, pressing the button once again. I was getting weird. It was a wonder Anders wanted anything to do with me, much less wanted to bond himself to me.

The tub in our room was fabulous, and so was the room service. Because I never did get the lobster I'd threatened to order in New Orleans, I had a selection of shellfish on ice. It was delicious. Even Anders' sushi, which normally did not interest me at all, looked appetizing. I put the covered container into the mini-refrigerator to keep it fresh for whenever he returned.

He'd made me ditch my e-reader in Texas because it could possibly be traced, but I'd picked up a paperback at a truck stop on the Nevada border, so I pulled it from my pack and read in bed for a while. The book was funny and well-written and had some pretty darn hot kissing scenes. By the time I set it on the bedside stand and turned out the light over my shoulder, I was actually a little eager for Anders to return.

He was a good kisser. There was no denying it. It was empirically true. The two previous times we'd kissed, it hadn't felt like kissing Nic. But still, the close physical contact was nice—pleasant and comforting. I hoped, since we'd decided to go ahead and pull the trigger on this bonding thing, that someday it would be more than that.

But it was only a small hope. I needed to learn to be happy with what I had instead of wishing for what I could never have again. Nic.

Some time later, I woke to the sensation of raindrops falling on my skin. No, it wasn't rain—it was flower petals... or maybe...

My eyes opened, and there was Anders' face, smiling above me. He was standing on the bed, his arms outstretched, and he was dropping *money* on me in a steady sprinkle of green, floaty paper.

"Why is it raining dollar bills?" I asked in a sleepy slur.

He grinned wider. "Those aren't dollars, baby. Get the sleep out of your eyes and check again."

Coming to alertness, I plucked one of the bills out of the air and brought it close to my eyes. Eyes that threatened to pop right out of my head once they saw the denomination. I sat up straight, the sudden motion bouncing the mattress and causing Anders to brace himself against the wobble.

"Is this... is this *real* money?" I asked.

He laughed loudly. "It is."

"Anders. This is a one *hundred* dollar bill."

He laughed again and nodded. "It *is*."

"Oh my God." Scooping handfuls of the paper money covering the white comforter, I looked at them closely. "They're *all* hundred-dollar bills."

Anders kicked his feet out and plopped down on the bed beside me then stretched out with his hands behind his head.

"They. Are." He looked over at me and raised a brow. "What do you think?"

For a moment I shook my head at him, staring in awe. "I think... I think you're *amazing*. And I think they're going to kick us out of Las Vegas."

Now he waggled both brows. "Well then... we'd better enjoy it while we can." Without any further prelude, he rolled toward me and slid a hand around the back of my head, pulling my face to his.

For some reason the kiss surprised me. It wasn't our first —but it wasn't *like* our first kiss, either. That one had seemed like sort of an accident, like it had surprised him as much as me. This one was purposeful, *planned,* and executed with confidence. And this time we weren't in a crowded stadium surrounded by thousands of other people. We were in a hotel room—alone—in *bed*.

This time, Anders had abandoned that sense of caution he always seemed to wear around himself like a bulletproof vest. When I didn't stop him or pull away, he deepened the kiss and pulled me closer, causing our bodies to align, almost touching but not quite thanks to the bedding—and money— still covering my legs and abdomen.

His chest rumbled with a sound of satisfaction, and his hand slid from my nape over my shoulder and down my back to my waist and hip.

"You taste good," he murmured. "And you smell incredible."

He smelled like cigarette smoke—unavoidable in this city of constant second-hand exposure—but underneath that, there was the alluring fragrance I always detected when I was near him. Beachy and fresh, it was like sunshine you could smell. And it was nice.

His hands felt nice, his mouth, too. I started waking up— in more ways than one. For the first time since losing Nic, I started thinking I might *actually* be able to move on—at least in a physical way. This... *thing* with Anders was a sweet distraction. And he was sweet. Sweet, and loyal, and fun, and yes... sexy. He was also eager to move things to the next level based on the way his hands were roaming.

My heart raced with equal parts excitement and panic. I wasn't sure I was ready for this. Yes, we'd discussed upgrading, but here in the actual moment it felt like maybe there should be *more* discussing. Instead, Anders shifted so he was over me, the hard weight of his lower body pressing me into the soft mattress. It felt good. And terrifying.

Oh God. I'm not ready. Am I? Maybe. Yes. No. No, I'm not ready.

I turned my head to break the contact with Anders'

mouth. He took it as an invitation to apply kisses to my neck instead.

"Wait—Anders. Can you... wait... a minute? Please?"

He didn't lift his head, just kept nuzzling my neck and collar bone and shoulder as he responded in a raspy voice. "What's the matter? Am I too heavy? My little pixie..." he crooned, shifting a bit to take some of the weight of his body from me.

"No. It's not that, it's... could you stop that for a minute so I can think?" I begged.

"Stop what?" he whispered, pressing his lips to the base of my neck and dragging them down so the top of my sleep shirt stretched and revealed my upper chest.

I placed a hand on his shoulder, exerting gentle pressure. "That—right there, what you're doing with your mouth. It's very... distracting, and I want to talk to you a minute."

Finally he lifted his head, his eyelids looking heavy, and the rest of his face looking very, very happy. *Wow.* Is this what they called "bedroom eyes?" *They* were quite distracting.

Belatedly responding to my plea, Anders rolled to his side again, not moving far away, but staying close and keeping one hand on my hip through the sheet. He dipped his face to bring his eyes even with mine.

"What's wrong? Are you too tired?"

"No. Not exactly." Actually I felt like a live wire, charged with enough nervous energy to light up the entire Strip should the electrical power fail. "It's just... I'm not sure we're prepared for this."

His brows pulled together then relaxed as he understood—or thought he did. "We don't have to worry about condoms. We're both virgins, so STD's aren't an issue, and it's basically impossible for me to get you pregnant the first time. Maybe you don't know this, but

Elves have major reproductive 'challenges.' It takes bonded couples decades—sometimes a century or more to conceive."

"But I'm not Elven. I'm human."

"I think the same rule would still apply. Hmmm... actually, I should ask Hakan, our court's healer about that one. Anyway, the odds against it are so high I don't think even Vegas would take the bet."

He moved toward me to kiss me again, as if the issue was settled.

I put a palm on his chest. "That isn't even my concern."

"So what is?"

"Well, I mean..." I blushed as I said it. "We haven't even said, 'I love you' or anything. It seems strange to be taking this step without any sort of..."

Now he rocked back and regarded me with a look of exasperation. "If it's commitment you're worried about, there isn't any bigger commitment I can make. I literally cannot bond with another person after I bond with you, so you've got me for life. I'd never leave. And as far as the 'love' thing goes, we already talked about that. You know I care about you. You're one of my best friends, I'm crazy-attracted to you, and I really like being with you."

He brought a fingertip up to stroke my cheek. "It doesn't matter if we don't have the whole mythical true-love-soul-mates thing. It's the perfect relationship—mutually beneficial. I'm going to stay with you forever, take care of you, treat you like the treasure you are. *And* if you'll let me... hopefully give you a lot of pleasure. Or at least I will once I get some practice under my belt. I promise to keep trying until I get it right."

He offered a persuasive smile. "I'll be a good bond-mate. I'll make you happy."

Studying his sincere face, I was conflicted. Inside I knew

the only thing that could make me completely happy was also completely impossible—having Nic back.

But maybe I could have happiness-light. Maybe a friendship-with-benefits-for-life with Anders would be the next best thing. He certainly seemed to want it. Enough to make an eternally-binding decision here and now. I couldn't help but be flattered.

"And you're *sure* it's going to be enough for you?"

"I am sure. You're the one who keeps making excuses. The question is—are *you* sure?"

I hesitated, but then I said, "Yeah. I think so." When he tried to draw me against his body again, I added hastily, "But I *do* want to use a condom. You never know about that baby thing."

He grinned ruefully, letting his chin drop to his chest. And then he chuckled. "Okay, you win." After a second, he rolled from the bed and re-adjusted his clothes, grabbing his wallet from the TV stand.

"Wait—are you leaving? Where are you going?" Had I hurt his feelings? Made him angry? The thought freaked me out—he was my best and only friend these days.

He extended a hand as if to help me out of bed. "To find a drugstore. And you're coming with me."

I took his hand and let him pull me up. "Why?"

"Let's call it a… test. Something to make sure you actually want to do this thing. If we get to the drugstore to the 'family planning' aisle and you can't pull the trigger on buying condoms, then I'll have my answer."

In the elevator on the way to the lobby, I thought about what Anders had said. It was a good test. And it was extremely understanding and honorable of him to suggest it. A lot of guys would've dashed from the room and come back with condoms as quickly as possible, purposely *not* giving me time to re-consider. He really did care about me. Maybe that was more important in a life partner than actually being "in love?"

I turned to him as the car descended. "You know what?"

"What?"

"You're a really good guy."

He broke into a surprised smile. "Thanks."

"No, I mean it. And what I said in New Orleans—I actually meant it. You are pretty perfect."

His eyes warmed with genuine happiness. That made me feel good. I stretched my arms up around his neck and looked him directly in the eye, standing on my tiptoes to get closer to my target. "Any girl would consider herself very lucky to be with you, Anders. *I'm* lucky."

He dipped his head down to position his mouth right over mine, not touching but hovering just out of reach. "No," he whispered. "I'm the lucky one, remember?"

And then our lips met in a sweet, warm, very "mutually beneficial" kiss. We pulled apart as the elevator doors opened. I hadn't even realized we'd reached the lobby. Still looking into Anders' eyes, I giggled.

He grinned at me, stretching a hand toward the control panel. "Want me to push the button for the top floor?"

Laughing, I raised a brow suggestively. "No. I have a *test* to ace—come on. Let's go shopping."

"You don't have to ask me twice. After you, my lady."

I turned to get off the elevator and stutter-stepped, my heart shrinking to atom-size then expanding to the point of bursting within the space of a half-second. There was a man there—standing in front of the bench opposite the elevator banks, and he... he...

My legs re-discovering their ability to function, I ran into the small lobby, turning one direction and then another. He was gone.

Anders followed close on my heels. "What is it? Did you

see someone from the Ancient Court?" He gripped my shoulders, turning me to face him. "Macy—what is it?"

"Did you see that guy?" I sounded asthmatic.

"What guy?"

"There was a guy—outside the elevator. He... I don't know."

Anders looked perturbed. "I didn't see anyone. Did he get on one of the other elevators? What did he look like?"

Nic. That's what he looked like. After this past year of feeling like he was with me everywhere I went, now I was actually *seeing* his ghost. I couldn't say that to Anders, though.

"Well?" he demanded, his expression on high alert for danger. "Was he Elven? Could you tell?"

"I..." I shook my head. "Yes. I think so. He was very tall, (like Nic) dark-haired, (like Nic) with a tanned, olive complexion." *Like Nic's.* "And he had a beard."

Anders seemed to relax a fraction. "Oh. Well, Elves don't typically wear facial hair. Maybe it was another hotel guest. He probably got onto one of the other elevators as we got off ours."

I craned my neck back toward the bank of elevators, searching the closed doors for answers. I was starting to feel dizzy. My stomach turned in a nauseating flip.

"Maybe. I guess so."

That made sense. But why was my heart burning like a bucket of acid had been poured directly into my chest cavity? Why had my brain nearly exploded when my eyes had connected for a split-second with that dark, intense gaze?

I closed my eyes and breathed, dismay creeping in and replacing the adrenaline that had flooded my veins. I was still so messed up.

I'm not over him. Not at all.

How could I do this with Anders—go on this "shopping

excursion" when the mere glimpse of a man who resembled Nic was enough to throw my entire body and mind into a frenzy?

"Macy—are you okay?" Anders sounded truly concerned now. Not that there was any danger here in the lobby—he'd obviously ruled that out—but that there was a problem with *me*—inside of me. He was right.

"I'm fine. No, actually, I'm not. Listen, I think I *am* too tired to go out right now. Or maybe I'm sick or something. Can I get a re-take on the test maybe?"

His brow creased. "Of course. Don't even worry about that. Come on, let's go back up. All you need is a good night's sleep—*without* some idiot waking you up and pouring money on you and trying to seduce you in the wee hours of the morning." He gave a self-deprecating laugh. "I should be shot."

"No, Anders, it's not you," I protested as he led me back onto a waiting elevator. "It's me."

Now his laugh was a bit more pronounced. "That's usually *my* line. Come here."

He drew me against his side, wrapping a comforting arm around my shoulders. Feeling drained, I rested my head on his chest. "You're not mad?"

"Of course not," he said, and his tone told me he meant it. "Above all else, Macy, I am your friend. Whatever's wrong we'll fix it."

"My friend," I repeated. He *was* my friend. And I believed he sincerely wanted to help. Unfortunately, what was wrong with me, no one could ever fix.

13

NIC

I staggered down the walkway and through the blinking, blaring machines past the blackjack tables, bumping into people without apologizing, fighting to stay on my feet and not collapse, trying to reach the back entrance of the casino without actually knowing how to get there.

It's too late.

At long last I'd found Macy. And it was too late.

When the elevator doors had first opened, I'd forced my bleary eyes upward to do a perfunctory check of its occupants, not really expecting anything after doing this very thing hundreds of times today with no results.

It *was* a couple—a tall guy and a short girl—but the wrong one. This girl had platinum hair and the guy was dark-headed. They were kissing. Happy. In love. *Lucky bastards.*

But then the girl had giggled, and I'd recognized the voice in an instant. Bolting to my feet, I'd stared, cataloguing everything about her to be certain. And then she'd turned to face me. For a split second I'd seen her eyes. *Those eyes.* The eyes I'd dreamed of nightly, desperate to see them once more, desperate to see myself in them. A silent scream had ricocheted through my body, bouncing off my bones and shredding my organs.

The next thing I knew my feet were moving. Nox had been right. It *was* too late. Macy had moved on and fallen in love with someone else. A moan built in my chest, demanding I let it out, pounding at the insides of my head and pressing against my eardrums. Reaching the casino exit I burst through the doors to the sidewalk and shouted. Actually, it might have been more of a roar. I couldn't hold it in. The emotions roiling inside me were two powerful, too violent to contain.

People moved away from me on the sidewalk. The crowd was not thick this early in the morning, but there were still pedestrians about. They gave me plenty of space and some wide-eyed looks.

"He's insane," one woman muttered to her boyfriend.

I didn't argue, and I didn't take insult. She was right. I *was* insane—with grief. With loss. With a sense of disappointment so dense it felt like a heavy metal beam trying to crush me into the cement. Lowering my head, I ran down the sidewalk, away from the observers.

Away. I had to get away.

I ran until I reached the end of the Strip and stood staring at the entrance to the Stratosphere tower. Tipping my head back, I looked up and fought to catch my breath. From this close angle, I couldn't see its famous needle-like top. A nearby sign proclaimed it the tallest structure in Las Vegas and the highest free-standing observation tower in the U.S. It also advertised the Air Bar, the highest bar in the city.

Yes. That's what I need.

In my current state I wasn't sure which I needed more—the "air" part—or the bar. I stepped inside, vaguely conscious of my wild appearance. My hair was windblown from running the two miles here, I was soaked with sweat, my suit was no doubt ruined, and who knew what my eyes looked like. I knew what they felt like. They felt like they were holding back a body of saline worthy of the Hoover Dam.

I've lost her.

That's all I could think, the words repeating again and again as I rode the elevator to the top. When I reached it, I found the Air Bar and outdoor observation deck both had closed at two. I laughed quietly to myself. It was probably for the best that I be nowhere near a tower ledge at this moment. The enclosed Sky Lounge was still open, though, and that's where I went.

It was actually quite busy. The interior was dark and noisy with the sounds of pounding dance music and people talking, and laughing, and dancing. New York was apparently not the only American city that never slept.

Finding an open barstool, I ordered a tequila neat and stared out at the view of the Las Vegas city lights. Macy was down there. *With him.* The pain sliced a new opening in my chest. I wouldn't be surprised to find my cocktail leaking out of it when I took the first sip.

I had been replaced in her heart while I could not even *see* another woman, couldn't tolerate the thought of being with someone else. I had known it was a possibility, but I'd been unable to predict how this moment would actually feel.

My plan had been to find her then stay nearby and protect her, whether she still wanted my love or not. But now... did she even *need* my protection? She'd survived on her own for a year, and she had Anders. I supposed I could be a sort of Phantom of the Opera figure, staying in the shadows and watching her love another guy, waiting and wishing for a change in her situation. But it wasn't even like Anders was human and would eventually die. He was Elven as well. They'd have eternity together, while I spent eternity —alone.

"You look like you lost your best friend," a soft female voice said.

I jumped a little, becoming aware that someone had taken the stool beside mine at the bar. "Oh. Yes. It's been a... rather bad night."

"Oh no," she cooed, resting a beautifully manicured hand on my forearm. "Did you lose big?"

I nodded. "I have lost *everything*."

"Poor guy." The hand on my arm rubbed in time to her soothing words. "Not *everything*. You're still the hottest guy I've seen all night, so that's something. And you sound like you're foreign, too. Italian?"

"French," I corrected, though she was partly right. I didn't have the energy to explain.

The rubbing increased and moved from my arm down to my thigh. "I *love* an accent," the woman informed me.

Shifting to move my leg away from her, I said, "I'm with— I'm bond—" And there I stopped. I *wasn't* with someone. I wasn't bonded to someone. Well, I was, but she wasn't bonded to me, so it didn't matter. I wasn't engaged or married or any of those things that kept men in committed relationships from accepting invitations like the one this woman was clearly extending to me.

I lifted my eyes from my glass to look at her. She was attractive, honey blonde, looked to be in her mid-twenties. She looked tired. I didn't try to use my glamour on her but my guard was down thanks to the alcohol and mental stress, not to mention physical exhaustion. The deepest desire of this woman's heart was to find a good man for a long-lasting relationship.

I inhaled. Exhaled. "You're looking in the wrong place."

Her head snapped back, causing her dangly earrings to swing back and forth. "What?"

"For a relationship, for commitment."

She sat up straight, an offended frown replacing the seductive pout she'd worn at first. "I don't know what you're talking about. I only want to have some fun."

I shook my head. "No. You want a long-term relationship with a man who'll love you and treat you well. You're lonely and tired of waiting, and you hoped by coming here tonight and wearing that skimpy dress and offering someone your body for the night you might be able to fast-track it and find what you've been longing for. But it hasn't happened yet. Now it's nearly four am, closing time, and you're becoming desperate. But it's not going to work. There is no fast-track. Even if you find someone to go home with, you're only going to wind up hurt and disappointed."

She slid off the stool in a furious movement and picked up her half-full drink, tossing its contents in my face. Hers was red and shaking.

"You're a jerk! What—do you think you're psychic or something? You don't know anything about me. Weirdo." She spun and stalked away.

The bartender handed me a stack of napkins to dry off with, the bored expression on his face never changing. "It always gets crazy around closing time," he told me. "You want one more before last call?"

I shook my head with a wave and slid from the stool, pulling a few bills from my wallet and laying them on the counter. "Thanks," I said.

"Yeah." Then he saw my ridiculous overpayment. "Oh—wow. Thank *you*. You have a good night. Listen, it's gonna get better," he added. "This is Vegas. Your luck could change at any time."

I nodded and shuffled toward the door. He was a nice guy. He meant well. He was wrong. I had been dealt the worst hand of all time. To find the love of your life and have her ripped from you before you could ever really begin your lives together was worse than never having found love at all. And now it would never happen. For all practical purposes, my life was over.

Making my way to the elevator, I noticed something unusual. One of the glass doors to the observation deck was open a crack. Something small was propped at the bottom of it, holding it slightly ajar. Either a staff member had gone out to clean up from the night's revelries or someone had found a way to bypass the two a.m. closing time. Maybe someone had put the object there earlier, planning to return for an after-hours private rendezvous out on the deck.

The opening called to me like a siren song. Slowly, I walked to it, put my hand on the cool glass. A faint whistle of wind passed through the gap, and the night air smelled fresh and alluring. Grasping the handle, I opened the door and stepped outside.

Though it had been scorching during the daytime, it was quite cool out here—maybe because of the elevation—maybe because we were in the desert. I didn't know, but it felt good. I roamed farther onto the deck, past the sleek leather lounge furniture and art deco cocktail tables toward the white metal railing at the edge of it.

The Strip lay below, its lights twinkling quietly. Its usual noises were tempered at this height. A faint light was beginning to show in the sky. Sunrise. The beginning of the first day of the rest of my eternity without Macy. I grasped the metal railing, gripping it hard, my muscles shaking with tension.

How am I supposed to do this? How will I live without her?

Truth be told, I didn't want to. There was a second railing outside of this one, no doubt to protect tower visitors from falling to their deaths. Or to deter people who were having thoughts like the ones I was having at the moment.

I didn't *want* to die. I wanted to live. With Macy. But that was impossible, and I truly didn't know what the next step was. Dropping my chin to my chest, I finally allowed myself to cry.

I didn't even speak to her.

All my fantasies of revealing myself to her, seeing the light and the love that would flood her eyes when she saw my face for the first time—they would never come true. The tears came fast and furious, blowing across my cheeks in cool, wet tracks. My chest heaved with deep sobs.

When my phone rang, I almost didn't pull it from my pocket. There was nothing anyone could say to make me feel better. There was no one I wanted to speak to, even if I had been in any condition to have a conversation.

But knowing Estelle was here in the city and that there *was* the possibility of another Ancient Court hunter team here as well, I answered.

"Hello?" my voice croaked.

"Nic? Nicolo, what is wrong?" my sister demanded.

"Nothing. What do you want?"

"Where are you? I checked the lobby, and you were gone."

"I'm fine. I'm... at another hotel."

"Well get back here as quickly as you can. I've found Macy's room number, and I have something very important to tell you."

I shook my head, unable to stop a new sob from cracking my voice. "It doesn't matter anymore. It's too late."

"It's not too late. There is a way to stop the plague and save the humans. But we must get to Macy—*soon*. She is the key to everything."

Swiping away what remained of my tears, I took in a new breath, my heart rate picking up, and my mind coming to full alertness. "What are you talking about?"

"I've gotten some new information. I've found out why it's so important to Alessia to find Macy."

"I already know why—she's furious with me over the broken betrothal and wants to punish me and experiment on her."

"No, you *don't* know. There's much more to it than that. Now get back to our room—or tell me where you are so I can come and get you. There is no time to waste."

I pulled my phone away from my ear and looked at it in astonishment. "I'm on my way."

1 4

NIC

W hen I barreled through the door of our suite, my sister waited on the other side, ready to explain to me how she'd wheedled Macy's room number from the hotel staff.

After speaking to her contact back in Italy earlier, she'd paid another visit to our friend Lorenzo last night. Turned out, he had spotted Macy and Anders together, and still under the influence of her Sway from earlier, he'd asked one of his co-workers in reception about them. Being a music fan —and a woman—the desk agent had recognized and remembered Anders.

She'd told Lorenzo the false name the famous musician had given when checking in—Tolkien. It had taken an additional dose of Sway and the promise of a date tomorrow, but Lorenzo had given Estelle the information. Too bad for him we'd be long gone by tomorrow. *Sorry Lorenzo, buddy.*

My sister insisted I shower and eat something before we went to drop the bomb—series of bombs, actually—on Macy and Anders.

"You look horrible. As far as I know, you haven't eaten in

the past twenty-four hours. You're going to faint before you even see her. And you *will* shave," she added. "It's the first time your bond-mate will see your face in more than a year. She should *see* your face. If she turns out to be a fan of facial hair, you can grow it back."

Weak with shock from the news she'd given me, and yes, with hunger, too, I obeyed. Twenty minutes later I was showered, dressed in clean clothes, freshly shaved, and about to see Macy, for better or worse.

My stomach boiled with nerves as Estelle and I stood side by side in the elevator on our way down to their suite. After the things she'd told me, there was no choice anymore. We *had* to make contact. If Macy had no interest in seeing me, it didn't matter. We'd have to find a way to work together for at least a short while until we accomplished what needed to be done.

The elevator opened. We stepped out and consulted the sign on the wall to see which way to turn for Macy's room number. As we took a left, Estelle reached for my hand and squeezed it.

"You will be all right," she said. "No matter what. I am here for you."

I nodded, too nervous to speak. When we reached the door, the two of us stood in front of it for a long moment, neither one reaching up to knock.

Estelle looked at me, "Are you ready?"

I nodded and squeezed my eyes tightly shut, focusing on breathing. I felt like I might pass out.

"You do it," I said. My hands were shaking so hard I feared the rap of my knuckles would sound like a woodpecker at the door.

She knocked. It was only about six a.m., so it was likely they were still sleeping. But within a few moments, a male voice answered from inside.

"Who are you? What do you want?" Anders demanded, obviously seeing Estelle's face through the fish-eye lens of the peephole.

There was murmuring on the other side of the door. I assumed he was informing Macy there was a woman outside, and they were debating whether the Ancient Court would send a female hunter.

"I am Estelle Buonoccorsi, Nicolo's twin," she answered. "I'm a friend—an ally. I'm here to help, and I bring news of great importance."

More murmurs. Then, Anders said, "How do I know I can trust you?"

If Macy had spoken, it wasn't loudly enough for me to hear her voice. I felt like I might explode if the door between us didn't open soon.

Estelle turned to me. "What do I say? He's not going to open the door."

"Tell them the first time I kissed Macy was just after I'd given her poppies… and made her cry," I whispered. "No one knows about that but the two of us."

She nodded. "Nicolo and I have always been completely loyal to one another. He told me about Macy. He told me about their first kiss. He'd given her poppies, and she cried." She paused. "You must believe me. I would never do anything to harm the girl my brother loved."

We waited for what felt like fifteen minutes before the deadbolt lock clicked. The door opened. Anders large frame filled the doorway, blocking my view into the room. As I'd realized after my initial moments of confusion seeing them in the elevator, he'd dyed his hair dark.

For long moments he stayed in place, his eyes on Estelle, never veering toward me. Though he hadn't seemed to even notice me standing behind her, he still looked like he'd seen a ghost. He stared at my sister in utter wonderment. His jaw actually dropped.

And then he stepped backward. Staggered backward would be more accurate, actually. He said absolutely nothing.

Estelle moved into the room, and I followed. At first I thought Macy wasn't there. And then I spotted her. She was on the bed, under the covers up to her chin, sitting against the headboard with her knees scrunched up to her chest—a small person trying to make herself even smaller.

No longer conscious of where my sister and Anders were or what they were doing, I moved deliberately toward Macy, my gaze locked with hers. As I got closer, I saw she was trembling, and her wide dark eyes had filled with tears. My eyes were wet, too, forcing me to blink repeatedly to clear them. I couldn't let anything blur this much-longed-for vision of her.

When I reached the bedside, my mouth opened, but no sound came out. What did you say to the girl you loved who believed you to be dead?

I'm not a ghost? No, you're not crazy? Please don't scream or pass out?

Finally, I uttered the only word I could force from my tightly constricted throat. "Macy."

Her stricken eyes widened, and her body quivered. She drew in a large, loud breath, as if she hadn't actually inhaled during the past few minutes and was desperate for oxygen. Very slowly, she reached toward me with a shaking hand.

"Nic?" The whisper was followed by a sob. "Am I dreaming?"

I clasped my hand around hers, and my eyes closed momentarily. The physical contact was almost too wonderful. Her soft skin, the tiny, delicate fingers wrapped in mine, the slight coolness in contrast to my heat. All of it was the stuff of my own dreams.

Opening my eyes again, I pulled her hand to my chest and pressed her palm to my rapidly beating heart, seeking to calm her obvious fear. "No. It's me. I'm here, piccola. I have come back to you."

Suddenly she burst into tears and wracking sobs. I dropped to the bed beside her and pulled her to me, wrapping my arms around her shaking shoulders and back and holding her head to my chest, rocking her the way one might a distraught child.

"What is happening?" she pleaded between sobs. She lifted her head to look at my face, reaching up to touch it. "They... told me you were dead."

I shook my head, smiling down into her streaming eyes. "No. No, I was only sleeping. Dr. Schmitt sedated me, and I was unable to move, unable to speak... unable to get to you."

"When—how long—how did you—"

She couldn't seem to finish a question, all of her tangled thoughts rushing through her brain faster than her tongue could convey them.

"I woke about eight weeks ago. Dr. Schmitt had come to kill me and taunt me by threatening you. Instead, I survived, and he is dead."

"Oh, Nic," she said, fighting a new round of sobs. "I knew it. I knew it all along. I could *feel* that you were still alive, but I convinced myself it was my imagination." She dropped her forehead to my chest again and wept. "I gave up on you. I should have been trying to help you, trying to free you from Dr. Schmitt."

Petting the back of her head, I lowered my mouth and spoke into her hair. "No. No, don't say that. You could not have known. And that castle was the last place in the world I wanted you. There was too much danger for you there, piccola."

"I don't care," she wailed. "I should have done something."

Grasping her shoulders, I set her back slightly so I could look into her eyes. "There was nothing you could have done for me. But you *can* do something for your people—for the humans, I mean. That is why Estelle and I are here."

For the first time since entering the room, I glanced back at my sister. She stood watching us, as did Anders. Also for the first time, I realized how inappropriate it was of me to be holding and touching his girlfriend like this. I was shocked he hadn't intervened or protested. Had I been in his position, I wouldn't have been able to stop myself. Perhaps he was in shock. He had just now learned of my "return from the dead" as well.

Trying to be mindful of their relationship, I let go of Macy and shifted back a bit, allowing some space between us. The absence of her skin against mine left me cold and hungry.

She stared at me in bewilderment. "What do you mean? *What* is why you're here?"

I drew in a breath before beginning. It was a lot to lay on a person, especially one who'd recently endured a shock. But as Estelle had explained to me earlier, there was no time to waste.

I wanted desperately to take her hands in mine, but I forced myself to ignore the urge.

"Macy… there are some things I must tell you. They are going to be surprising, perhaps even frightening. But please try to remember you're not alone. Estelle and I will do everything in our power to help you. And you have…" I glanced back at the concerned face of her boyfriend. "…you have Anders."

"What is going on, Nic?"

"There is so much to say. I guess I should start with this—you are not human."

"What?" She gasped, understandably stunned.

143

Anders moved for the first time since seeing Estelle and me. He stepped closer to me and Macy. "What are you talking about?"

As considerate as I wanted to be of their new relationship, I did not address him when I answered. Macy was my main concern. And I still felt like he had taken something away from me, though the rational part of me understood he had not meant to do me any wrong. You couldn't cuckold a dead man after all.

I'd vowed to be polite to him, but I might not be able to manage more than that. Besides, this information was primarily about her, and she was the one whose help the human race needed.

I kept my eyes trained on hers. "You are not human, Macy. Dr. Schmitt ran tests on your blood. You are a nymph. It is one hundred percent certain. I remember you telling me you were adopted. You were raised by humans, but your birth mother was undoubtedly a nymph. Your father, too. There is no human DNA in your body."

MACY

I couldn't respond, only shake my head slowly side to side, my mouth opening to speak then closing again as no words formed.

I still wasn't convinced this wasn't all a dream. When the knock at the door had woken us, Anders and I had assumed the worst—the Ancient Court had found us, and we were trapped, twenty-four floors above the ground in a room where the windows didn't even open.

It was only when Estelle had mentioned that first life-altering kiss with Nic that I'd motioned for him to unlock the door. He didn't like the idea, but he'd thrown on a shirt and done it anyway while I'd shrunk into the bed, bracing myself to see the face of Nic's twin and the inevitable pain that would cause.

But when she'd stepped to the side and Nic had entered the room, all anticipation, all fear, every thought had flown from my mind, the empty space filling with heart-stopping shock.

For a split second I'd thought that perhaps Estelle was an Ancient Court agent and had shot me or done something else to end my life instantaneously because it was the only way my mind could explain the sight of him before me—so real, so physical—so beautiful. Not like the hazy memories I held of his face and beautiful form. I was in the afterlife, and paradise was being with him again.

But then, no. He *wasn't* a spirit. His sparkling dark eyes, his thick, unruly hair, his tan, touchable skin, the thick muscle of his body—even the delicious scent of him—it was all undeniably corporeal.

Only in my dreams where I was once again able to touch him and hold him were my memories of Nic this vivid and tangible. So that was where my mind went next. I was dreaming. The entire sequence of events from the knock on the door to Nic approaching the bedside were part of a sweet, torturous dream that would wake me crying and haunt me for days to come.

And then he'd spoken—said my name. His voice, so lovingly remembered and desperately longed for all these months, was the sweetest sound I'd ever heard.

And when he touched me, it was like epinephrine had entered my body at the sight where skin met skin. The adrenaline flooded from that point throughout my bloodstream, waking me fully, bringing me back to life when I hadn't even realized I'd been a walking, talking dead person all this time.

That new life was accompanied by such a flurry of emotions I wasn't sure my heart would ever stop racing. Perhaps it would adopt this Elven-like speed as its own, and my pulse would finally be a match for Nic's.

But now Nic was saying things that had me re-examining the dream thing. A nymph? I didn't even know what that was.

"Nymphs are extinct." Anders voice sounded dazed and

very far away. I couldn't see him, unable to pry my gaze from Nic's face in front of me.

Estelle was the one to respond to him. "That's what everyone believed. But the test results are irrefutable. And we've already seen proof beyond that. Nic should have died the morning you and your bandmates left the castle and rescued Macy. Her blood saved his life."

Her words snapped me out of my stupor. Still sitting close to Nic, I grasped his wrist. "What? What happened to you? I thought you said the doctor sedated you?"

He looked down at my hand on his arm and swallowed. "Yes. He did. But first I tried to overtake him. I was determined not to let him use me in his plan to impregnate the fan pod girls. We struggled, but he overpowered me. As he was about to inject me, I attempted to take my own life."

"No." My hand covered my mouth in horror. The thought of Nic killing himself to protect Olly and the other girls ripped my heart out.

"I saw no other choice," he explained. "I had discovered some glass vials in his clinic, and I broke them with my teeth, swallowed the broken glass. It should have killed me, but... well... the vials were filled with your blood. Instead of dying... I healed instantly."

"Whoa," Anders said on a long exhale. "So the legends are true, then. Nymph blood heals."

"Yes," Estelle said. "And not only that... I have learned today it may also *prevent* disease—as in the Plague. That's the reason Alessia is so determined to find Macy. Dr. Schmitt was terrified her blood could be used to make a vaccine or an antidote against his terrible creation. That's why we had to make contact with you."

Had to. She'd said, "... *had* to make contact."

I looked away from Estelle and back to Nic's sorrowful

eyes, trying to make sense of it all. "That's the... only... reason?" I asked.

Had he not wanted to see me again, then? Had he not even planned to tell me he was still alive until Estelle had gotten this information?

He didn't answer, just stared at me with that haunted look.

"Were you... were you there last night, outside the elevator?" I asked him, barely able to breathe. "Did I see you? Did you see me... and then *leave?*"

The thought was crushing. If he could see me after all this time, after all we'd shared, and walk away without even speaking to me, then perhaps I'd been wrong about him. Maybe he *hadn't* felt the same way about me as I'd felt about him. Or maybe the knowledge that I was a nymph—not a human—had changed his feelings for me. Were nymphs disgusting to Elves? I didn't know anything about the Fae lore on this subject, if there even was any.

His face contracted in a pained-looking scowl that answered my question. The bearded man *had* been him. We'd been *that* close to each other, and he'd left without a word.

Estelle came to stand close to us, laying one hand on her brother's shoulder and one on mine. "I am sorry to rush this. I know all of this comes as a shock to you, to say the least, Macy. But we must hurry if we are to prevent a catastrophic loss of human life. Dr. Schmitt infected all of the fan pod girls with the Plague before releasing them to go back to their homes around the world. Alessia has the power to trigger the virus at any time. I believe all she is waiting for is your capture and return, but she may grow weary of waiting and do it even without having you in hand. She is highly unstable."

My head whipped around to face her. "*All* the fan pod

girls are infected? So they're not... or did they already have the babies?"

Now Nic's hand reached to cover mine. It was the first time he'd touched me since our initial contact. "No. No, it didn't work. I have no offspring. Dr. Schmitt did perform the procedures—against my will—but none of the girls were impregnated."

Relief rushed through me like a sudden rain shower. "Oh thank God. So, your glamour isn't what he thought it was then. Or..." I was confused. Dr. Schmitt was supposed to be infallible at detecting physical gifts and maladies in others. How could he have been so wrong about Nic's fertility?

"No," Estelle corrected. "Dr. Schmitt was right—about both of us. Nic's genetic matter was ineffective with the fan pod girls because—"

"Estelle." Nic grabbed his sister's hand, cutting off her explanation. "We will discuss this later. Right now we need to help Macy and Anders pack. We must move quickly if we are to beat Alessia to the punch."

He stood and began searching the room. "Where is your backpack? Anders—do you have luggage?"

Anders blinked at Nic's question. He seemed to be emerging from a fugue state that had swallowed him the minute Nic and Estelle had entered the room. "This is all going a little fast for me. Where exactly are we going? I'm supposed to perform at the Grammy awards in two days. Macy and I were planning to leave for L.A. tomorrow."

"Macy is not going to L.A.," Nic informed him. "She's going to Mississippi—with me."

"Mississippi? What the hell is in Mississippi?" Anders stared at Nic like he'd lost his mind. I was also puzzled. I'd never even visited the state. I was as eager to hear the answer as Anders was.

"Altum. And its healers," Nic said. "Nox says they need to

study her to find out the full extent of her powers. They may even be able to use Macy's blood to make an antidote for the Plague—possibly even replicate its makeup and create a vaccine to prevent new infections."

"I'm surprised the Light Elves are getting this involved," Anders said. "They're not usually interested in the humans."

"Yes, well, apparently the Light King has his reasons. But we need to give the healers there time to work, which means there is no time to waste. Alessia could choose at any time to visit any one of the fan pod girls and use her glamour."

"You mean her musical glamour?" I asked, truly baffled now. "What harm would that do?"

"It's not her only glamour," Nic said. "Not many people know about it, even within the Ancient Court. She has another one. She can make people sick. In fact, it's not even a choice. Unless she avoids physical contact with them, people —and Elves—become ill around her. Whatever damaged or genetically pre-disposed cells are already present in their bodies become activated when she is near. I used to think she was just a cold, standoffish person—until I read her deepest desire—to be rid of her glamour."

"Wow." Anders let out a low whistle. "That sucks. Can you imagine? You could never even kiss someone, or hold hands for very long. It's so lonely."

"It's also very dangerous," Estelle said. "Nox asked me to bring some blood samples to L.A. as well, so his healer there can work on a cure from a different angle. Would you be willing, Macy, to let me draw some here—this morning before you leave?"

"Wait a minute now." Anders stepped forward, finally acting like himself again, being the friend and protector he was. "I'm not sure about letting people 'study' Macy and take her blood."

Nic bristled at his tone, his body going rigid and his eyes

hard. "I would *never* let anyone harm Macy in any way. Your *king* assures me we can trust these healers. He knows them well and has given me his vow that Macy will not only be unharmed, she'll experience no pain. And in Altum she'll be completely safe from any Ancient Court agents who may still be in this country hunting her. "

The creases of concern on Anders' forehead softened a bit. "Well, all right then, if Nox vouches for them. I guess I'll… I guess I can tell him to find another keyboard player to fill in for me at the Grammys."

Now it was my turn to speak. I slid from the bed and went to stand in front of Anders. "No. You *have* to go to L.A. You guys are nominated. You have to perform at the awards, and what if you win? You wrote most of the songs on that album. You're up for Song of the Year. I will *not* let you miss that moment, the experience of being there and being honored in front of all your peers—in front of your *father.*" I gave him a significant glance.

During our time together, we'd discussed our families, our pasts, our disappointments, and hopes and dreams. I knew it was Anders' ultimate dream to win a Grammy *and* an Oscar, something even his multi-awarded father had not achieved. He sometimes still wrangled with feelings of inadequacy, though I'd reassured him repeatedly his musical gifts were as good as—if not better than—musical glamour. In my opinion this awards ceremony was critical for him. That was why I'd agreed to woman-up and drag my country mouse self there to support him. Now I had no choice but to miss the event, but there was no way I'd let him pass it up.

"I know. But… how can I go without you?" he asked, looking torn.

"Estelle can go with you. Right?" I turned to her. "Didn't you say you have to go to L.A. anyway? You guys can travel together, and she can be your date and your cheering section in my place. I'll bet she actually even has something appropriate to wear for that kind of thing. I was going to have to go shopping—which you know I hate."

His eyes went from mine to Estelle's, giving her a questioning look. Her surprised face morphed into a smile.

"I do, actually. I always pack too much, because, you never know. And well, with modeling and everything, I'm given a lot of designer samples." She shrugged.

Now Anders' eyes glinted with something that resembled satisfaction. "I *thought* that was you."

Her eyes went wide, and her smile even wider. "You recognized me?"

He gave a wry chuckle and looked away, clearly abashed. "Yeah. But *don't* ask me how—please."

ANDERS

I t took me a full ten minutes to recover from the staggering vision that greeted me when I'd opened the hotel room door. Not Nic-back-from-the-dead. I hadn't even seen him at first.

No, what had me reeling was coming face to face with the real-life version of the girl whose photos I collected like a middle-school fanboy.

Known simply as "Estelle" in her modeling career, her last name was not available in any of her online profiles—I knew because I'd looked. Before this assignment to protect Macy had come up, I'd been entertaining the idea of having my agent contact hers and trying to set up a meeting or something. Yeah, I was *that* pathetic when it came to my cyberstalking of this woman.

But of course I'd put that aside, and rightly so, when I'd started traveling with Macy. It had been a silly idea anyway. Nothing ever came of those celebrity setups. And Macy was a *real* girl—someone I could relate to and be friends with— not some goddess who was drooled over by men around the world and who probably wouldn't give me the time of day or even recognize my name when my agent called.

Even more shocking than the flesh-and-blood sight of her—which far exceeded her photographs, by the way—was what I'd *heard* when she'd stepped into the room.

Music.

Not a few notes.

Not a riff of melody or a jingle or even a song.

A symphony.

I'd heard a freaking *symphony*—full-blown, note-by-note, completely composed in my head as if an angel had unzipped the top of my skull and dropped the whole thing in there.

It's real.

That was the only coherent thought I'd been able to form. That whole cockamamie story my father had told me about the moment he'd met Mom had not been a crock after all.

And now, apparently, we were traveling to L.A. together today, and she was going to be my *date* for the Grammys. I wasn't sure whether to pinch myself or run around giving everyone hi-fives. Probably neither if I didn't want to look like a complete idiot.

Estelle saved me from having to react by laughing. Oh God, she even had a great laugh. Inside my head, the symphony played louder. I was going to have to get out my music writing pad and get this down soon, or I wouldn't be able to hear anyone over the masterpiece playing between my ears.

Estelle laughed again. "It's so funny that you recognize me from my modeling work, because I am one of your biggest fans."

"What?" My voice sounded choked, like I barely had enough air in my lungs to respond. Because I didn't.

"I love your music. I have been to some of your shows—

when you played in L.A. while I was working there, and in Paris as well. I have your Hidden albums and your jazz one as well."

I did a double-take, feeling my eyes bulge from my head. Either I was suffering from shock, or someone had slipped me a roofie downstairs in the casino in order to steal all my chips and I was in a deep hallucinatory state, because this was *not* actually happening. *No one* knew about that solo album. Well, not many people, anyway.

I'd done it on the side, produced and released it myself, and not even bothered to promote it because it was such a departure from my work with The Hidden. And here my dream girl was telling me she had heard it—that she owned it?

"I love that song, 'Midnight Masquerade,'" she continued. "Oh, and 'Last Night is This Morning'—that one gives me the *feels* like you would not *believe.*"

Oh. My. God.

I was starting to think I was going to have to excuse myself and go to another room or maybe jump in the rooftop pool to regain control of myself. Something *I* did had given this *goddess* the "feels."

"Oh," I managed to force words from a throat that seemed to have shrunk to the diameter of a toothpick. "That's... good to hear."

She blushed. *Even prettier now. Great, I really* am *going to have to excuse myself.*

"Forgive me for gushing. I know I am embarrassing myself, but I am such a fan. I even subscribed to your You Tube channel so I'd never miss any of the acoustic versions you post there."

Okay, that does it.

"Um... could you excuse me? I need to... I'll be right

back." I spun and fled from the room, speed-walking down the hall until I reached the door to the stairwell. Once inside it, I ran up and down several flights of stairs and then I let it all out in a stream-of-consciousness rant that exploded from my lungs.

"Oh my God Oh my God Oh my God this is happening—freaking *Estelle* knows who I am and likes my music—no—loves my music—and I gave her the feels—and she's watched my acoustic videos—and she's going with me to the Grammy awards—and I am *not* dreaming or on mind-altering drugs—and I heard a freaking *symphony*."

Running out of breath, I bent forward and rested my hands on my knees, hanging my head as my pounding pulse finally began to slow.

"And now," I added, "she thinks I'm a lunatic because I ran out of the room in the middle of a conversation."

I hadn't been able to help it. It was either that or lose my shit right there in front of her, which was probably worse. Maybe. I didn't know. Running away was pretty freaking bad, too.

Macy was right.

Dad had been right, and Mom was right, and Macy was right. What if the two of us had bonded last night, and then I'd met Estelle this morning? Would it have felt the same? I didn't know, but I had never felt anything close to this with any girl—hadn't believed it was even possible.

Now that I'd experienced it, I wanted to feel this way every day for the rest of my life. No drug could ever be as exhilarating and addictive as being in Estelle's presence. Standing up straight again, I drew in a deep breath and let it out.

"Okay then. Time to go back and act like a normal, *sane* person and get packed and ready to head back to Los Angeles. For the Grammys. With Estelle the supermodel."

I leapt up and touched the ceiling of the stairwell with my fingertips, letting out one more whoop before jogging back downstairs to our room.

17

MACY

The plane touched down at around two p.m. in a small, private airfield in Oxford, Mississippi, a nice-looking small town near Deep River, where Nox had directed Nic and me to go. Apparently, Altum, the traditional home of the Light Elves in this country, was deep under the earth on the outskirts of the rural main-street community.

Nic had slept for nearly the entire three-hour flight. I tried not to be hurt by that. Estelle had told me he was exhausted, having slept very little during the past few days. But really? It was the first time we'd been alone together in more than a year. So much had happened, and I *really* wanted to talk to him about it all.

It seemed like he should want to talk to me, too. And other than the initial embrace to comfort me when I was crying, he hadn't touched me, hadn't even tried to sit close. I got the distinct impression he was trying to keep his distance from me.

Again, the suspicion that nymphs were somehow distasteful to Elven people crept in. That hurt, too. It wouldn't matter to me if Nic were a troll or a bogeyman or a two-headed cyclops. I'd love him till my dying day no matter what mythical creature he was or wasn't.

And no matter what he'd said to me a year ago or what I *thought* I'd seen in his eyes when we'd first seen each other this morning, now he was acting as if my nearness was some kind of threat to him. Maybe that was it. Were nymphs harmful to his people? Were nymphs and Elves natural enemies?

"Nic," I said as we climbed into the back of a waiting car that the Light King had sent to pick us up. "What are nymphs to Elves? Is there some sort of... bad blood between our races?"

His expression was careful as he finally looked at me. "You could say that. You see... in ancient days, Elves... hunted nymphs."

"Hunted them?"

"Yes. Nymph blood was highly sought after. It was said to have great healing power—which appears to be true—as well as..." he didn't finish.

"As well as what?"

"It's been used to... enhance... male virility." He coughed into his hand and looked away uncomfortably, gazing out the window at the small houses in the neighborhood we passed through as he continued. "As you may know, there is a highly sexual connotation associated with the word 'nymph,' even among humans. That's most likely where it came from. Although you *do* have a particular... allure about you. That is undeniable."

"Oh." The information caused me to sit back and take a breath. I was starting to figure out what was wrong with him, why he was acting so different. "So... you believe the only reason you were attracted to me, then, was my nymph-ness. You don't think your feelings for me were real."

He jerked back around to face me. "What? Where on earth did you get *that* idea?"

"Well… it's been over a year since we've seen each other. The last time we were together you said you loved me. And when you showed up this morning and said you'd been searching for me, I thought it was because… but then you said the only reason you came to find me was so I could help stop the Plague, and you're acting so distant, and you don't seem to want me to touch you. I figured that maybe Elves think nymphs are gross or something. But I guess it's more that you feel like you were tricked into liking me by some nymph blood-chemistry thing."

For a long moment he just stared at me. Then his head started shaking slowly back and forth, a small, sad smile bending his lips.

"How your little brain works, I will never understand. No, Macy—I did not feel *tricked*. And the possibility of a plague cure was not the only reason I came looking for you. It wasn't even the primary reason. I've been… keeping my distance today because I don't want to overstep bounds."

"What? What bounds?"

"You buried me in your mind a year ago. Since then you've created a new life for yourself. I don't want to interfere or cause you problems."

"Interfere? How can you possibly think like that? *You're* the one with the indecipherable brain." I reached out and touched his hand.

A jolt passed through his entire body. But instead of pushing my fingers away in repulsion, he grasped them inside his and squeezed.

"Nox tells me Anders is a good person. And he is Elven. Which means the two of you could have an eternal future together, as nymphs are also immortal Fae."

Now the thunderbolt passed through *my* body. "They *are*? I mean, I am?"

"You are. And if you and he have bonded, I would not try to—"

"Stop right there." I cut off Nic's sentence, touching a fingertip to his mouth, not wanting him to think for one more minute that I'd bonded with Anders.

I was crazy about Anders, and he had been a true friend to me, but the instant I'd seen Nic's face—or rather the instant I'd finally accepted that he was real and not some figment of desperate imagination—I'd sent rocket ships of gratitude to the stars for keeping Anders and me from taking that step together and upgrading our relationship from friendship to something more.

Conscious of the intimacy of the touch, I removed my finger from Nic's lips before explaining my interruption. "Anders and I have not bonded."

His chest rose and fell in an abrupt inhale and exhale. "But you've been traveling together for two months. And there was only one bed in the room."

I nodded. "Yes. *That* room had only one bed—because we were exhausted when we checked in, and they didn't have a double room available. It's the first time in two months we've slept in the same bed. And we *slept*."

Nic looked puzzled. "Does he not like girls, then?"

I laughed. "No. Anders likes girls. A *lot*. He and I are just friends. Well, we thought about taking it beyond that, but neither one of us really wanted to."

He shook his head in denial. "I don't believe that. He must have wanted you."

"Because I'm an irresistible nymph?" I smirked.

"Because you're *you*. Look at you." He reached out to cup my face in his hand. "You are even more beautiful than you were before. Everything about you is… perfect. No man alive could fail to see that."

"Oh Nic." The words were a sigh.

"He cares for you," Nic insisted. "And… I *saw* you kissing."

I let out a breath, wondering how much to tell him. "Yeah. About that. When I believed you were dead, that I'd lost you, it… affected me deeply. I was barely alive myself. I wasn't fit company for anyone, so I went out on my own again. But Nox got information that the Ancient Court was after me and some agents had gotten close in New York City, so he assigned Anders to watch over me. At first I was angry. I didn't want him around. I didn't want *anyone* around. But after getting to know him, we became friends. Good friends. And then…"

"And then you started falling for each other. I understand. He's very… handsome, if you go for that golden god look."

I couldn't help but laugh at his surly pout and his attempts to be a good sport about this.

"Let me finish please." He nodded, and I went on. "And then we had a discussion about whether to take things beyond friendship. Anders thought it was a good idea to go ahead and bond because—"

"I knew it," he snapped.

Silencing him with a warning glance, I continued. "Because he believes himself incapable of love, and he knew I would never feel about anyone the way I felt about you. He said it made sense for the two of us. Knowing that a love match was impossible for both of us, he thought a permanent friendship-with-benefits was the next best thing."

"And you?"

"I considered it," I admitted. "But I kept putting it off. It felt wrong to me, and honestly, Anders feels more like a brother to me than a life partner. Besides, I believe *everyone* is capable of falling madly in love. I think someday he's going to meet a girl who blows his little surfer-boy mind."

"I think someday might have been today," Nic said.

"What?"

"I didn't get a clear picture because I was so focused on you, but Anders had an extreme reaction to meeting my sister. Even a glimpse in his direction revealed it to me."

"Really?" I asked, a swell of delight lifting my heart.

He nodded. "What's especially interesting about that is I read her greatest longing the day before when we were discussing him. She's always wanted to meet him. It actually quite annoyed me when I thought you were in love with him, too. I sort of hated the guy."

"Oh Nic, that's wonderful. I am *so* going to enjoy telling him I-told-you-so." I giggled.

"Then you're not upset about the idea of him reacting to another girl?"

"No. Not at all. I hope something works out between them."

For a few moments he said nothing, then he lifted his gaze to mine. The look in his eyes was guarded. "You said... Anders knew you would never... feel about anyone the way you felt about me."

"That's right." I smiled softly, watching the realization take hold in him. "He knew you were the love of my life. That I'd never fall in love with anyone else—because *no one* could ever compare to you."

"Macy..." His hand enclosed mine. "Is there... a chance you could feel that way about me again? Because nothing has changed for me. I still love you desperately. I came to America to find you—not to help anyone else or save humanity, but to help myself, to save myself. Because I need you, and I love you, and I want you more than ever."

He sat back and blew out a breath, his chest rising and

falling rapidly. "I'm sorry. I didn't mean to say all of that. That's putting a lot of pressure on you."

Unbuckling my seatbelt, I crawled across the seat and into his lap.

"Crazy boy," I murmured affectionately. "I've spent a hundred nights dreaming of you saying those words. I always woke up crying because I knew my dreams would never come true. You've just given me my future—my whole life—back. I've thought about you constantly, taken you with me everywhere I've been for the past year. I want to be with you forever. I love you, Nic. I never stopped loving you."

He stared at me in wonder. "I'm afraid to believe my ears. It's too good to be true."

I smiled slyly. "Use your glamour on me."

Nic took me up on my offer, focusing intently on my eyes. Air burst from his mouth in a gasp of emotion, and he wrapped his arms around me, pulling me tightly to himself, bringing his mouth to mine.

All my senses swelled wth the glorious reality of him, the sweet taste of his mouth, the solid strength of his body beneath me, the enticing and entirely unique scent of his skin.

I inhaled deeply, melting into him, saturated with relief, and happiness, and overwhelming love. My heart wasn't dead. It had just been in a coma while waiting for Nic to emerge from his.

As our lips met for the first time in more than a year, the world slipped back onto its axis and began turning again. And in the place of bleak despair, the future once again held promise.

18

NIC

Our passionate reunion was interrupted by the driver's voice. "We're here."

Feeling like I was coming out of a daze, I raised my head and pulled away from Macy, taking in her soft smile, her loving eyes.

She loves me. Not him. Me.

When I'd accepted her invitation and used my glamour, I'd been overwhelmed by the power of her desire for me. What she'd said was true—*I* was her greatest longing.

It was hard to release her and attend to the business at hand, but there was no choice. We were guests of the Light King. It wouldn't exactly do to send word that we were busy making out in the car and would be there when we were good and ready. Besides, I'd *never* be ready to let her go.

The car had come to a stop in front of a rambling log cabin surrounded by tall pines and numerous other species of trees and underbrush.

"This is Altum?" I had expected the Light Elves' home to be somewhat… grander.

The driver laughed. "No. This is the closest place one can drive a car. We'll get out here and walk the rest of the way."

As we passed the house, a middle-aged couple sitting on the porch lifted their hands to us in greeting. They sat, drinking iced tea and looking wholly unconcerned about the two exceedingly tall men and one very short girl traipsing across their property.

I lifted a hand in return, feeling strange about the intrusion. "Hello... thank you," I said awkwardly then looked away and focused on our guide's back, taking care to follow in his footsteps and make sure Macy didn't step into a hole—or on a snake. This place was rather rustic compared to what I was used to.

I never let go of Macy's hand as we made our way through the dense woods. Every time I glanced at her face, I couldn't stop myself from smiling. And her expression took my breath away. I could only describe it as pure happiness. She was the loveliest thing I'd ever seen.

"What are you grinning about so big over there?" she asked. "It's my hair, isn't it? I know it's weird. I'm going to dye it back to my natural color as soon as possible."

"It's not that. You are beautiful no matter what color your hair is. I'm smiling because of you, piccola. Us. The fact that *my* greatest longing has been satisfied—forever."

She nodded in understanding and squeezed my hand. But a trace of worry creased her brow. "There won't be much of a forever if we don't figure out how to stop the Plague."

"It won't affect you. You will be immune," I assured, addressing the concern that was first and foremost in my mind. "You have never been sick, have you?"

Glancing off to the side then up at the treetops, she said, "No. I guess I haven't. The only times I've ever been treated by a doctor were when I had injuries from gymnastics, and even then I healed quickly. I thought I was just really healthy

—and that my parents were always on the ball about getting me and Lily flu shots and vaccines and stuff."

She took a quick breath and threw me a miserable look. "Oh Nic—my parents. *Lily.* What does it matter that I'm immune if they die, along with all the other innocent humans who'll be wiped out? I have to stop the Plague for them. I don't even want to imagine a world without them."

"I understand, and I agree. That's what we're doing here."

Before meeting Macy, I might not have been all that concerned about the humans who would die without ever being aware of the immortal intrigue behind the scenes. Terrible to admit, but it was true. I had been selfishly wrapped up in my own little miseries. But now—now I understood exactly what was at stake. I was determined to do whatever was necessary to save the humans who were so important to the girl I loved.

"These are the people who can help us." *I hope*, I added internally.

I didn't have much experience with Light Elves, but Nox assured me the Light King was completely trustworthy and had more reason than most Elvenkind to care for the human race. If I hadn't been confident in that, I would never have agreed to bring a nymph into the presence of so many Elves.

After walking for what felt like miles, we came to a stop at the base of the biggest tree I'd ever seen in my life, in a photograph, anywhere. It was a magnolia with a trunk like a grain silo and branches spreading overhead like a giant, fragrant green umbrella.

"This is it," the driver/guide said.

"What is it?" I looked around us.

"You'll see." He gestured for us to follow then squatted and disappeared from view, sliding into a hidden opening in the ground, tucked beneath one of the tree's mighty surface roots.

"Wow," Macy said in a whisper.

"You said it," I whispered back. Loud voices seemed inappropriate as we followed the man down a long, winding tunnel slanting deeper and deeper into the earth.

It was dim but roomy enough for me to walk upright. Macy, of course, had plenty of head room. The earthen walls were studded with some sort of glowing stones—the source of the light we navigated by.

The tunnel ended, and we emerged into a vast, wide-open space. It was an underground cavern like nothing I'd ever seen. It sort of seemed impossible that something like this could stand without caving in.

But when I looked at the ceiling high above, I understood. The whole thing was interwoven tree roots and rock, and interspaced throughout the cavern were mammoth columns stretching from the roof to the stone-and-earth floor. I was filled with admiration for the Elven architects responsible.

Not only had I never seen anything like it, I never could have *imagined* such a place. *This* was worthy of being the headquarters of my people's counterparts in the Light Court on this continent.

I knew little of them, save for the fact they shunned human contact and were the craftsmen among our race. There was evidence of that all around us as we traveled through the underground kingdom toward the royal residence, where the Light King and his bride lived. It was also where we'd be meeting with the Elven healers who would study Macy and try to produce a miracle cure from her blood.

Cave-like openings in the cavern walls revealed men and women hard at work, and a number of huts in the center of the cavern floor housed what appeared to be workshops or perhaps places of business.

Throughout the whole cavern ran a wide, clear river.

Bridges crossed it at regular intervals, and on the far side of it I spotted workers drawing water and carrying it away.

As we made our way down the path, most of the Elves I saw minded their own affairs, but a few looked up and observed our party, showing keen interest.

Glancing from them to Macy, I realized many of the residents here had probably never seen someone so small, except for children of course. She was smaller than the average human, and Elves were much taller and more powerfully built than most humans, so she was a novelty for certain.

Macy noticed the staring as well.

"Don't worry about it," I whispered, bending to her ear. "They don't get out much. The Light Elves don't mix with the rest of the world. They keep to themselves. They also speak mind-to-mind only, so get ready for the silent treatment."

She nodded, clearly fascinated by everything she saw. "I remember you telling me that."

The palace was even more captivating than the rest of the kingdom. Tasteful and obviously very old, it was decorated with elaborately carved art objects and hand-made wall hangings, more glowing colored stones, and tall, heavy doors with intricately carved scenes from ancient Elven life.

A man greeted us inside the great hall. He had wavy, shoulder-length hair and wore leather breeches and a gauzy-looking shirt. He was typically Elven in his build and bone structure but looked quite different from the Dark Elves I'd spent my life around.

While my people adhered to the standards of fashion admired by the human world and "wore our wealth," so to speak, this man looked very primitive and yet elegant at the same time.

He didn't speak aloud, but to me he said, *Welcome to Altum. I am Langnon, personal guard to the king. He is occupied at the moment and will greet you later. I am to escort you to the offices of our healers. Would you follow me please?*

He turned and led us down a corridor, and I filled Macy in on what was happening. "Langnon is taking us to the healer now. We'll meet the Light King later."

She nodded, continuing her perusal of the fantastical surroundings. "The human population of the world would be in complete disbelief if they had *any* idea this place existed. Of course, some scumbag would probably lock up the residents and turn it into a tourist attraction, complete with a 'freak show' of Elves in captivity."

She shivered at the mental image. "I think I'm starting to get why you all protect the secret so closely."

We finally reached our destination, a warmly lit room featuring floor-to-ceiling shelves holding bottles of various sizes and labeled earthenware jars.

Several empty beds stood in a row, covered in crisp, folded-down sheets, ready for anyone who might need the services of a healer. Of course, Elves didn't usually suffer from illness, but I supposed since I'd been injured from time to time in my life, injuries occurred here as well. And perhaps there were some maladies that were exclusive to Light Elves?

Waiting inside the room were not one, but two healers, a middle-aged man, and a guy about my age. He was unique-looking with black hair and brilliant turquoise eyes. If I wasn't mistaken, he wasn't full-Elven but a hybrid of some sort.

"Hi Macy. Hi Nic." He shook each of our hands. "I'm Asher. This is Wickthorne. He is Altum's healer. I'm his apprentice. Like you, I grew up in the human world, so I can relate to the way your head's probably spinning right now, Macy. I remember the first time I saw this place. Don't worry. You'll get used to it pretty quickly."

I liked the guy instantly. He had a nice way about him and a thick Southern accent that was fun to hear.

Macy laughed, visibly relaxing as well. "Yes. It is all a bit overwhelming. And I've had an overwhelming day. Nic and I were reunited after a long separation."

"Yes, I've been informed," the young healer said. "I'm happy you found each other again. And we're happy you're here. There are many people I care about in the human world—my mother and grandfather, for instance—all my friends in town. Many of us here in this kingdom care deeply for the human race and don't want to see it wiped out. We'll do our best to try to stop it."

"Thank you," she said with sincere gratitude.

"I am also grateful," I said. "It shames me that my people created such an agenda and that so many in the Ancient Court seem to support it. I assure you my family and I do not. Not anymore, anyway."

"That's good to hear. There are good people everywhere —even in the darkest places—I've learned that. And we've all made mistakes. It's what we do from this point forward that matters. Speaking of which…"

He turned to listen to the older healer, then back to Macy again. "I know you're tired. We'll take it easy on you today, just take a few blood samples, if you don't mind."

She started pushing up her sleeves. "Whatever you need. I'm used to it by now."

Before he touched her, I reached out and gripped his shoulder lightly. I'd been right about his mixed heritage, but I hoped he could communicate in the Elven way. *Be careful with her. Nothing is more important to me than her safety—not even the human race.*

He gave me a smile of reassurance. *Message received loud and clear, my friend. She's in good hands here.*

I nodded and released him, and he went to work,

inviting Macy to sit on one of the tables then glancing at the bandage on the inside of her left elbow before reaching for her right arm instead. He spoke to her as he applied a band of cloth tightly to her bicep. His tone was calm and relaxing.

"So, I understand you've been doing quite a bit of 'donating' lately—this guy's drop-dead gorgeous sister is transporting some blood samples to L.A., right? My father lives there and serves Nox."

"Yes, but you might be too late to get in on that one," she teased. "Nic's sister Estelle is traveling there with a friend of mine, and he had his eye on her *big-time*."

He laughed. "Oh no—I didn't mean it like that. I'm very happily bonded to the most beautiful girl in the universe."

He glanced between Macy and me. "I recommend it by the way, if you're on the fence because of the whole star-crossed-races thing. I've never been happier, and my being half-human has never been an issue here. I feel completely welcome. Unlike the Ancient Court rulers, you'll find the Light King to be quite open-minded about the issue."

I moved closer to Macy and enveloped her hand in mine. "There is no 'on the fence' here. I jumped off that fence with both feet the moment I saw her face."

"Awwww," she purred and tilted her face up for a kiss.

Completely unable to resist the invitation, I bent and pressed my lips to hers, encountering softness and warmth that drew me deeper and made me want to lift her up and carry her away to some dark corner of this subterranean world, where I could have her all to myself.

"Okay, you two," Asher teased. "Langnon will show you to your rooms shortly—as soon as we're done here."

Finishing with the final blood draw, he pressed his thumb to Macy's arm while Wickthorne removed the tight cloth from her bicep and busied himself with the samples. He hadn't yet engaged us in conversation, keeping to himself on the other side of the office.

"Okay, one more thing before we let you get some rest," the younger man said to Macy. "We need a sample of infected blood before we can begin testing. You spent some time with the other fan pod girls, right? Do you know where to find any of them?"

Infected blood. Of course. They'd need a sample of the virus to create an antidote or vaccine for it.

Olly immediately came to mind. But I knew Macy didn't want to involve her. The Ancient Court had already tapped into her social media accounts and emails, and any further contact between them could make the girl a target. They might even torture her for information if they believed she might know of Macy's whereabouts.

"There was a girl from Australia," she said. "She was the one who initially got me to go to Corsica. Her name's Ella, but I don't know her last name or her hometown. And Australia's kind of... big."

He chuckled. "Yeah. Kinda. Anyone else you can think of?"

Macy gave me a miserable glance. I couldn't read minds, but I knew what she was thinking. We'd have to get the Plague-infected sample from Olly. There was no choice.

"There is... one girl. In England. I know where she lives," Macy admitted with obvious reluctance.

"Excellent. Nox was able to convince some of the Dark Court members in England to break with the Ancient Court and give up their fan pods. We'll have to prevail upon one of them to collect the sample. They'll have to sway the girl afterward, of course, because it's all too much to explain and we're not allowed to reveal the secret to humans anyway. Just tell us where to find her, and we'll take care of the rest."

"Oh. Sway is not going to work in this case—it doesn't

affect her," Macy said. "That's what actually drew us together in the first place. We were the only two in Nic's fan pod who were lucid—the only two who wanted to leave."

I backed her up. "It's true. It's unusual, but it happens. Some humans can't be swayed."

"That is odd," the young healer said. "Someone once tried using glamour on me—back before I knew about my true heritage—and it didn't work. But of course, I later learned why. Are you sure she's human? If not, her blood may not be helpful after all."

"I'm pretty sure of it. I'm adopted, but she's not. She knows her birth parents. They're regular people." Macy thought for a moment. "She's been begging me to visit her. I can use that as an excuse and go collect the sample myself. She trusts me, so it's probably best that I go. She'll help if I ask her too, even if I can't explain the reason."

Asher's brow furrowed. "I'm afraid we'll need for you to stay here a while." He turned to me. *Can you go instead?*

"No," Macy blurted, apparently guessing what he'd silently said to me. "You can't send him away." She slid from the table and flung her arms around my waist, surprising me with her vehemence. I liked it.

"You can't leave me—not now," she commanded. "Not after all we've been through and all you did to get to me."

My heart melting, I wrapped both arms around her small form and pressed a kiss to the top of her head. "I don't *want* to leave you, piccola. Ever again. But you said you'd do anything it took to save the humans. This is necessary. It will be only a short separation."

The frown she wore told me what she thought of the idea, but she said no more in protest.

"How quickly do you need it?" I asked Asher.

"The sooner the better. It will take us a week or two to do the necessary research and find out if Macy's blood can even counteract the virus. And according to what Nox said, every minute counts at this point."

I nodded. That was it then. I had to leave for England tonight— early evening, if it could be arranged. No rest for the weary. No sex for the weary, either, apparently. I was desperate to seal the bond with Macy, but there was no way I'd make our first time a quickie and then run off to another country and leave her behind. It would have to wait until my return.

We'll have plenty of time for that, I reminded myself. *We have eternity.*

My body wasn't as convinced as my mind. Maybe it was having been forced to spend so much time away from her. *And* the fact that while I was bonded to her, she wasn't bonded to me. Not yet. As soon as it was feasible, though, I'd change that. I'd bind her to me with every convention, law, and physical act I could find. Now that I had her back in my life, I was never letting her get away.

I turned back to Macy and took her pouting face between my hands. "I'll take Nox's jet. I'll go there and come right back. You'll hardly know I'm gone."

"I'll *know* you're gone," she grumped. "I don't like this —at all."

"I know you don't, piccola, but it's a necessary evil. And when I return... we'll take care of... unfinished business."

That drew a reluctant smile.

"Okay," the young healer said. "Time to make arrangements then. Macy, you'll have to contact her and gain her cooperation. My grandfather still has an old wall phone at his house. There is no digital signal to trace, and even if someone managed it, it would lead them to a property that is quite... well-protected from Dark Elves. I think it'll be safe for Macy to use it for one phone call to this girl, if you can keep it kind of short. You can let her know Nic is coming.

That way she won't be alarmed, and she can make herself available for the blood draw."

She nodded, liking that idea. "Good. And we'll need to make the arrangements on our end for the clinic appointment. She's only fourteen."

"No problem. I'll drive you both to my family's home in a little while, and you can make the call," Asher said.

Langnon returned to lead us to our guest room within the palace so Macy could rest and I could shower and change before setting off again. Before I left the medical office, the voice of the older healer, Wickthorne, stopped me.

If I could speak with you a moment, your highness.

I looked into his serious brown eyes and knew this would not be a casual chat.

"Macy." She turned back around to look at me. "You go ahead and get settled. I'll be right there."

She looked worried but nodded and continued following the guide. When she'd gone, the older healer walked over and offered me his hand.

It's good to meet you, Nicolo. Nox has informed us you are an ally in the Ancient Court, and those are too few and far between.

Yes, I have... broken with most of them recently. Thankfully my father has re-thought his path, and my sister and mother are on our side as well. They are, literally and figuratively, an island of compassion in a sea of animosity, I'm afraid. What is it that I can do for you?

Well your highness... I'm actually going to ask you not *to do something.* He looked uneasy.

Oh?

Yes. Pardon my forwardness, but I perceive that you and the nymph girl have not bonded. Am I correct?

I hesitated before answering, not sure where this was going. *That is correct. Not physically anyway.*

I have been reading up on the nymph lore we have on hand—

I've also requested materials to be sent from Europe—older texts that may be more accurate. He paused again, looking acutely uncomfortable.

Go on.

I hate to intrude, and I certainly don't want to impede your relationship with your betrothed, but what I have read strongly suggests that not all nymphs possess healing power in their blood.

Oh. And you're worried that Macy might not?

No. I feel sure that she does. My concern is... that could change if she... if you two were to... you see... all the lore suggests it is only the nymphs still in possession of their... virginity... whose blood is capable of healing and enhancing health.

Wham. A great, heavy door shut in my mind.

Perhaps it is only legend and not truth, but it's mentioned in several accounts, and the possibility is there, he said. *I apologize for eavesdropping, but I could not help but overhear the two of you a few minutes ago, and your comment about "unfinished business" concerned me. I know it is a lot to ask, but if you could possibly...*

I interrupted. *I know. I get it. You want us to wait to bond.*

He heaved a visible sigh of relief at not being forced to say the words. *Yes, your highness. Thank you, your highness. If that is at all possible, it could make all the difference to our cause. Otherwise, I'm not sure that anything my apprentice and I do in our laboratory will have an effect.*

I understand. I paused, deciding how to word my next question. *I wonder... that is, how long exactly do you think you'll need to create this... cure or vaccine or whatever?*

He let out a long breath. *It's hard to say. This is something entirely new for me. We're dealing with very old magic—and modern technology as well. At the very least... a few weeks?*

And at the most?

He flinched. *It could take us years to land upon the correct combinations and create enough vaccine for the whole human population.*

Years. I let out a laugh born more of despair than humor. *Okay then. I'm glad you warned me—I think. I'll... take this information under advisement.*

Yes, your highness. He gave a curt bow and went back to his bottles and tubes.

I headed for our guest room, where my irresistible fiancée waited. My irresistible fiancée whom I would *somehow* have to find a way to resist. For weeks. Possibly for *years.*

Though I was eager to see her as always, I dragged my feet and slowed my pace. How was I going to tell her this piece of news? More importantly, how was I going to keep my *hands* off of her?

When I reached the room, Macy was not in sight, but the clothes she'd been wearing were draped on the bed. Hearing the sound of running water, I turned and saw a closed door, most likely to an attached bathroom.

I stared at the bathroom door. Stared harder when I heard the sounds of someone stepping into a bathtub. It was utterly impossible to keep from imagining Macy in there, slipping into the bathtub with nothing on. *No.* I shook my head, actually debating slapping myself. I had to put those thoughts out of my mind for now. I had to ignore the fact that every cell in my body demanded that I walk through that door, pluck her from the water, and throw her onto that very large and very comfortable-looking bed. Right. Now.

No no no.

I was two years past Elven bonding age. I was five feet away from the girl I loved, who loved me back, who *wanted* me back. *Who was naked.* And I couldn't have her—unless I was willing to sacrifice the lives of every human being on the planet.

The gods hated me.

19

MACY

Our room was the perfect honeymoon suite. Well, okay, maybe I was rushing things a bit, but it *was* a lovely room. It was cozy and beautiful with an incredible carved wooden four-poster bed and an upright chest for storing our clothes.

I'd gone straight for the bathtub once Langnon had left, planning to be clean and sweet-smelling for Nic when he arrived. Thirty minutes later, I emerged from the steamy room, pink-skinned and fresh-scrubbed and wrapped in a thick towel. Nic was sitting on the bed. *Was* sitting. When he spotted me, he sprang off the mattress and started pacing.

"Hi. Everything okay back there?" I asked. I didn't like the look on his face.

"Um… yeah. Wickthorne wanted to tell me some things about… what they're planning to do." He finally glanced at me but then darted his eyes away again quickly.

"The tub is awesome," I informed him. "I wonder where they get the hot water?"

"There are hot springs running beneath the earth. They tap into them for bathing and cooking."

"Oh. Cool."

Nic was definitely acting strange, not quite looking at me. Was he thinking about the flight to Europe tonight? Or maybe he was as nervous as I was about all the possibilities now that we were finally alone together and clear on where our relationship stood. We'd spent plenty of time together but never under circumstances with this much… potential. Even on our spontaneous holiday in Italy, we'd had separate bedrooms.

"It's a nice room, isn't it? I feel like I'm in a fairy tale," I said, walking over to him, running my hand down one post of the bed and across the elaborately stitched blanket on top of it as I went. I was a little nervous myself but eager all the same.

He cleared his throat and moved away, going to open the armoire and examine the clothing someone had hung there for us. "Yes. It's… lovely. I'll be staying in a similar one down the hall."

"What? I thought this was *our* room—they put your clothes in the chest there."

"I'll have someone move them." He glanced around. "Is my overnight bag here somewhere? I should pack." He was acting as if he was ready to move his things down the hall right this instant.

"Nic." I closed the distance between us again and touched him on the arm.

He flinched.

"What's going on? You're acting funny."

Finally he made direct eye contact. "You're in a towel," he informed me, his voice sounding tight.

"Yeeeesss?" I dragged the word out into a question. "I just got out of the bathtub. Do you want to take a bath now? I'll wash your back," I teased. Sort of. Actually the idea of sluicing hot water and soap over Nic's body had me ready to jump right back into the tub with him.

"No thank you. I mean, I will—bathe—in my own room."

"What's wrong with this one?"

"Macy I… can't stay in here with you. I can't… take a bath —in here—with you—in here."

Something was terribly wrong. When we traveled together in Italy, Nic hadn't been able to keep his hands off me. Now he was acting like I'd bathed in liquid kryptonite.

"Nic—what happened? Do you not… want me like that anymore?" And then a horrible thought occurred to me. "Did what Dr. Schmitt did to you make you unable—"

He whirled around and caught my shoulders in a crushing grip, molten emotion flashing in his eyes. "No. No, Macy. Believe me, I am ready, willing, *and* able. And now that we're actually in the same place at the same time and I've determined you are *not* in love with another guy, I would love nothing more than to rip off that towel and *bond* with my bond-mate." He let out a growl of restraint. "I don't know how much longer I can stand to wait."

Shaking my head, I started to say, "You don't *have* to wait, idiot." But then his choice of wording struck me. I blinked at him. "Your bond-mate? I thought it was called 'your betrothed' before the actual wedding, or am I messing up the Elven lingo?"

Nic's dark eyes shuttered again. "I… didn't want to mention this before I was certain that you actually did want to spend your life with me." He licked his lips, hesitating. "I don't want to make you feel… obligated to be with me."

"Don't be silly. You know I want to be with you forever. *What* did you not mention?"

"Macy… I am already bonded to you."

I blinked. Blinked again. "How is that possible? Did we… um… did something happen that I don't remember? Maybe I had a few too many glasses of Romigi's wine or something and passed out?"

"God no," he exclaimed. "How could you even think something like that?"

"Well, I don't really. I didn't. But I thought to be bonded to someone you had to... you know..."

"Yes. That is how it works—in every case I've ever heard of before ours."

"So how did we become bonded then?"

"*You* are not bonded to *me*," he corrected. "You are still free to choose. I'm not even sure it works the same way for nymphs as it does for Elves. Regardless, I *am* bonded to you —for eternity. Apparently during my suicide attempt, when I swallowed the glass vials filled with your blood, not only did your blood heal my injuries, it *changed* me. It convinced my body that you are already my bond-mate. That's why the procedures on the girls didn't take. My genetic matter could have no effect on them... because it's programmed to respond only to you."

As the truth sank in I began smiling. And couldn't stop. "So you're saying you're stuck with me, huh?"

He nodded. "And apparently you are stuck with me. Because no matter where you go or what you do, I'll be driven to follow you around declaring my undying love for the rest of our lives."

I gave an exaggerated frowny-face. "Oh that's *horrible.* An international heart throb wrapped around my little finger? Everyone will feel so sorry for me." Growing more serious, I added, "I do feel sort of bad, though. You were worried about making me feeling obligated—you didn't choose this—you're obligated to me by virtue of biology. That evil doctor took away your choice."

He drew me close again and kissed the tip of my nose. "Piccola, my choice was taken away from me the second I met you. I was utterly lost, and I wouldn't have it any other way."

Running my hands up his abdomen and chest, I began to work on the buttons of his shirt. "Then we might as well go ahead and make it official."

Nic pulled away from me with a groan of frustration. "We can't."

I was swimming in confusion. He seemed to want me as much as I wanted him. He said he was *bonded* to me for eternity. "Are you worried about me losing *my* choices? Because you shouldn't. I'm ready to be with you—only you —forever."

He gave me a weak smile. "That is very good to hear, though I'm not even sure it works the same way for nymphs as it does for Elves. You might be able to take multiple partners throughout your lifetime. You might be driven to."

"Well, I'm not going to. Is *that* what has you worried? You think I'm going to leave you—or cheat on you?" My tone sounded as indignant as I felt.

"No, no, piccola. I am sorry. Sit down and let me explain."

I sat on the edge of the bed, waiting. And fuming a little bit, if I was being honest.

"I spoke to Wickthorne. There is not much reliable information available to us about nymphs. They've been ex— we all *believed* they were extinct for hundreds of years now. Obviously, that isn't entirely true."

He gestured toward me as if I were Exhibit A in a courtroom. "But what limited information he does have suggests... well, it indicates that your blood is only useful in healing illnesses and injuries as long as you remain... as long as you're a virgin."

My mouth dropped open with an audible click. "A... *wow*. That is not what I was expecting you to say." I wasn't sure *what* I'd been expecting, but it wasn't that. "So then… if we were to bond before they figure out the cure…"

"There might *be* no cure. Ever," he said, looking tortured. "The Plague will be activated and continue unabated until all the humans are dead."

"Oh Nic," I sighed. "I'm so sorry."

Smiling and coming to sit next to me on the bed, he opened his arms in invitation. "So am I—for myself, mostly." He laughed. "At least we have eternity together. We've waited this long to bond, we can wait a little more I suppose."

"How *little* is that, exactly? Did Wickthorne say?"

"He doesn't know—no one does. Hopefully it's soon, because there's one thing I *do* know."

"What's that?"

"You look too good in that towel. You need to put some clothes on." He ran his eyes over my bare legs and feet then up to my shoulders and exposed upper chest. "Now please."

ONCE I WAS DRESSED, Nic's hurry to evacuate my room evaporated. We lay together on the bed, holding each other and talking, my head resting over his heart.

"Have you visited the Light Elves before?"

He nodded. His voice rumbled pleasantly in his chest beneath my ear. "Not here. But in Europe. We went to an Assemblage there. It's a gathering they hold every ten years. The place was something like this one. The king there is very old, though. Here, the Light King is our age—his father died not that long ago, so he stepped up to rule."

"How sad. That would be weird—to be running a kingdom at our age. Although, I guess there have been teenaged kings throughout history. It's so much responsibility, though."

"I have a lot of sympathy for him. I've grown up knowing

my future would be much the same—though in the Ancient Court, there are more individual ruling families. Here, the king rules the entire Light Court, and Nox rules over the whole Dark Court—it's a larger area than in Europe where it's divided by countries."

"Alessia's family is royal as well, right?" I asked. "Do you think she will sit on the Dark throne eventually in Italy? I mean... even if she doesn't marry?"

"I'm not sure. I'm not sure about anything when it comes to her. She's very mixed up right now." His tone was thoughtful. And sad.

"It seems clear enough to me what she wants—capture the nymph, drain her blood, kill the humans."

He squeezed me tighter. "I still cannot believe she is behaving this way. I thought the danger would end with Dr. Schmitt. But apparently, he really got into her head and twisted her all up. And of course there's what I did to her. That—on top of the way she's always been treated by her family. She used to be... normal. Now... I don't know... I guess it was all too much for her, and she snapped."

"What do you mean 'how she's been treated?' She seemed like the stereotypical spoiled princess to me."

He nodded. "Yes, she was given *things*. But she's never had the kind of affection and nurturing you and I had. Her parents always kept her at arm's length because of her glamour. Since reaching maturity, she has kept others away for the same reason—and possibly because she's become so accustomed to being alone and to thinking of herself as 'untouchable.'"

I thought about it for a minute. It *was* a sad story—I couldn't imagine growing up without any physical affection. Touch was supposed to be vital for a child's development. Bearing that in mind, it probably would've been nice of me to feel some compassion for the lonely young girl Alessia must have been.

My grandmother would no doubt have said, "Bless her heart—we should pray for her." But I just wasn't able to muster any positive feelings—or pleas for divine intervention—when it came to that girl. All I had ever known was the vindictive person she was now. And she was *hunting* me. She was threatening my family and friends.

"Um… yeah. Well, her 'snap' is about to end the world as we know it. I know a couple of broken engagements has to suck, but that's no excuse for ending mankind," I said. "You fell in love with someone else—it happens. In my book the *only* reason to marry someone is if you feel like you absolutely cannot live without them. If you have *any* reservations—which you obviously did—I believe you should call it off."

He lifted his head and looked at my face speculatively. "What about you?"

My eyes met his. "What about me?"

"Do you have any reservations… about marriage?"

Sliding my hand from his chest up to his nape, I gave him a sly smile. "Are we talking in general terms here, or did you have someone particular in mind?"

He squeezed me against him and tickled my side, making me squeal and squirm. "You know what I'm asking, you little nymph."

"No. I don't. I think you'd better spell it out for me."

"Being married to a nymph is going to have its challenges, I see," he said.

I gave him a sassy cocked eyebrow. "I don't remember a proposal. You'd better get to work on that, big guy."

His eyes widened at my words. He broke into a scrunched up grin and shook his head as he lowered his mouth to mine.

"You're going to be the death of me. How am I supposed to wait?"

And then he was kissing me, and I was kissing him back and doing everything in my power to express my complete and thorough *lack* of reservations when it came to him.

There was no controlling myself with Nic. The scent and feel of him were dizzying, intoxicating. I wanted to hold him with every part of me, the sheer pleasure of his nearness driving me mad.

A knock at the door caused us to jump apart. I hadn't realized his body had shifted until he was mostly on top of me, pinning me to the bed. We looked at each other, smiling ruefully. Well *I* was smiling. He grimaced. The knock came again.

Sighing, he rolled off the bed. "I'll get it."

When he opened the door, the young healer stood outside. "Hope I'm not disturbing y'all. Ready to go make a phone call?" He held up a set of keys and jingled them.

Nic's shoulders sagged, and he nodded, answering in a tone that could only be described as disgruntled. "Sure. Let's go. It's not like we've got anything better to do."

He cast one last longing look at the rumpled bedcover as we left the room.

20

MACY

A sher drove us to his family's farm on the outskirts of Deep River. It was a charming place with groves of pecan trees and acres of pasture land enclosed by white-railed fencing.

He took us onto the property through a gravel road back entrance, pointing out the crops and the livestock standing in clumps together, enjoying the late afternoon sun. It wasn't Tuscany, but it was beautiful in its own way, peaceful and remote.

"You'll have to come back here another time when everything's a little less crazy. We can do some pecan picking." He grinned.

"Are you sure your family won't mind us showing up at dinner time?" I asked. "I hate to impose."

"I called ahead," he assured. "My mom's happiest when she has lots of mouths to feed. Besides, we're on a mission. We can't wait. We have to do this now, no matter what time it is."

In England where Olly was, it was six hours ahead— kind

of late on a school night. I hoped she was still up and would answer her phone. If her "mum" answered, I wasn't sure what I would say to explain a phone call from a stranger in America.

Once inside the white-painted farmhouse, Nic and I met the healer's mother and grandfather then got down to the business at hand—making the phone call. Nic assured Asher's grandfather he'd cover the long-distance charges incurred, but the old man brushed it off in his thick Scottish brogue.

"Never you mind that. I'm happy to be of help to my grandson's friends."

The receiver felt heavy and odd in my hands—I was so used to using cell phones. My parents had gotten rid of their landline years ago. My nerves sang with tension as I waited for the overseas call to connect. Thankfully, Olly was the one who answered.

"Hello?"

"Olly, it's Macy. How are you?"

"Oh Macy," she squeaked. "I'm so happy to hear from you. Where are you now?"

Instead of answering her question directly, I side-stepped it and got right to the point. "Still traveling. How are you feeling?"

It wasn't just the usual nicety. There was actual reason to be concerned about her health. If Olly had taken ill, it might mean we were already too late for a Plague vaccine and would be scrambling for a miracle cure instead. But Olly was her usual cheerful, carefree self.

"Oh, I'm aces. Very sound. How are you?"

"Good. That's so good to hear. I'm fine. Listen, I do want to catch up, but it's late and I'm sure you need to get to bed. I'm afraid I don't have long to talk this time anyway. Are you alone where we can talk privately?"

"Yeah, hold on, let me shut my door." There was a click. "Okay, now I'm good."

"Olly, listen—this is going to sound really strange, but I promise you it's important. I need you to do something. Your life and the lives of everyone you know could depend on it."

"Well that sounds scary."

"No, there's no need to be scared. Everything's going to be all right. Just do exactly as I say and tell no one. I don't usually condone keeping secrets from parents, but in this case it can't be avoided."

"Is this about the fan pod? Because they already know."

"It's *related* to the fan pods, but it's much more serious than that. Here's what I need you to do. There's a clinic within walking distance from you—I looked it up."

Actually Asher had looked it up for us and would be calling early tomorrow morning to notify the clinic to expect her.

"Tomorrow after school, go by there and let them draw some blood," I continued. "They'll be expecting you as a walk-in patient."

There was a pause before Olly responded. "I don't like having blood drawn."

"I know. You and me both, kiddo—especially after what we went through in Corsica. I hate needles, but I promise it's for a good cause."

"This is kind of weird, Macy. What are they going to do with my blood?"

Withholding information from her felt terrible, but I knew it was for her own good. Any human who knew the truth about the existence of Elves was at risk.

"I know. I know it seems weird. I can't tell you exactly what's going on, but no one's going to do anything bad with your blood sample. It's something very, very good. Remember how you told me I came to the fan pod for a reason? I argued with you at the time, but I believe it now. And I think *you* were there for a reason, too. This is it. There is something in your blood that can help us save millions of lives from the bad people who were keeping us in the fan pod. But my friends need the chance to test it as soon as possible. Can you do this for me? Can you trust me?"

She let out a shaky-sounding breath. "Okay. I do trust you. I'll do it. For *you*. When are you going to come see me, Macy?"

"As soon as I can. As soon as it's safe for both of us. I promise. Unfortunately, I can't make it there myself this time, but a friend of mine will be coming to help you." I thought for a second then decided to share my good news with her. "Can I tell you a secret?"

"Okay."

"It's Nic. He's okay. He came and found me, and he'll be getting on a plane soon to meet you at the clinic. He'll bring your samples back himself, to make sure they get here safe and sound. And as soon as we can, we'll come see you together."

"Yay! For a honeymoon?" she asked eagerly.

"Maybe," I said, then looked up at Nic's watchful face and felt myself blush.

"I hope it's soon," she said. "Okay, I'll go to the clinic right after school. I could even skip and go in the morning when it opens if you like."

"No, don't do that. I don't want you to get in trouble for playing hooky. The afternoon will be fine."

"Okay," she said, sounding slightly disappointed.

"If there's any problem, make a collect call to this number and let me know, okay?" I said. "And take care of my boyfriend for me."

Olly assured me she would, and we hung up. I felt the eyes of everyone in the room on me.

"I think it'll work," I said, and there were sighs and nods all around. "She said she'd do it today and didn't seem to think there'd be any issue with her family." I turned to Nic. "So now I guess it's up to you two."

"Great. We'll get it done, I promise."

"I didn't have time to make anything fancy, but I fixed y'all some sandwiches," Asher's mom said, carrying a tray into the dining room. "My son said you've had a long day and might be hungry."

"Actually, I'm starved," said Nic. "But I want to stay with Asher while he makes the call to the clinic. I'll be there in a moment. Macy, why don't you go on ahead and eat?"

I followed her to the dining room where Asher's grandfather joined me at the table. Asher's mom went back to the kitchen for water and tea.

"So where are you from, young lady?" the old man asked.

"Missouri. The Joplin area."

"No—I mean where are you *from*? Your people?" He gave me a nod and a knowing wink.

"Um…" I wasn't really sure what he was getting at. "I don't know exactly. I'm adopted. I've never met my biological family."

"Oh, I see. Well, when you go lookin'—if you ever do—I'd suggest startin' in the vicinity of the Scottish Isles. I grew up around those parts, and you have the look of a local."

A bit taken aback by his suggestion and knowing manner, I smiled tightly. "Okay. Thanks. I'll do that."

Within an hour we'd all been fed, the arrangements were made, and we were on our way—first to take Nic to the airport for his flight to England—then back to Altum where I'd have nothing to do but play my role as a human, oops— nymphian?—pin cushion and wait for him to return.

I walked with Nic to the bottom of the jet's boarding stairs.

"I wish you didn't have to go."

"I wish you could come with me." He looked exhausted. And sad.

"You'll probably sleep all the way there and back. You won't even miss me."

"Oh, I'll miss you. More than you can possibly imagine," he said, punctuating the vow with a deep kiss. He lifted his head again. "But knowing you're waiting here for me—and that you love me—will make it bearable. And the sooner we get the healers in Altum what they need to create the cure, the sooner your 'duty' will be done, and we can move on with our lives and seal that bond."

He kissed me again, until I pushed at his chest and smiled against his lips. "You'd better get on that plane then—instead of kissing me senseless all night long." I took a step backward, wiping a tear from my cheek.

He backed up the steps, smiling. "I love you, piccola."

Though the airfield was brightly lit, his figure blurred before my eyes. "I love you, too. Come back to me."

"Always."

21

NIC

Macy was right about the sleep thing. I did doze almost the entire eight-hour flight from Mississippi to Bristol.

She was *wrong* about me not missing her. Even in my sleep, I longed for her. My dreams were *all* her—the sound of her laugh, the way her eyes lit up when I walked into the room, the way she'd pouted on the plane ride to Mississippi from Las Vegas when she thought I wasn't looking… the way her body had looked in that towel.

I woke frustrated and filled with pent-up energy with zero outlet for it. Hopefully this trip would speed things along. The reason I'd agreed so readily to be the sample-delivery-boy was to ensure that Olly's infected blood made it to the right people in as short a time as possible.

Though… maybe my being half a world away from Macy was for the best. I wasn't sure I'd be able to keep from ruining the host of the miracle cure if I stayed in close proximity to her. Who knew how long it would take the healers to complete their work. I was praying for "weeks" rather than "years." The human race might not even *have* years, and I was at serious risk of spontaneous combustion.

When the plane landed in Bristol, I saw I'd missed a call from Estelle. At first I was hopeful—was she calling to say Nox's healer had made a breakthrough? My heart sank, though, when I heard the message she'd left.

"Nic. Call me as soon as you can. I've gotten some new intel—and it's not good."

She answered immediately when I dialed her back, though it was very late at night for her in California. "Nic— hi. Where are you? Are you okay?"

"I'm good. I'm in England, actually. Just landed. What's happening?"

"Bad news, I'm afraid. Or, it might be bad, I'm not sure. I spoke to my source in Italy tonight. Alessia is on the move. She's left the palace in Rome. According to several people who were around at the time, she said, 'It's time,' before she left."

"*Merda.* You're right—that doesn't sound good."

"No, not at all. And no one is quite sure where she went. She didn't use her usual driver or pilot. She must be onto the fact there's a leak. She could be anywhere, Nic."

She could be in America. The short hairs at the base of my scalp lifted. Had Alessia given up on her henchmen and come to hunt Macy personally? Or equally as frightening, had she set out to "visit" the fan pod girls, activating the Plague virus they carried with her glamour—her own personal poison touch?

Either way it wasn't good. Either way, I was more determined than ever to do my job well here and do it quickly. I needed to get to Olly and bring the blood samples right back here to the airport as soon as possible and then fly back to make sure Macy stayed safe.

"Well, keep working your sources to see if you can find

out where she's gone. Macy and I are doing what we can on our end."

"How's it going with your reunion?" she asked. "Are things… okay between you?"

I smiled. "No. They're better than okay. She still loves me."

"Oh, I'm so glad for you, Nic."

"Estelle?" I hesitated before asking the question. "Have you ever thought about… marriage proposals?"

"What do you mean? I've gotten lots of them."

"I know, but I mean… have you ever thought about how you'd *want* someone to propose? You know… the ideal."

When I wasn't sleeping on the flight, I'd thought about what Macy had said. I *hadn't* actually proposed marriage to her. I'd declared my love and been overjoyed to hear that she still loved me, too. And she'd seemed happy when I'd admitted I was bonded to her for life. But there *should* be a wedding proposal. It was much more a human thing than an Elven one, as our marriages were typically arranged by our parents—especially in the Ancient Court. But now that I thought about it, I was actually starting to get a bit excited. A proposal. This could be fun.

"I haven't really thought about it. You know I'm going to be stuck with whichever toady little prince Papà picks for me. Although *you've* gotten out of it well enough." She laughed. "Maybe I should have someone put *me* in a coma for a year so our parents will let me do whatever I want, too."

"Don't even joke about it, Estelle," I warned. "I nearly lost everything. Macy was close to deciding to move on."

"I know. I was only kidding—I was as scared as they were of losing you."

Now that we were on the subject of guys who were interested in Estelle, I had to ask. "How *is* Anders? Does he… talk about her?"

"About Macy? Sure. They're good friends. But if you mean 'is he in love with my bond-mate?' the answer is no."

"You sound very certain of that."

"I am," she said with cheery frankness. "I asked him."

Bearing in mind her glamour gift, his answer to her would have to have been the truth. "And he said..." I prompted.

"He said, 'no,' silly. He's never been in love... before," she added the last word belatedly.

It took a moment to register. "Hey—what's going on between you two?"

"I've got to go, *mio fratello caro*," she chirped, sounding younger than she had in years. "*Ciao.* Keep me updated." And she hung up.

BRISTOL, England was known for its bustling historic harborside, its plentiful artists and activists, and the Clifton suspension bridge spanning the Avon river gorge. It was a popular spot for conferences and weekend holidays.

The area near Olly's house was quieter. Well-kept and charming, it was clearly targeted more toward locals than tourists, with a bakery and several brick-fronted shops lining the intersecting streets of the city center. The sidewalks weren't crowded, but there were people about, walking, chatting together, shopping.

Though Bristol was one of the sunniest and warmest cities in the UK, it *was* February and not exactly warm out today— probably only about eight degrees Celsius, or around forty-seven degrees Fahrenheit, as Macy would think of it.

I shivered and buttoned the top button of my coat as I walked toward the address Asher has supplied for the clinic. Spotting the small, blonde girl leaning against the outside wall, I felt a wave of relief that nearly lifted my feet from the pavement.

When Estelle had said Alessia was on the move, my first fear had been for Macy. My second was that Alessia had decided to follow Macy's digital trail and come after Olly.

She looked up as I got close, recognition warming her eyes. "Nicolo!" she said, popping to attention and moving toward me, but stopping short of hugging me. We hadn't really known each other, except through Macy.

"Hello Olly. It's good to see you. I think you're actually taller than Macy now and much more grown-up than the last time I saw you."

Her cheeks reddened to match the tip of her nose, which was pink from the cold.

"You look a lot *better* than the last time I saw you. I thought you were dead, you know." Her little face scrunched. "I'm sorry I told Macy you were dead. I hope you're not mad at me."

I reached out to ruffle the top of her hair. "Of course not. You saw me in pretty rough shape, and you were trying to be a good friend. All's well that ends well." Tipping my head toward the clinic doors, I asked, "Have you been in yet?"

"Yes. I did it already." Obviously used to the chilly temperatures, she wore no coat, only a sweater. She pushed up one long sleeve to show me the small bandage. "I just wanted to wait and see you. So... you can't tell me what's happening? Macy said millions of lives could be in danger."

"I'm afraid not. It's better for you if you don't know everything. But I will tell you this—you might very well be saving every person you know—and lots of them you don't. Thank you for what you're doing."

She shrugged her narrow shoulders, causing the scarf around her neck to hide her chin. "I didn't do much. Just stuck out my arm. Nic—" She peered up at me, searching my face. "Is there something wrong with me?"

Heat crept up my neck. How did I answer that question? "No. You're perfectly healthy." *For now. As long as we can keep the time bomb inside your body from going off.* "Why do you ask?"

"Well, Macy and me were the only girls who didn't get hypnotized in your fan pod. And my family were really, *really* angry when I told them where I'd been and told them about your guards and your palace and your family—sorry, I had to tell them—if you ever met my nanna you'd understand. She told me I was lucky to 'be who I am.' And now... you say my blood might help save people's lives."

Perplexed, I shook my head. "You'll have to ask your mum about what she said. I don't know what that means. But there *is* something in your blood that's like... a puzzle piece. When we put it together with Macy's, we'll be able to unlock a weapon that we can use to protect the world. That's really all I can say. And Olly—if you can help it—don't tell your mum what I said, okay? I don't want her worrying about you unnecessarily."

"Okay. I'll try. Are you getting married soon?"

"What?" Her lightning-fast changes of subject were giving me whiplash. "Oh, maybe. Hopefully."

"Macy said maybe you could both come and see me on your honeymoon. I miss her so much."

An upsurge of guilt soured my stomach. This sweet child had been lured into *my* fan pod for use in Dr. Schmitt's plan. How many more like her had been victimized by my people worldwide? Brimming with determination to protect her and those like her, I made her a promise.

"I know she feels the same way. We'll come back together as soon as we can. You can count on it."

Her face gleamed. "Okay good. Well, I've gotta get home

or I *will* have to come up with some sort of story for where I've been."

"Be safe, little one." As she skipped away, something occurred to me, and it caused a wintry chill to slither down my back. "Olly."

She turned back around. "Yes?"

"If an Italian woman calls on you—a young, pretty one, tall like me—*don't* let her in, okay? She's not your friend."

She rolled her eyes. "I feel like I'm in a James Bond film on the telly."

"I'm serious."

She bobbed her head in a repeated nodding motion. "Okay. Okay, I get it. No pretty Italians in our house—except for *you*," she added with a giggle, then turned and ran away.

I stepped into the clinic and told the woman at the counter I was there to pick up a sample for delivery to the States.

"Your name, sir?"

"Nicolo Buonoccorsi."

"Oh—there's a football star with that same name. You even look a bit like him."

I smiled. "I get that a lot."

She looked at me straight-on then, studying my face. Thankfully, her strongest desire at the moment was to get out of work and to her daughter's piano recital, so she turned and went to the back without quizzing me further. Returning with a package wrapped in ice packs, she handed it over. "Blood sample for patient..." Looking down she checked the name. "Rowan. Correct?"

I took it from her. "Yep. That's the one. Thank you so much. Have a good evening."

I signed a form then left the building, walking swiftly to where I'd left my car and driver. The sky had clouded over and a frigid raindrops were beginning to fall. Sliding into the backseat, I said, "Airport, please. Take the fastest route possible. I'm in a hurry to get home."

Home. I wasn't thinking of Altum as my home, was I? Upon further reflection, I decided no, it wasn't the place. It was the person. Macy was my home, and wherever she was, that's where I wanted to be.

22

MACY

I knew it the minute Nic returned to Altum. Don't ask me how I knew, but I did.

It was nearly nine at night, and I was hanging out in my room, reading in bed. Suddenly, I had the strongest urge to go to the palace entrance. Throwing on a jacket and some shoes, I hurried through the halls. Just as I arrived, Nic shuffled through the doors, bleary-eyed, travel-rumpled, and completely beautiful.

His eyes lifted and connected with mine. His smile was so big it must have hurt his cheeks. I ran to him, leaping into his arms.

"You're here," I said in a joyful laugh-sob.

"I am. Oh, piccola, I'm so happy to see you. What did you do today?"

"Worry about you. Did everything go okay? Did you get it?"

Nic held up the package in his hand. "Right here. Come with me to the healer's office. We'll deliver this, and then we can catch up. Do you think they're still working?"

"The last time I saw them they said they'd wait up all night for you. They're *that* convinced that we need to work fast on this. You made great time."

"The flights were smooth. Traffic wasn't too bad in Bristol—about a half hour each way to and from the airport. I saw Olly—she's adorable."

"Isn't she? How did she look?"

"Older. *Healthy.* She's done some talking to her family about the castle and the fan pod situation, but I don't think any harm will come of it. As long as no one in the Ancient Court realizes she was never swayed. She asked me about that."

"About Sway? I never told her anything about the—"

He held up a hand. "I know. She didn't call it by name. She was curious about why you two were the only ones unaffected."

I lifted my shoulders and let them fall. "I understand now why I wasn't, but I have no idea about her."

"You don't think—nah," he shook his head.

"Think what? What were you going to say?"

"You don't think she's like you, do you? A nymph?"

"I *really* don't think so, Nic. You said nymphs were all supposedly very small—in the history books? She was only thirteen and already almost my height last time I saw her. And like I said, she lives with her birth family. She even mentioned a grandmother. If she was a nymph, wouldn't she know it?"

"I guess so. And you're right. She's grown even more in the past year. I'd say she's several inches taller than you now."

"Is it possible she's part-Elven, and that's why she was immune? Asher said his Elven heritage made him resistant to glamour."

"Maybe. Who knows? But she's not *that* tall, and she said

she described us—my family and my guards—to her mum, and her family didn't say anything about Elves to her. If they had, she wouldn't have been asking me about herself, still wondering why she was different from the other fan pod girls."

"Well, anyway, the main thing is she's safe and still healthy."

"Right. She looked great. And she was very eager to see you again. We'll have to go back as soon as we get the chance."

Hands clenched together, we walked through the passageways of the palace, which glowed with colored stones. By now I'd gotten used to the dusky half-light of this underground kingdom. It still amazed me that the Elves who lived here could tell the difference between day and night. Nic and I entered the medical office to find Wickthorne and Asher hard at work.

"Ah—Nic." The younger healer strode forward and shook Nic's hand, accepting the wrapped package with care. "Fantastic. We're at the point where we're ready to test the formula we made with Macy's blood on an infected sample. Without it, we were stalled out. Any trouble? It stayed in ice the whole trip?"

Nic nodded. "Yes. I was careful with it. They drew a half-pint. I hope that will be enough."

"More than enough. Thank you so much. I can't wait to get to work on this."

"So what now?" I asked the young healer.

He turned to me. "Now, we try everything in our power to kill the virus in these samples. You might want to say a prayer or two if you're into that kind of thing. Hopefully, the concoction we've already created will work to eradicate the virus. If it doesn't, we'll at least know how to start tweaking it. I'll get a sample out to California as well so my dad can work on it." He smiled and went back to hand the sample to Wickthorne.

Nic and I left the clinic together, walking through the halls of the palace.

"What do *we* do now?" I asked.

Sliding me a side glance, he waggled his eyebrows in a silly, suggestive way.

I laughed. "I don't think *that's* on the menu for tonight. I've been thoroughly warned today by pretty much everyone who speaks English that I cannot *compromise* the 'cure.'"

He took my hand. "I know. Wishful thinking. Actually, I'm about to fall asleep on my feet. But I was thinking tomorrow we might take a walk in the woods. The people here say there's a double waterfall not too far from Altum. Would you like to see it—if it's still warm enough, that is?"

"I didn't realize you were a hiker."

"Not usually, but without my regular football practice, I've got to do something for exercise. And it's best if we stay busy. Too much time alone in a room with you, and the human race can kiss its collective behind good-bye."

I laughed. "Good call. A hike it is. And maybe we could go into town for some lunch—or shopping in Oxford or something. I could use a few new things, and I'm told it's a great town."

Nic's gaze came back to mine. It wasn't encouraging. "I think we'd better stick to the woods. I heard from Estelle, and… well, we should keep a low profile. Alessia has left the palace in Italy for parts unknown. She could be anywhere. It's unlikely anyone in a small Mississippi town would recognize me from my European sports career, but I suppose it is possible there are some soccer fans here. If Alessia were to get a report on where *I* am, she'd know where to find *you*."

"I see. So we're in hiding then."

"Basically. Are you okay with that?"

I squeezed his hand tighter and wrapped my other hand around his wrist, leaning against his arm as we walked. "As long as you're with me, I don't care if I see another soul for weeks."

23

NIC

*T*wo weeks later

THE KNOCK CAME EARLY in the morning. I opened the door of my room to find a servant standing in the hall with Macy. A look of concern creased her face. I stepped out of my room, took her hand, and interpreted the servant's unspoken request.

"She says we're wanted in the medical clinic."

"Do you think something's gone wrong with the samples?" Macy walked quickly to match my hurried stride.

"I hope not," I said. "They've been working non-stop. If this isn't working, I'm not sure what the next step would be."

When we reached the clinic, both Wickthorne and Asher rushed forward.

"It works," the younger healer declared, nearly shouting the words. "It works. The new formula completely cleared the virus from the infected blood. We should be able to administer this to anyone who's been infected and see a complete reversal in their carrier status."

He looked elated, though a bit worn out. He and Wickthorne had been toiling tirelessly to create the right formulation of Macy's blood, coming close several times but failing until now. Macy had been extremely patient, submitting herself for additional blood draws again and again.

"The next step is creating a vaccine to prevent further infections," Asher explained. "But at least the fan pod girls can be treated now. We have enough for a couple hundred of them. Wickthorne and I are working to create duplicate batches for the rest."

Wickthorne spoke up, though only to me and mind to mind. *This is good news, of course, but there's something else you should know. We noticed something strange when working with the British girl's sample. The amount of virus contained in her blood continued to increase over the course of time we've been working on it. I've never seen anything replicate that quickly.*

He shook his head, rubbing the tension lines on his forehead with one hand. *The sooner this treatment is administered to the infected girls, the better. They are not just ticking time bombs—they are the equivalent of nuclear weapons. Any human near them would be instantly infected and virulent within hours. Once this thing starts, it will move fast and devastate every population in its path. And if it's true that the Italian Dark Princess can activate the virus simply by touching one of them...*

I nodded, understanding his meaning completely. I'd already directed Estelle to get to work compiling a list of the fan pod girls who'd been at the castle during the time of my betrothal to Alessia and up until Dr. Schmitt had released them. She'd told me last night she was nearly finished pinpointing all of their locations.

Very well, I told him. I *will leave today to take the treatment to the girls. I'll have to visit each of the fan pod girls one by one, moving from country to country until I get to all of them.*

I only hope what we have on hand will be enough for all of them, he said. *If the Plague starts to spread to the general population before you reach all the infected girls... well, let's hope that doesn't happen. Macy has only so much blood, after all.*

I shivered at his silent words, thankful she couldn't hear them. There was no way I'd let this turn into a situation like those in the Elven histories, where my people used nymphs as sacrificial lambs, draining them dry for their own purposes. I was concerned for the human race, but if it came down to a choice between them and Macy, there was no choice. I'd grab her and hide her away somewhere until the carnage was complete—with or *without* her consent.

Nox had offered to let us keep one of his jets at the airport in Oxford in case we had a need for a quick escape or for any other emergency. Asher had shipped some of Olly's blood to his healer in L.A. as well, but as far as I'd heard, he hadn't made a similar breakthrough. Now it was time to call my friend in the Dark Court to tell him of the healers' success here and prevail upon his generosity—and his pilot— once again.

"I need to go to the surface and make some calls," I told Macy. "And I'll be leaving immediately after that—as soon as I can pack."

"Leaving? Altum?"

"The country. Wickthorne says the danger from the infected girls is even greater than we thought. I must take the treatment to Europe and begin treating the girls as soon as possible. Estelle is still in L.A. We'll send her a portion of the cure, and she'll take care of the few American fan pod girls who were infected and returned to their homes stateside."

"I'm going with you," Macy said, her eyes wide with fear. "I want to go to Olly first, if there's that much of a hurry."

"No, piccola. It's too dangerous for you to be in Europe—"

"I have to go," she insisted. "She trusts me. It *has* to be me. And she can't be swayed, remember, so I need to be the one to take her the cure."

I heaved a sigh. "I thought you might say that."

Reading the determination in her eyes and knowing my inability to refuse her anything she wanted, I caved in. "I'll ask the pilot to make England the first stop on our flight plan. Why don't you go ahead and start packing. It could be an extended trip. I'm not sure how many countries yet—I'll need to ask Estelle when I speak to her."

I held up my phone. "Going up to call her now. Can you be ready to leave in about an hour?"

"Sooner," Macy vowed.

AN HOUR later we were boarding the plane, preparing for the eight-hour flight back over the pond to England. It would be eleven p.m. on Friday night when we reached the UK—too late for a visit. Olly's treatment would have to wait until morning. I had something different in mind for tonight anyway. Nox and Estelle weren't the only phone calls I'd made before our departure. I instructed the pilot to land at London City airport. In the morning, we'd make the short hop to Bristol, where Olly lived.

Once we were in the air, Macy and I both relaxed a bit. In fact, she was a little *too* relaxed, sitting close to me and draping her legs over mine, resting her head on my shoulder and playing with my fingers. It was messing with my very tightly held self-control.

Over the past two weeks, we'd kept ourselves busy—and surrounded by other people. It was the safest thing to do. Every time I was alone with her, my natural inclination was to kiss her, and once I started kissing her, I didn't want to stop. I wanted more—of everything.

So I'd been as chaste as I'd ever been in my life, keeping our physical contact brief and avoiding being alone with her at all costs. The fate of the world literally depended on me keeping my hands—and the rest of me—*off* of her.

But now... now we had eight hours of alone time. And the desires always simmering at the back of my brain had crept to the front, drawn there by her tempting nearness, her sweet, captivating scent. She stretched up and planted a warm kiss on my neck.

"You smell good," she murmured in a sexy purr, stealing the words from my brain.

I'm in so much trouble.

I sat straighter and shifted slightly away from her, looking out the window at the landscape spinning by in a dizzy circle as we lifted off and the plane turned.

"I'm surprised a town this small has an airport," I said, trying to distract her—and distract *myself* from the overwhelming desire to attack her.

It worked—at least the part about distracting *her.* She leaned across me to peer out the window at the town growing ever more distant below us. "It must be because of the University here. See? There's the Lyceum building—and the stadium. A lot of alumni fly in for football weekends— you know, the *real* football kind, not the soccer kind," she added with a flirty smile.

I smiled back. "There are millions of football fans across Europe, Africa, Australia, and South America who would argue with you about which is the *real* football."

She reached down and released her seatbelt buckle then scooted onto my lap, her impulsive nature taking over. "You are *so* cute when you get all 'snooty French-Italian' on me."

Sliding her fingers through the hair at the back of my

head, she pressed her lips to mine. The pent-up heat inside me exploded. I was like a wild creature that had been deprived of food for too long and had just spotted a helpless prey animal. I basically attacked her with my mouth, my hands, devouring her sweet softness, fighting against a ravenous hunger that threatened to steal all reason and ability to control myself.

A battle raged between my mind and body. The healers *had* formulated a cure, but Wickthorne had hinted that Macy's part might not be done yet. My mind pointed out they might still need her healing power. I'd never let someone drain her completely, but I knew I'd have a hard time stopping her from donating more blood if it was necessary to create additional doses for the suffering humans. And her blood might become useless to the cause if I allowed myself to cave in to the compelling desire that only grew each day I was with her.

On the other hand, my body argued, I'd already waited a *long* time. I'd been patient, and I was at this very moment on the way to begin administering the cure. There probably wouldn't be a need for additional doses. I'd done my part without (much) complaining. I had the girl I loved this close to me, and I wanted her. *Needed* her. In fact, if she had my glamour gift, she'd probably be terrified to see exactly how strong *my* greatest desire actually was.

Macy was not helping Team Brain one bit, squirming on my lap then shifting and turning so she sat facing me and returning my kisses with a passion that told me the waiting had been equally as difficult for her.

Every nerve ending in my body was on high-alert—some were reaching critical mass. Her weight on my lap and the feel of her soft curves in my hands was setting off a series of connected explosions inside me, each of them destroying the parts of my conscience that cared about the fate of the world and leaving gaping holes for my self-centered hormones to rush in and take over. I had to stop this before the invasion was complete and my desire obliterated the human race's chances of survival.

Drawing on every shred of moral decency I possessed, I pulled my mouth from hers. Team Body objected immediately, but I forced the ragged words out.

"Macy. Piccola. Wait a minute, *mi amore*. We need to slow down."

"No." She breathed heavily. "The cure works. It's okay. We can be together now." Her soft lips came back to mine, and I felt myself melting back into a brain-surrenders-body-is-winning-the-battle state.

Holding her shoulders, I exerted enough pressure to break the contact again. "We can't. Not yet."

I was reluctant to tell her what Wickthorne had said. Knowing her, she'd immediately volunteer to give up every ounce of healing blood she possessed. I wanted to reserve the right to save her from herself if it came down to it, so I wouldn't mention what he'd told me about what would happen if the Plague was released before we got to all the girls.

"Why not?" she asked.

"We're... not married. We should wait."

She wrinkled her nose and smiled. "What? Is that an Elven thing or something? I don't remember you being all that concerned about your marital state when we were in Italy."

"I know—but I've had more time to think about it now. And now that we're talking about eternity, I think we should do things the traditional way. Don't you?"

She sat back a bit and let out a long breath. "I guess so, but—wait—are you having second thoughts about us? Do you think you're going to change your mind or something?"

She hadn't come out and asked, but I knew Macy had been wondering why I hadn't proposed yet. My glamour told me it was her strongest desire, but I'd been waiting for an appropriate moment. I wanted it to be special, and while we were hiding out in Altum the perfect moment had not presented itself. I was hoping it would tonight.

"No, definitely not." I reached up to take her face between my hands. "I just don't want either of us to have any regrets when all is said and done." She would have *eternal* regrets if our inability to wait led to the demise of the human race.

Gripping her waist, I lifted her from my lap and deposited her back into her own seat. "With that in mind, I think we'd probably better keep to our own seats for the remainder of the flight." There was a small pout on her face, until I added, "You are a little *too* persuasive when you want to be."

She nodded and gave me a sheepish grin. "Okay."

I laced my fingers through hers and smiled back, then turned to the window again and focused on soccer stats as I willed my inflamed hormones to recede.

After a while, Macy interrupted my (mostly) successful self-talk.

"Nic… how do Elven people get married? I mean, within the Ancient Court, is there a certain ceremony or way of doing things?"

"It's usually a grand ceremony in the castle of the bride's family—sometimes the groom's, if the location suits better. Why do you ask?"

She shrugged. "Just curious. I was thinking about Olly, and I realized she's going to think we're on our honeymoon. I told her that's when we'd visit."

I nodded. "I see." It was killing me not to blurt out my plan for tonight, especially when I could tell what was on her mind. I held my tongue though, determined not to ruin the surprise I'd arranged on the phone this morning.

A car met us at the airport and drove toward our hotel in the city. Macy gazed out the windows at the impressive city skyline, smiling. "I loved being in London last year. What a great city," she said. "Where are we staying tonight?"

"The Shangri-La. It's supposed to have unbelievable views."

"Oh wow. That's great."

After a few minutes, as if it was a spur-of-the-moment decision, I leaned forward and spoke to the driver. "You know what? I think I'd like to get out and stretch my legs a bit before we go to the hotel. Could you drop us off in front of St. Paul's?"

"Really? You want to walk... now?" Macy asked.

"I do. It's a beautiful night, and I've always wanted to see St. Paul's. It was designed by Britain's most famous architect, Sir Christopher Wren."

"I'm sure it's closed at night, though."

"That's okay. We can see it from the outside."

The driver did as I asked, and we got out in front of the majestic English Baroque style structure. Macy stared up at it.

"Wow. I didn't see this when I was here before."

Before he drove away, I leaned back into the car and handed the driver an enormous tip, asking him to meet us later in a different location. Then Macy and I began our walk around the cathedral. The entire majestic building was fully lit by spotlights, from its colossal dome to its columned porticos, the white stone glowing and visible to nearly the entire city from one angle or another.

"It's beautiful," she said, her warm breath leaving a cloud in the cold night air.

It was beautiful, but seeing this place was only my cover

story for what I really had planned. After only a few minutes of exploring the grounds and admiring the building's facade, I took her hand.

"Come on, let's go for a walk."

"You don't want to see the other side?" she asked, obviously confused.

"I'll see it another time. I just want to walk with you through the streets of London as the snow falls."

She grinned at that. "Okay."

Thankfully we were both wearing appropriate coats, and Macy had gloves and a hat as well, because it was cold. But it was the kind of calm, still cold that wasn't uncomfortable, and indeed there were light snowflakes falling all around us, lending exactly the sort of magical air to the night I'd been hoping for. Occasionally other couples would pass on the sidewalks, usually giving us an isn't-it-lovely smile.

After a few blocks, we reached a small, lushly planted park tucked into a street corner among the multi-story buildings around it. It was contained by a low stone wall and featured a variety of trees and shrubs and plantings, many of them retaining their leaves even in this season.

"Oh, look—it's William Shakespeare," Macy cried, pointing to the bust of the famous playwright rising from the greenery.

"It is. Would you look at that?" I said. "Hello Will, old boy. Nice work."

On the other side of the street, a group of four young men ambled along together, or staggered, rather, down the pavement, talking and laughing loudly. They appeared to have just left one of London's many pubs and had been *very* good customers, from the looks of things. One of them still held a large bottle, in fact.

When we reached the corner of the park's hip-level outer

wall, I stopped and leaned against it. "Let's stop here for a minute."

Macy complied, stepping between my spread legs so she could burrow against my chest. She pressed the tip of her nose into the warmth of my neck. "I'm starting to get a little cold."

I wrapped my arms around her, pulling her closer. "Okay, we'll head for the hotel in a minute then."

"It is beautiful, though. Did you arrange for this snowfall?" She looked up at the sky then narrowed her eyes in feigned suspicion.

I raised my hands above my head. "You caught me."

Just then, Macy looked down and spotted the black and white block-lettered street sign affixed to the stone wall.

Finally.

"Oh my gosh, Nic. Look at this. We're on Love Lane!" She giggled in delight.

I slid from the wall and stepped back, pretending to have only now noticed the sign myself. "Wow. How funny. We should take a picture. Go stand in front of the sign."

I pulled my phone from my pocket and focused on her, framing her up with the iconic street marker.

"Hey, what is that?" I lowered the camera and took a step toward the wall, pointing out a wrapped package partially obscured by an overhanging shrub.

Macy went to it and pulled it out. The white square box was topped with a white satin bow. There was no tag, nothing to indicate what might be inside.

She lifted it and turned it around. "What do you think it is?"

I shrugged. "Open it, and let's see."

"Okay." Her tone was eager and she pinched the end of the bow, prepared to pull it, but stopped. Her brows pulled together beneath the brim of her fuzzy knit hat. "I probably shouldn't. What if someone put it there for somebody to find?"

"You mean like a drug money drop or something?" I smiled. "It has a white satin bow. Maybe it's a gift someone dropped while walking through the park. They're probably looking everywhere for it, trying to figure out where they lost it. We should open it and see what it is—then we can return it to the rightful owner."

"You're right."

The excitement of the mystery returned for her, and she carefully set the box on top of the wall, untied the bow, and lifted the lid. She looked up at me.

"It's… a cupcake."

"A cupcake? What flavor?"

"I don't know." She lifted the elaborately decorated treat from the box. It was topped with at least a thousand calories worth of creamy white frosting and crowned by delicate flower petals made from either white fondant or white chocolate—I couldn't tell. Macy pulled back the edge of the cupcake liner to see beneath the swirl of white frosting. "It's red velvet," she exclaimed. "That's my favorite."

"What are those little colored things on top?" I asked, leading her into it.

"Rainbow sprinkles." Her eyes veered back to mine and bulged in shock. "Nic—did *you* put this here?"

I only smiled. The chimes of Big Ben sounded in the distance, ringing the midnight hour. As if on cue, the intoxicated bar patrons crossed the street, starting to pass us. Suddenly they all stopped in place. And started singing. Because it *had* been a cue. And they weren't intoxicated bar patrons.

Macy's shocked face swiveled to stare at them, then she searched my face again. "Nic… what's happening?"

As the hired quartet serenaded her, I dropped to one knee

on the snowy pavement and took her hand—the one *not* holding the cupcake—in mine.

"Macy, I love you—more than I know how to express. I know we're not out of the woods yet, so to speak, with the Plague. I know we have many challenges ahead of us. But I'd rather face them with you than anyone else in the world."

Macy's shoulders began shaking as she realized what was happening. Her eyes glistened with unshed tears as I continued.

"You know I'm already bonded to you, so no matter what you say, I'll always want to be with you and keep you safe. But it would make me the happiest man on earth if you'll say you love me too, and agree to marry me, and spend eternity as my wife."

"Oh Nic," she whispered. "I love you so much." After pausing to swallow and blink back tears, she said, "Yes. Yes of course I'll marry you. You are the only person I could imagine spending eternity with."

Overjoyed, I got to my feet and lifted her, swinging her around and kissing her hard. Off to our side, the singing stopped, replaced by applause and the loud pop of a champagne cork. I lifted my head to see two of the singers approaching, one holding the bottle, the other offering two filled flutes.

"Congratulations," they both said, smiling widely.

"Thank you. Excellent job, gentlemen. Thank you."

The two joined the other singers, and the four of them walked off down the street together, leaving Macy and me alone. Macy waved good-bye and then gazed up into my eyes. "How did you... when..." She shook her head in wonderment.

"Well, I *may* have spent a considerable amount of time researching, 'World's Most Romantic Places to Propose,' on the internet. And I made a few phone calls this morning once I learned we'd be heading for England."

"Thank you. It couldn't have been more perfect."

I grinned down at her and kissed the tip of her cold nose then her lips. "Well, it *could* be… if there was a ring."

She shook her head vigorously. "No, don't even worry about that. You haven't had time to shop for rings, and I don't even need one. I—"

"Piccola," I interrupted. "Take a closer look at that cupcake."

Frozen for an instant, she blinked several times then followed my instructions, bringing the flower-topped confection closer to her face. Her eyelids flared, and her lips formed a small "o."

Reaching into the whorls of the center flower's petals, she pulled out the ring. The golden band was encrusted with tiny, glittering diamonds in an ancient Elven pattern. A much larger radiant-cut diamond was set into the top.

"Oh my… wow. This is the most gorgeous ring I've ever seen in my life. When did you…"

"I *procured* it in Altum. The day after we got there—those Light Elven craftsmen are incredible."

"You've had it all this time? Wait—how did you get it to England?"

I smiled, rather pleased with myself and how my grand plan had worked out. "The ring flew here with us on the plane. When I leaned back into the car to 'pay the driver,' I gave it to him and he drove over here and put it in the cupcake while we walked around the cathedral. The driver was a plant—like the flash mob singers. And… here he is now."

Right on schedule, the car pulled around the corner and came to a stop.

"Ready to go to the hotel?" I asked, opening the back door for Macy. "It's not far."

"I'm ready to marry you right here and now," she said. "Too bad the cathedral's not open for business."

I laughed, thrilled by her eagerness—and a bit regretful I hadn't thought of that one myself.

"It is too bad. Unfortunately we do have to wait. You think Alessia's vicious? You wouldn't want to see my twin sister if she were left out of such an important occasion. Our eternity together would come to a very abrupt and painful end."

Tapping on the back of the front seat, I indicated to the driver we were ready to go. Then I shifted and took my fiancée into my arms and kissed her all the way to the hotel. Figuratively we had a long road ahead of us, but at least now I was confident we'd be facing it together.

24

MACY

The next morning, I woke with a start, wondering if it had all been a dream. Drawing my left hand from beneath the covers, I held it up to check. And smiled. The magnificent ring glittered in the small beam of light penetrating a gap in the hotel draperies.

Turning my head, I saw Nic still asleep beside me, fully clothed, on *top* of the covers. And I smiled even wider. There was the real priceless jewel. This guy was unbelievably gorgeous. And sweet. And good. And he was *mine.* Forever.

When the group of "drunken carousers" had abruptly stopped in the street and turned toward us last night, I'd been frightened at first. But then they'd placed their hands dramatically over their hearts and started singing, and my head had started spinning. It all happened so fast—the surprise box, the incredible cupcake.

I was thrilled when I'd thought that was all there was to it. But then Nic had encouraged me to look closer at the beautiful confection, and I'd finally spotted the ring. My heart had nearly burst with happiness.

Were elaborate proposals common in the Ancient Court?

I didn't know, but I assumed I'd learn all these things in time since I'd be spending the rest of my life—of my *eternity*—with an Elf. The thought made me giddy. The only thing that could have been better than learning Nic was alive was learning that our time together was unlimited and knowing we'd soon be married. I was too grateful to even put into words.

And that was one *more* reason I had to do anything necessary to help the humans. I had been blessed beyond measure—how could I not want to pay it forward? I'd start with Olly.

Even if the worst happened and we didn't reach all the fan pod girls before the Plague was activated, at least Olly would be saved.

"Good morning," I said, leaning over to wake Nic with a kiss to the cheek.

His eyelids fluttered open. For a moment there was disorientation in the liquid brown depths, but it was quickly replaced by warmth. "Good morning, piccola. Did you sleep well?"

"Best night of my life—so far." I added a flirty tone to those last two words. Soon we'd be married and we'd truly be a bonded couple. Before we could get to that, though, we had to complete the task of treating all the girls who carried the Plague virus.

"It's nearly eight o'clock," I told him. "We should probably get up and going."

"You're right. We've much traveling ahead of us. The sooner we treat Olly, the sooner we can get to the other girls."

He rolled out of bed and sauntered toward the bathroom, pulling his shirt up and over his head as he went. *God help me.* If the fate of the human race hadn't been hanging in the balance, he'd never have made it to the shower without me tackling him and dragging him back to the bed.

As it was, we both showered and dressed quickly, picking up pastries downstairs in the hotel coffee shop to eat on the short plane trip to Bristol. From the airfield there, we took a taxi. A few streets from Olly's, Nic handed me his phone so I could text my young British friend. I tapped in the words, grinning with eager anticipation.

Macy: Hi, it's Macy. What are you doing?

The answer came across the screen moments later.

Olly: Just finishing my porridge.

Macy: Are you dressed or still in your jammies?

Olly: Dressed. Why? You want to Skype?

Our car pulled up to the curb in front of Olly's address, a two-story stone-front row house with a tiny front garden and leafy green vines growing up and over the blue-painted front door and the bay windows.

Macy: No, I want you to open the door.

Nic and I got out of the back seat. Moments later, the front door flew open, and Olly's wide-eyed face stared back at us.

She screamed and ran down the steps toward me, dressed in leggings, an oversized sweater, pink socks, and no shoes or jacket. "I can't believe it! I can't believe you're really here." She turned to Nic. "You weren't lying—you really did come back with her."

"I told you so." He grinned.

"Are you married?" she squealed, hopping on her toes.

"Not yet," I told her. "But look at *this*." I held out my left hand, knuckles up, for her inspection.

"Oh wow. That is the most brilliant thing I've ever seen. It's like a fairy tale ring. I bet Princess Kate's ring isn't even this big."

"You shouldn't have come out with no coat and no shoes on," I said. "You must be freezing."

"I am." She took my hand and started pulling me toward the door. "Come in. You have to meet my mum. Dad's gone out, but Nanna lives with us, and you can meet her, too. They've heard all about you. They're dying to meet you. You two can stay in Wes's old room, and we'll have dinner tonight at my favorite restaurant. I'll wear the new dress I got for my birthday, and..."

I turned and grinned at Nic over my shoulder as Olly dragged me through the vestibule into the entrance hall, chattering nonstop. We wouldn't be staying the night, but I didn't want to throw cold water on her happiness. I'd tell her later.

I'd never been in an English household. All my time in London I'd spent visiting tourist attractions and stayed nights in a youth hostel. Olly's home wasn't large, but it was nice, smelling of herbs and coffee, and decorated with a pleasant clutter of tchotchkes and numerous potted plants in each room I could see. The walls of the entrance hallway were covered in a fascinating running mural of vine-covered tree trunks and gnarled limbs.

Olly led us to the kitchen, where the first thing I noticed were the floor-to-ceiling glass-fronted cabinets that occupied an entire wall. Inside were shelves displaying bottles of every imaginable shape and size—hundreds of them. Some had faded, handwritten labels, most did not. Someone in the family was obviously a collector of antique bottles.

A long wooden work table centered the room, and behind it stood a middle aged woman with a short-cropped pouf of blonde hair and a big smile displaying prominent front teeth that were slightly crossed. A pot rack hung over her head and from it were suspended a variety of drying herbs, making it seem as though she were standing between curtains of fragrant greenery.

"For mercy's sake, Olly, you didn't even invite them to remove their boots and cloaks?" Wiping her hands first on a dish towel, she came forward and extended a hand.

"It's lovely to meet you, Macy. I'm Ciarra. I am so grateful to you for being a friend to Olly when she was in that dreadful place. And I'm so happy the both of you were able to escape. I'm not fond of those fan pods—or of that horrible Buonoccorsi family." She turned to Nic. "And who is this handsome young man?"

"Nic... Bonneaux," he said, altering his last name at the last second. "I'm Macy's fiancé. We met in France." Technically true, as the island of Corsica *was* a French territory. I noticed he added more of a French flair to his accent than he usually allowed.

"Well, Nic, you are lucky to have gotten your young lady back. I hope from now on you two will listen to your parents when it comes to these things." She wagged a finger at me and Olly, causing us to cut our eyes at each other in commiseration. "Now, who would like a cup of tea?"

Olly led us to the sitting room and invited us to sit on a sofa in front of the tiled hearth. Floor-to-ceiling built-in bookcases flanked it, which drew my attention instantly. I was always fascinated by other people's books. These were interesting. Some of them looked ancient, and there seemed to be quite a few about botany. They had titles like *Natural Cures for Common Ailments* and *Plants, Herbs, and Flowers and their Practical Uses.*

Ciarra came in with the tea tray, setting it on a low table in front of the sofa before seating herself opposite us in a chair. "Now, we must all get to know one another properly."

Nic and I made small talk and answered her questions as best we could without revealing anything classified. After a few minutes, an older woman descended the central staircase and entered the room.

She wore a simple blue cotton dress, belted at the waist. Her gray hair was styled in a casual twist. She was of average height and weight, like Ciarra. Unlike the younger woman, she did *not* wear a welcoming expression. Her blue-gray eyes bored into Nic as if she could see directly past his handsome camouflage and directly into his Elven nature. When her eyes turned to me, they changed, narrowing and growing warmer, almost… appreciative looking. I wondered how old she was and if, perhaps, she suffered from a bit of dementia.

Ciarra stood. "Mother, come and meet Olly's friend Macy and her fiancé Nic. Macy, Nic, this is Olly's grandmother, my mother, Fenella Rowan."

We both stood. Nic offered his hand first, but she bypassed him and reached toward me instead, walking up to me until she was uncomfortably close. She looked me over, smiling.

"It's *very* nice to meet *you*. Where are you from? Where is your family?" The woman spoke so close to my face I could smell the scent of her flowery skin cream and black licorice on her breath.

I sat back down before answering, reclaiming my personal space. "I'm American. My parents and sister live in Missouri."

"Ah," she said, continuing to stand directly in front of me —which meant she now looked down at me. "And do you have a large family?"

"Um…" I slid a glance to the side toward Nic, who returned my *this is bizarre* look. "Not really. Just kind of the normal size. Some cousins on my mom's side. My dad's family lives in Texas."

"Yes. Good. And they are small—like you?"

What? This was one of the strangest conversations I'd

ever had. It didn't feel like a conversation at all—more like an interrogation.

"Macy is adopted," Nic interjected. "She's one of a kind." His tone was jovial, but his smile was too tight. I could tell he was as disconcerted by the woman as I was.

"Oh how lovely." Ciarra emitted a forced laugh, acting as if the scene in her sitting room was just an ordinary chat over tea. "Arthur and I considered adopting, but then Olly's brother Wes had such health problems, and it was all I could handle, honestly. How do you like your tea, Nic? May I pour for you? Mother—why don't you have a seat?" she gritted between clenched teeth.

"I don't really care for any. Thank you anyway," Nic said.

"Oh no. I insist now. You must try it. I make the best pot of tea in South Gloucestershire."

He nodded, giving her a reassuring smile. She was obviously nervous over her mother's inappropriate social behavior, and being the nice guy he was, he accepted.

"How can I resist then? Thank you. Only a little sugar for me."

Olly's grandmother finally stepped back and went to a chair of her own. She never took her eyes from me, though. Dementia, definitely. That must have been difficult for the family. I decided to follow their lead and pretend like I didn't notice the bizarre behavior.

"I can make my own." I reached for the teapot when Ciarra finished pouring Nic's cup.

"It's no trouble, at all," she said. "You must let me serve you—you are an important guest."

"Thank you." I sat back and smiled, watching as she added a spoonful of sugar to my cup followed by a dose of cream. "It smells delicious. I love tea in England. It's such a nice tradition, and it just tastes better than it does in the States for some reason."

She gave me a grateful smile. "Well, Arthur has gone Yank on us and started drinking coffee. Wes, too. He takes it as strong as can be. I don't know how they drink the stuff. Cream for you?"

"Yes please. Where is Wes? Away at university?" I asked. Olly had mentioned her brother was much older but hadn't said where he lived now that he'd moved out.

"No, his health condition forced him to leave the mainland. He can't be around a lot of people, you see, so he lives a very quiet existence off the coast on one of the Scottish small isles. We miss him terribly."

"Oh, I'm sorry to hear that."

Olly listened intently while she made her own cup, adding sugar and cream until the concoction was nearly white.

"Not so much sugar, dear, you'll rot your teeth," her mother scolded.

"Her teeth are fine," Fenella corrected. "Let the girl be."

A dark look passed between the two Rowan women. Suddenly, I became very thankful we *didn't* have time to spend the night with Olly's family. I lifted the cup to my lips and took a sip of the hot liquid.

"It's very good," I said to fill the uncomfortable silence.

"I'm so glad you like it," Ciarra said. "Well then, Macy, you must tell us all about your exciting travels. Olly is very jealous of the places you've seen. How did all this come about? Were you an exchange student?"

Before I could answer, Fenella interjected. "Why don't we talk about what's really going on here instead?"

Every head in the room turned to her.

"Mother—"

"Nanna—"

Olly and Ciarra's words stepped on each other as they each began to protest the rude—and very odd—remark.

"What? Is it bad manners to ask *why* there's an Elf and a nymph in our sitting room?"

My jaw and Nic's dropped simultaneously. I wasn't sure about anyone else's expression in the room because I was looking only at him, desperately searching his face for clues as to our next move. What was *up* with this old lady? How could she know what we were?

"Oh dear." Ciarra shot out of her chair and moved toward her mother, throwing an apologetic glance back over her shoulder toward me and Nic. "I am *so* sorry. My mother grew up out in the country in a very small, very superstitious village, and I'm afraid that sometimes these days, with her age and all, her mind goes back to the wild faerie stories she heard as a child. Do please forgive her remarks."

She put a hand under the older woman's elbow. "Mother, why don't you come help me in the kitchen? I have some fresh biscuits in the oven, and we must get them ready for our guests. Olly, dear, why don't you show Macy your room? Nic—I'll be right back. Feel free to explore the conservatory if you like—Mother grows some interesting plant species in there."

She led Fenella quickly from the room. Olly and I stood slowly, staring at each other, not quite sure what to say.

She took a couple steps toward the front hall. "The stairs are this way."

I got up and followed her, glancing back at Nic.

The cure, he mouthed to me, and I nodded, patting my purse. He was right. It was the perfect opportunity to give Olly the treatment for her Plague infection. I wasn't sure *what* else was going to happen when we got upstairs behind closed doors. She was bound to have questions. Should I tell her the truth or deny it all?

"So this is my bedroom," she said at the top of the stairs, gesturing for me to enter. Once we both stood inside, she shut the door and turned to me, her blue eyes wide with wonder.

"Is it true? *Are* you really a nymph? Is Nic Elven?"

"I…" I sat on her bed hard, my legs suddenly weak. "I don't know what to say, Olly."

"The truth. You can trust me, Macy. I knew you were different as soon as I met you in Corsica. I'm different, too, though I'm not quite sure how."

For long moments I sat staring at her sincere face as a battle waged inside my head. It *would* be easier to get her to simply take the cure if I told her the truth. But then Nic's people required complete secrecy when it came to their real identities. Of course, Nic's people wanted to capture me and drain all my blood, so…

"It's true. I am a nymph. And Nic's an Elf. He told me about himself when we went away on our holiday in Italy. I found out about my heritage only a few weeks ago."

"That is so *cool*," she gushed, her face glowing with delight. "What can you do? Like, do you have special powers or anything?"

"I'm not sure. I don't really know much about being a nymph. I don't know any others to ask—I was adopted by humans. There is one thing I *can* do." I pulled my purse to my lap and withdrew the case containing the tiny vials we'd brought along for treating the girls.

Extracting one small vial from its padded compartment, I said, "I can give you this."

Olly reached for it eagerly. "What is it? Magic elixir?"

"Sort of. It's medicine. I brought it for you because Dr. Schmitt injected all the fan pod girls with something very bad—a plague virus."

Her eyelids flew open.

"It's dormant right now, but it could be activated at any time. That's why you need this. It will clean the virus from your blood so you won't get sick and you won't infect anyone else. Without it, the plague could kill you and spread to your family and your neighbors and friends. And they'd spread it to more people."

"What about you?" she asked.

"I'm fine. I'm immune to it. But the other fan pod girls are in danger. That's why Nic and I have to leave right away. I'm sorry I can't stay the night, but we have to go and find them and give them the cure as well."

She nodded. "I understand. Is this why you needed my blood?"

"It is. Without you, we wouldn't have been able to find the cure. Some doctors put your blood and mine together in a bunch of tubes and dishes, and they finally created this medicine out of it."

"That is so brill! You were right—I *was* meant to go there and meet you. So is Nic not like the other Elves then? He doesn't want to kill us?"

"No, he's not like them at all. And he has a very nice sister as well. They're not all bad. There are many Elves in the States who are trying heroically to save all the humans."

She nodded. "That's good. I'd hate for all of them to be evil as Nanna says."

"Nanna. She's told you about Elves, huh? I wonder how she knows. It's a very carefully protected secret."

"I don't know, but she's always told me stories about them, and they're always scary. They hurt people, and they stole things from the good Earth-wives who tried to heal them."

"Who are the Earth-wives?"

She shrugged. "Good women who were the healers in their villages. They delivered the babies, helped people find lost things, helped the farmers by predicting the weather."

"I see." That sounded a whole lot like a description of

witches to me, and very *pro*-witch, as if it were right from a recruitment brochure. "And what did the Elves steal from them?"

"I don't remember exactly. Just certain things they needed to make their best healing potions. The Elves used to let the Earth-wives have some in return for helping to keep their secret, but then the Elves got greedy and took it all. They became competitors and enemies instead of friends."

"Wow. That's quite a story. Your grandmother has quite an imagination." *Or some personal experience.* I was starting to understand why Olly had been immune to Elven glamour— her grandmother must have cast some kind of protection spell over her. I couldn't wait to tell this to Nic and see what he thought. Maybe he knew something of an ancient quarrel between Elves and witches?

"She does. She's really nice, you know," Olly explained. "She didn't mean to be rude by announcing that in front of Mum and me. It's just that she's old now, and sometimes her thoughts come out of her mouth instead of staying put in her brain."

"I understand. I have grandparents, too." I wiped my brow, my hand coming away wet. It was *really* hot upstairs in Olly's house. I even felt a little light-headed. I was eager to get back downstairs and let Nic know what I'd learned from Olly. It would probably be a good idea to make our departure even earlier than we'd planned.

"Okay then, let's get you healed. Need me to open that for you?"

"I can do it," Olly said. "You don't have to give me a shot, do you?"

"No, you drink it."

"That's good. I like that much better," she said as she unscrewed the vial's top.

"The healers in America thought it would be easier to

treat the girls without them knowing it if we could pour the cure into a drink or something. We might even be able to sneak the cure to most of them."

Olly nodded in understanding and put the vial to her lips, tipping her head back and emptying it.

"How is it?"

"Not bad," she said. "There's no real taste to it. It just feels warm in my mouth."

"Speaking of warm," I said, "I am roasting up here. Your family likes it toasty inside in the winter, I guess."

She cocked her head. "I don't feel warm at all. Want to go back downstairs?"

I nodded and rose from the bed, swaying slightly as my feet struggled for balance.

"Maybe you're sick," she suggested. "Sometimes people get germs on airplanes."

I shook my head. "I don't think so. It was a private plane, and I can't get human illnesses. Let's just get back downstairs to Nic."

Olly offered me her hand for support as we made our way to the stairs and down to the ground floor. Nic was waiting in the entrance hall, wearing a troubled expression.

"We need to go," he muttered. "Something's not right here."

I nodded my head, my eyelids growing heavy. "You're right. And I don't feel well."

His brows drew together in instant concern, and he slipped an arm around my back. "Olly, it was good to see you. I'm going to take Macy to our hotel and let her rest. Tell your mother and grandmother good-bye for us, okay?"

"I wish you didn't have to go so soon," Olly said. "I'm sorry about Nanna. She gets a bit addled at times."

Before the last few words left her mouth, Ciarra and Fenella returned, rushing into the entrance hall.

"Oh, you cannot leave so soon. Nic hasn't drunk his tea yet," Ciarra said. "And you haven't even had any biscuits. We made them specially."

Fenella glared at Nic, making no attempt at hospitality. "Where are you going with that nymph? I know what *you'll* do with her. She needs to stay *here*. I need her."

"Mother, please," Ciarra pleaded.

Nic placed himself between me and the two women. I clung to the back of his shirt, trying to stay on my feet. My eyelids were heavy, and I felt as if I might faint at any moment.

Reaching behind him and taking my hand, Nic backed toward the front door. "I'm afraid Macy and I must be going. She's taken ill suddenly. Thank you so much, Ciarra for your hospitality. Mrs. Rowan, you needn't worry about Macy. I'd lay down my life for my fiancée."

Turning quickly he opened the door and guided me through it just as Fenella charged him, screaming, "That can be arranged, you Elven filth."

Keeping a firm grip on my hand, Nic led me down the front steps. We were closely followed by all three Rowan females, Fenella shouting threats, Ciarra sobbing apologies, and Olly yelling, "What in the bloody hell is going on here?"

The whole procession stopped dead in its tracks as someone stepped into the narrow gap between the garden hedge and the stone gatepost, blocking our path.

It was Alessia.

25

NIC

Of all the times for Alessia to catch up to us. Even before Macy had staggered down the stairs, obviously drugged, I'd decided it was time to abandon ship.

All during the bizarre teatime ritual there had been one desire in Fenella's heart—Macy's blood. All I could think at the time was that she must have somehow sensed that it was important for her granddaughter. If she *was* a witch, perhaps she'd been able to detect the Plague virus Olly carried? Uneasy, I'd avoided drinking the tea, but Macy had sipped some before I could prevent it.

"Where do you think you're going?" Alessia snarled. "You have no idea how many stinking little villages I've visited, looking for you."

I pulled Macy closer to my side. Most of her weight was resting on my arm now, and her feet stumbled on the unbroken pavement. My mind scrambled for the best course of action. She was a world-class gymnast. Under normal circumstances, she'd have been easily able to vault the brick and iron fence separating Olly's garden from the neighbors.

But these weren't normal circumstances. Macy couldn't

vault anything in this condition—she couldn't even walk unassisted, and I couldn't hold her and make the leap. On our other side, the hedge was too thick to go through and too tall to go over. The only thing to do was pick up Macy and charge right into Alessia, running her over if necessary to escape the threat behind us and the one in front of us.

Before I could make a move, Macy's legs buckled. She'd passed out. I caught her sagging body and swept my other arm beneath her knees, supporting her now in a cradle hold against my body as my former betrothed glared daggers at us.

She took a step forward. "What is the matter with my nymph?"

From behind us, Fenella's voice rang out, sounding much stronger than it had when we'd first met and I'd thought she was just a doddering old lady.

"She is *my* nymph, and you are on my property, Elven she-devil."

"Oh my heavens, the neighbors," Ciarra cried, sounding like she was about to swoon.

Glancing down at Macy, I saw her eyes were closed. Whatever I did here, I'd have to do it without her cooperation. Deciding on the forward charge, I gripped Macy tightly and started toward Alessia.

She withdrew her hand from her overcoat to show me what she held in it—a gun. She aimed it at Macy's head, which rested over my heart.

"It would be poetic, would it not? The two of you with one bullet?"

"Alessia, please," I said but stopped speaking when she cocked the gun audibly.

Keeping it pointed at Macy and me, Alessia flicked a glance to the old woman on the front stoop and then back to

Olly, who'd come to stand at my side, striking a protective posture.

"Your property?" Alessia sneered. "Perhaps you should have done a better job keeping this little runaway witch on *your* property, old crone. Perhaps then she wouldn't have brought the source of your annihilation home with her onto *your* property. Oh, but I guess you don't know about the Plague, do you?"

She lifted the hand that didn't hold the gun, wiggling her fingers at Olly. "I could take out a few of you with bullets, but one touch from my hand to this scrawny girl, and everyone in this county is dead—every *human*, that is. You and your coven have powers, but you are only human, and your precious little English rose here is carrying a new Black Death—one that will make the plague that wiped out sixty percent of Europe's population in the fourteenth century look like child's play. No doubt my *darling* betrothed and his nymph plaything came here trying to save her, trying to hide her from me and my 'poison touch,' but there are too many of them, my darling."

She laughed. "Even if you'd managed to shield this girl, all it takes is one, and the whole world will eventually contract the disease. Why does it matter where it starts?"

I could have told Alessia about the cure—about the fact that we came here to heal Olly, not hide her, but not knowing how this would play out, I didn't want to give her too much information. For all I knew, a carload of her henchmen would show up in a few minutes brandishing guns as well, and she could order them to search us and take the cure from Macy's purse. Better that she remained ignorant of its existence for now.

Instead, I tried appealing to whatever shred of decency might be left in her. "You don't want to do that, Alessia. I know you're angry, but Olly is only a child, and the people in this neighborhood, this county—this country—have never done anything to you. These are the same people who buy your albums and cheer for you in concert halls. They're not your enemies."

"She is," Alessia said, waving the gun at Fenella. "She is," she said, shifting until it pointed at Olly. "As soon as she's grown and initiated, this *child* will hate you as much as the rest of her kind hate all of our kind. And *she* is definitely my enemy."

Her arm swung to aim the pistol at Macy again. My heartbeat exploded, pounding so loudly in my ears it was almost disorienting.

"Don't shoot the nymph," Fenella pleaded. "I need her. I need her blood to heal my grandson."

Ignoring her, Alessia continued to rage, tears running down her face, streaking her perfect makeup. "She's taken everything from me. Look at you—even now, you'd rather die with her than give her up and marry me."

Oh man, she was gone. How had she changed so drastically from the horse-loving fashionista princess, the talented and soulful singer she'd been when we'd first met?

She'd always been spoiled, but she hadn't been *evil.* Now there was a very high likelihood she'd go ahead and pull that trigger, killing Olly or me. Or Macy. I had to get through to her somehow. I had to get Macy away from danger. Using my glamour, I looked into Alessia's damaged, heavily guarded heart and unearthed her deepest desire.

"You're wrong," I said. Gingerly, I bent and lowered Macy to the ground. Then I raised my hands in front of me and paced slowly toward Alessia.

She waggled the gun. "Stop right there. What are you doing?"

"I'm coming with you. We'll go home together—right now. I'll marry you. You can keep that gun on me until the vows are said—I won't try anything. I won't back out on you. You have my word. If you leave Macy alone, if you do not harm this little girl, I will be your bond-mate for eternity."

Her watchful gaze, which had been trained on the collection of women behind me, flew to my face. "Do you lie to me, Nicolo?"

I gazed right into her fever-bright eyes and made my vow in a way she could not doubt. *I'm not lying. I will marry you. You know we won't be able to bond and have children, but I'll marry you tonight and never leave you. You won't have to be alone ever again. Let's go.*

Her eyes changed then, the rage and madness draining from them, replaced by vulnerability and hope, and a glimpse of the old Alessia.

I think it might be too late. I've gone to the homes of many fan pod girls.

Oh no—Alessia, what have you done?

I didn't mean to. I was looking for you. And her. Her eyes skipped to the side to see Macy lying unconscious on the grass. *I didn't touch any of them. I started to, but I couldn't do it.*

Alessia's eyes came up to meet mine, and they were haunted, frightened even. *But one of them touched* me. *I'm sorry. I have killed them all, haven't I?*

Maybe not. If you'll tell me where she is, we might be able to stop this before it gets out of control.

But how? Dr. Schmitt said it was unstoppable.

There is a way. If you'll trust me. And help me.

She nodded, and her hand dropped to her side. Relief burst through me like a broken dam releasing water—she was going to cooperate and stop this insanity.

The second her gun was no longer pointing at Olly, a strange shimmer shook the atmosphere around us. A low hum vibrated my eardrums, causing a piercing ringing that was almost painful.

For Alessia, it was more than "almost." She screamed and lifted her hands to clamp them over her ears. The gun fell from her hand to the pavement with a metallic thunk.

I scrambled to retrieve it. Alessia dropped as well, falling to her knees, then rolling onto the small patch of grass in the front garden, squeezing her eyes tightly shut and writhing in obvious agony.

"What's happening to her?" Olly asked, her young, high-pitched voice tinged with fear.

Her mother, who'd seemed like a sweet, nurturing stay-at-home-mum earlier, now wore a wild, vengeful expression. Her piercing gaze was trained on Alessia, and she muttered a stream of nonsense words under her breath, stopping long enough to answer. "I'm sending her *away*. I won't let her touch you, darlin'. Don't worry."

Fenella continued chanting without a break, standing beside her daughter, and staring steadily at Alessia's body twisting in pain on the lawn.

Olly ran to the steps of the house where the two older women stood. "It doesn't matter if she does, Mum. Macy and Nicolo brought me a cure for the Plague. I've already drunk it. The lady can't make me sick now."

"I'm going to make sure she can't make *anybody* sick," Ciarra said. "Where she's going, there *is* nobody to glamour."

"Mum," Olly said, apparently still upset. "What are you doing? I'm scared. Why does she look all fuzzy like that?"

My eyes went back to Alessia's convulsing form. She did look... odd. As I watched, her body seemed to lose substance, fading as if a low cloud passed in front of her, then she returned to clear view, then faded again. What *was* happening?

The chanting grew louder. My hair stood on end from the electricity in the air. I looked back at the front stoop where the Rowan women stood hand-in-hand, their eyes closed now. Though Olly did not join the mantra and appeared to be as freaked out as I was, one of her hands was now wrapped firmly in her grandmother's. It was some kind of ritual, and she was part of it, willing or not.

This was my chance. While their attention was solely focused on Alessia, I scooped Macy's unconscious figure from the lawn and ran toward the street. I'd have to leap over Alessia to get through the narrow garden exit, but with all the adrenaline charging through my veins, it would be no problem.

Just as I reached her and my feet left the ground, Alessia's body faded once again, flickered, and then disappeared entirely. I came down hard on the other side of where she had been lying and whirled back around, unable to believe what I'd seen with my own eyes.

Olly let out a high-pitched scream. "Where is she? Where did she go?" Tears ran down her red face.

The two women stopped their incantation and opened their eyes, fixing them on me and Macy. I didn't wait to find out the answer to Olly's question. I turned and ran, pounding down the street toward the village center, praying my inborn speed and endurance would be enough to let us escape a fate similar to Alessia's. Reaching the main street, I hailed a taxi and climbed in the back.

"What's the matter with 'er?" the driver asked, craning his neck for a look.

"Hangover," I said, and he snickered. "Bristol airfield please—and hurry. We've got a plane to catch."

As he pulled away from the curb and sped down the street, I kept my eyes on the rearview mirror, praying we'd seen the last of Olly's family.

Macy made a faint sound. I looked down to see her eyes flutter open.

"Nic... where are we?"

"We're in a car. On our way to the airport." For the driver's benefit, I added, "I think you had a little too much to drink." *Or rather—the wrong drink, as in, a witches' brew in your tea cup.*

"Is Olly okay?"

"I think so. Yes, she looked fine when we left. No need to worry." I decided not to mention her obvious distress at seeing a person disappear into thin air.

"What... was I hallucinating... or was Alessia there?"

"She was."

"What happened? Where is she now?"

I answered her as honestly as I knew how. "I don't know, piccola. I don't know."

"I'm tired, Nic," she said, her eyelids drooping again.

"I know. Rest again. You are safe." *For now.*

26

MACY

I woke with a start, lifting my head and looking around, not sure at first where I was. Seeing Nic's warm brown eyes looking down at me, I relaxed. Oh, the plane. We were on the plane. And it was on the ground.

"Where are we? Have we left England yet?"

He chuckled. "You slept right through England, piccola, and the entire Atlantic ocean. We are in the States again."

I nodded and sat up. I'd been sleeping with my head on a pillow in his lap, apparently. "Did you ride like that the whole flight—with me sleeping on you?"

He nodded and grinned. "You snore."

"I do not."

"Yes. You do. It was very entertaining."

I covered my mouth, partly from embarrassment, partly to shield him from my morning breath. "I'm so embarrassed."

He laughed. "I'm only kidding. And even if you did, I'm sure you'd have the cutest snore imaginable."

I scooted from our aisle and headed for the bathroom. When I got back, Nic had gathered our luggage and was waiting for me to de-plane with him.

"Are we back in Mississippi?" I asked.

He shook his head. "No. Wait and see."

I gave him a quizzical glance. "Why?"

Emerging from the plane, I had no more clue as to our whereabouts than I did before. But as the car pulled out of the airport property and onto a highway, I recognized the surroundings. I pivoted to face Nic.

"We're in Missouri? We're in Joplin. Why? Why are we here?"

"We're going to see your family. What is your address?"

In shock, I rattled off the street name and number. "Does my family know I'm coming home?" I had no idea what all Nic had been up to while I slept during the eight-hour plane flight, but apparently he'd been busy.

"They don't. I didn't know how to call them. But they'll be happy, right?"

I wasn't sure. And I wasn't sure if *I* was happy about this development. "I want to stay in a hotel—just for tonight, okay? I'm not ready to face them twenty minutes from now. I need to think."

He took my hand. "I understand. But I think it's important that we go there without delay."

"Why? What's happened? Did Alessia visit them or something? Are they okay?"

"Yes, yes, calm down. They're fine. Wherever Alessia is— I'm pretty sure it's not Joplin, Missouri. Olly's mother mentioned sending her to a place where she couldn't harm anyone with her glamour."

I let out a breath, experiencing a sudden influx of elation. "So it's over then? We got the cure to Olly, and if Alessia is gone, there's no way the virus will be activated in the other girls. Nic—this is great."

I hugged him, and he returned it, but when we pulled apart again, I could see he didn't share my sense of relief.

"Macy… I'm afraid it's *not* over. I should explain. Olly's house was not Alessia's first stop."

"What does that mean?"

"She told me she'd visited other fan pod girls, and one of them touched her. She didn't get the chance to tell me where. I spoke to Estelle on the phone before we left England, hoping she'd have some information, but so far, there are no reports of an outbreak—or at least it's not big enough yet to have made international news. But it's happening. The news will be coming at any time now."

"Oh no. We have to get to the other girls as quickly as possible with the treatment. *Why* did we come back to the States? The outbreak is happening overseas, isn't it?"

"Because there's more," I said, filled with dread at having to tell her the terrible truth. "Before we left Altum, Wickthorne warned me—if the virus was activated and began to spread, there would not be enough antidote to treat everyone in time."

I squeezed his hands. "Then we should be going to Mississippi, so they can *make* more. I can donate more blood, and they can create more antidote. Nox's healer can fly out and help, and maybe there are other Elven healers who can come and help as well. We should be going back to the airport." I leaned forward, intending to tell the driver exactly that, when Nic's touch on my arm stilled me.

"Macy—the problem is not a lack of healers." A long pause. "There is not enough *blood*."

"I said I'll donate more… oh…" My words dried up as I understood his meaning. It wouldn't be just a donation. It would be a total sacrifice. It would take all I had to give.

I drew in a shaky breath and swallowed. "It's okay." I nodded and made my voice stronger than I felt. "It's okay. I want to do it."

"No." The word was quiet and as solid as a stone pillar.

"Yes, Nic. There's no other choice. I *have* to. Do you really think I'd let the human race be wiped out so I can live?"

"No, I know better than that. That is why I've brought you back home."

My jaw dropped. "Were you planning to try to *hide* me here with my family or something? While the world dies around us?"

"No. Macy, listen to me. I knew, of course, that you'd volunteer to sacrifice yourself—but I will *not* allow that." He held up a hand to silence the protest that was already on my lips. "And before you tell me it's not up to me, hear this— even if you did give your life and every ounce of blood in your body, it would *still* not be enough to treat the whole planet. It would be a needless sacrifice, and most of the population would still die."

"I have to do *something*, though."

He nodded in agreement. "I know. And that is why we're here. I've brought you back to your family… so they can help us find your *other* family. The only hope we have left of saving the humans now—is finding your birth mother and the rest of your people. We have to find out where the nymphs are hiding… and beg them to share their magic."

A YEAR and a half after leaving to backpack around Europe, I stood once again on the covered front porch of my childhood home. It was almost surreal to be here. Nothing had changed. The wooden porch swing creaked on its chain hinges. A small placard over the mailbox read, "Moreno Family." In the summertime the porch would be hung with ferns, but now it held a tray for muddy boots and a blue doormat decorated in oversized snowflakes above the words, "Let it Snow!"

A grapevine wreath on the door was studded with sprigs

of evergreen and white ribbon—my mom hated that time after Christmas and before spring when the trees had no leaves and days were short. She'd always strived to hold onto the festive holiday feeling until spring arrived.

Fumbling for my house key, I noticed my palms were sweaty—in February.

I glanced up at Nic. "I'm not sure I can do this—not after what happened."

He smiled in encouragement. "They're your family. They'll be happy to see you. And a lot of time has passed. A lot has changed."

He was right. I wasn't the same girl I'd been when I'd left here. I'd been certain I could never take on any responsibility again. I'd believed everyone was better off without me. But thanks to my time in Nic's fan pod and the entirely new world he'd introduced me to, I had a whole new sense of purpose—a new understanding of myself. I *was* useful and responsible and valuable. Maybe even a little brave. I'd saved Olly's life. And I had no intention of stopping there.

Feeling a bit stronger, I inserted the key and turned, opened the front door and called out to my family as Nic and I stepped inside.

"Mom? Dad? Lily? Anybody home?"

There was a scurry of footsteps. My mother came into view, wearing the same cozy blue velour track suit and sheepskin-lined slippers she'd always favored on weekends. Her eyes and her mouth flew open wide at the same time.

"Macy! Baby, I had no idea you were coming home. Oh my word. Joel, Lily—Macy's home."

She hurried to me and embraced me, squeezing hard and letting out an abrupt sob. "I'm sorry. I don't mean to cry. It's just such a surprise. A wonderful surprise. I've missed you so much, honey." Pulling back and regarding my companion, she said, "And who's this?"

"Mom, this is Nic—"

My father jogged into the foyer, followed closely by Lily in her wheelchair. I hugged them both in turn. By the time we were all hugged out, tears were running down my own face. I stepped back, laughing with relief and joy. They were happy to see me—*truly* happy. I hadn't expected that. I had it so built up in my mind that they resented me or harbored some sort of wish that I'd just go away or something. It shocked me to realize how much I'd been missed.

And I'd missed *them*. Fiercely. "Wow, look at you," I said to Lily. "You look at least sixteen," I teased.

She beamed in return. "You look the same. Or, mostly— your hair is longer."

"You should have seen it a few weeks ago—it was platinum."

"Awesome," she exclaimed, clearly delighted. Grabbing my hand, she pulled it toward her face. "And you have a giant rock on your finger."

Of course she would notice—she was at eye level with my hand *and* completely obsessed with weddings.

"What?" Mom snatched my left hand and brought it up into view. "Oh my word. You're engaged?" She turned back to Nic. "I'm so sorry. We've all been so excited about seeing Macy again, we've been horribly rude to you. I'm Natalie. This is my husband Joel and Macy's sister Lily."

Nic smiled. "I feel as if I know each of you already. Macy has talked about you frequently." He offered his hand to my father then my mother, then bent to shake hands with Lily. "Nicolo Buonoccorsi. Macy's fiancé. Please call me Nic."

They all stared at him for a moment, as dazzled by his appearance as everyone was. My mom spoke first, stretching one arm around my shoulders and the other around Nic's back. "Well, let's get out of the foyer and into the den where it's more comfortable. Just leave your shoes on, honey, it's fine," she said to Nic. "We've got a fire going in here, and we can all sit down and talk."

Once we were all seated, Dad said, "I'm so glad to get a chance to meet you Nic. You're going to have to explain to us how you and Macy met. There's so much to ask, I'm not even sure where to start."

"I'll start," Lily said. "When are you getting married? And have you picked out a dress yet?"

I grinned at her. "No, I haven't. You have to help me with that." Addressing the rest of them, I gave a highly edited Spark notes version of our relationship. "We met when I was in France. Nic grew up there—on the island of Corsica. We spent some time together and really liked each other."

"I *loved* you," Nic corrected. "Almost at first sight."

I smiled and continued, blushing. "But then I came back to the States. We didn't reconnect until he came here recently. He found me, and the feelings were all still there. We got engaged two days ago."

"How wonderful." Mom clasped her hands over her chest. "You look so happy, Macy."

"Is that why you decided to come on home?" Dad asked. "Not that you need a reason. I was just starting to wonder if you ever would."

"That's part of the reason," I said, wondering if it was too soon to get into the rest. But time was critical. The virus could be spreading at this very moment. We needed to stop it before it got out of control, like a wildfire ripping through the population of Europe.

Nic and I had talked on the way here—we knew what we needed to accomplish, and we had a plan. We'd come up with a cover story for why I'd be asking about my birth mother now, after all this time, but I wasn't sure how it would fly with my parents.

"The other reason is that I wanted to find out anything you can tell me about... my birth mother."

"Oh." Mom sat back in her chair, clearly stunned.

"Why's that?" Dad asked. His expression and tone stayed neutral—he'd always been better at concealing his emotions than Mom had. "You've never even asked about her before. Are you hoping she'll come to the wedding or something, honey? Because you know she wanted it to be a closed adoption. She didn't want to be contacted. Maybe she's changed her mind by now, but she could be married, she could have other kids and never have told them or her husband she put a baby up for adoption when she was younger."

He turned to Nic. "If you're worried about medical history or anything, Macy's always been exceedingly healthy."

"Oh no, sir. It's not that." He launched into the fabricated story. "My family has a tradition of keeping a very detailed family tree. They present younger family members with their own updated and hand-painted version of it whenever one of us gets married. I thought it would be nice to have all of Macy's lineage included—for the sake of the children we may have someday. And I know my parents would appreciate it. They're from a very old European line, and they love genealogy."

Mom's brow furrowed. "Well, we'll try to help, but you realize... this path may not lead to any sort of prestigious family name, right? I hope your parents will be accepting no matter what you may find—if you can even track her down."

He nodded vigorously. "Of course. Nothing could change the way I feel about Macy—I am already committed to her for life. My parents have no say in that, though I'm sure they will love her when they meet her."

Well, that one was a bit of a stretch, but I realized he was trying to set my parents at ease, which I appreciated. My father nodded his head, apparently satisfied, and went to his desk in the corner of the den. He opened one of the lower file drawers and bent to shuffle through it. When he straightened again, he held a large envelope. Bringing it back over to the sitting area, he handed it to me. The paper was a faded yellow color and felt dry and brittle in my hands.

"That's all we have," he said. "Your birth certificate is in there, along with some documents from the lawyer who handled the adoption and your file from the hospital—one of the nurses made a few notes on it because your biological mother left without checking out. I don't know how much it will help."

"Thank you," I said, still staring down at it. "I'll open it later, after we catch up."

Mom smiled, apparently relieved I wasn't diving into the envelope's contents immediately. I hoped she wasn't hurt by my request, but either way, there was no help for it. It was literally a matter of life and death. We had to do anything necessary to find my birth family, and my real family could never know why.

Mom stood. "Well, why don't you come into the kitchen with me and Lily? We'll get some dinner started, and Nic and your dad can chat a bit."

I glanced over to him, checking his reaction. He nodded to let me know he was okay with that, and I rose to follow Mom and Lily. As I left the den, I heard my father's voice.

"Now, what do you do for a living, Nic? Or are you still in school?"

"Actually, I'm retired," he began to explain. "From a career in professional sports. But I plan to go to architecture school…"

Good luck, buddy. I chuckled as their voices faded from hearing. Before they were done, my father would no doubt know Nic's exact worth in cash and investments, making sure he could "afford" a jobless wife, rent, and tuition. Of course I had no intention of staying jobless forever. Once Nic and I were finally able to settle down in one place, I'd find something. I had even flirted recently with the notion of taking up gymnastics again. First things first, though. We had a world to save.

"So," Mom dragged out the word. "Nic is very handsome. And so tall. He's not like anyone you've ever dated before. He's not like… anyone I've ever *seen*." I could see the wheels turning in her head, trying to work out what it was about Nic that was so different.

"Is that what drew you to him?" she asked.

"Not really," I said honestly. "I didn't even really like him very much at first. I mean, *of course* I liked the way he looked, but really, I just wanted him to leave me alone—until I got to know him better."

"Did he get on one knee and propose?" Lily asked, giddy at the idea of it.

"Even better. He arranged for a serenade by a flash mob at midnight—on Love Street in London. And he gave me my ring… in a cupcake!"

She squealed and clapped, and my mind flashed to Olly. The similarities between the girls were striking—starting with their sweet hearts. *Olly.* I hoped she was okay. I knew my blood had healed her from the virus, but the situation with her mother and grandmother had been very strange…

My blood healed her.

I looked down at Lily sitting in the automated metal chair that had been part of her daily life for nearly two years now. Overwhelmed with love and gratitude, I hugged her, fresh tears springing to my eyes.

Why had I not thought of it sooner? Maybe it was because the permanence of her spinal injury had been sunk so deeply into my heart and brain where it had solidified into rock-hard guilt. I had not realized until this very moment what my nymph heritage could mean for my little sister. My blood had kept Nic from bleeding to death. It had healed Dr. Schmitt's head injury after he and Nic battled. It had been successful at cleaning the Plague virus from Olly's blood in the lab. Could it also heal my sister's severed spinal cord? It was definitely worth a try.

Standing again and facing my mom across the kitchen counter, I debated how to bring it up. If all else failed, I'd ask Nic to sway my parents into following my request.

"Hey, Lily," I said, grinning excitedly. "I want to show Nic my yearbooks and some of our old photo albums of you and me as babies. Would you go to my room and get them for me?"

"Sure." She wheeled around until she faced the hallway to our bedrooms. "I'll be *sure* to show him the ones of when you got your braces on. And cut your own hair," she teased.

"Not those," I pleaded as she giggled and rolled away. "Don't you dare, you little stinker."

As soon as she was out of sight, I turned back to my mother. "Mom? I recently learned about a new therapy for injuries like Lily's. It sounds really promising, and I think we should try it."

Her hands stopped in mid-motion, the knife she'd been using to chop lettuce hovering in the air above the cutting board. She darted her eyes at the hallway where my sister had disappeared.

"I'm sure it's interesting, honey, but you know the doctors have tried everything there is. They say what she has is beyond repair. It would take a miracle."

"Well, maybe this is it. Maybe this is the miracle that will work. There's no risk in it—according to what I read."

She gave me a wary grimace. "What is it? Not snake venom or anything, I hope."

"No. It's pretty simple, really. It's just a transfusion from someone else. Someone with exceptional health—like me."

Her head started moving in a dismissive gesture. I could tell her hopes were already dashed. "Macy, she had countless blood transfusions after the accident, during all her surgeries. From several different donors."

"But they weren't me. We didn't try *my* blood."

"Because you're not a blood relative. And from what I remember, you're not a match for blood type."

"We'll be compatible," I said, confident in my statement. Nymph blood was compatible with anyone, human, Elven, or otherwise.

"I'm not sure what good it would do—and it could do some harm to her morale. I don't want to get her hopes up only to have them come crashing down."

"Okay," I said, giving up trying to convince her. My poor mom had been through too many ups and downs with Lily. She didn't have enough hope left to try again, but I had enough for the both of us. We'd have to go with the Sway method.

"I'm going to go by the blood bank before I leave town and have some drawn and earmarked for Lily anyway—in case you change your mind and want to try it." Which she *would* as soon as Nic got through with her.

Her expression grew alarmed. "When are you leaving town? You're staying at least a few days, aren't you?"

"I wish we could. We'll spend the night, but Nic and I have to fly to Europe tomorrow. We have to tell his parents about the engagement as well. We'll be back before too long."

The cover story once again. In truth, we had to leave immediately in search of my biological family—wherever that might lead. It seemed to placate her.

"So we're the first to know?" She smiled.

I walked around the counter to hug her. "You're the first. And no matter what I find out about my birth mother, you will always be first in my heart. *You* are my real mom."

A sob shook her shoulders as she held me close. "Thank you, honey. I hope you've always believed you are our *real* daughter. You were my first baby girl and always will be."

Over dinner we talked and laughed. My parents and Lily really seemed to like Nic, and I was proud for him to get to know them. They were good people. I really did intend to come back soon, as I'd told Mom. It was *nice* to be here. For the first time in a long time, I felt like I *belonged* somewhere.

Sitting there with them all, soaking up the love and togetherness, I realized I'd blamed myself for Lily's injury much more than they had ever blamed me. They forgave me. They loved me. I had my family back. And I had Nic. My heart was whole.

But it wasn't enough for me to have a happily ever after ending because the lives of my human family—and the rest of the human world—were all still at risk. This happy interlude had to be a short one. I had a job to complete.

"Well." I pushed back from the table and stretched. "It's been a long day. I think I'm about ready for bed."

"Me, too. Thank you so much for the delicious dinner, Mrs. Moreno." Nic followed my lead and took his plate from the table to the kitchen sink.

Mom shooed us both away. "No, no don't do that. You're exhausted from traveling. And this is why God created dishwashers."

"Actually, the first commercially successful dishwasher was invented by Josephine Cochrane in 1886," Lily corrected.

"She collects facts about female inventors," I explained to Nic then turned to Lily, creeping toward her and pouncing.

"Who invented the first noogie?" I put her in a loose headlock, rubbing the top of her head with my knuckles.

She giggled and slapped at me, wriggling the top half of her body in an attempt to escape the "torture" administered by her older sister.

"Nic," she shrieked. "Save me."

He laughed and got into the game, coming up behind me and lifting me from the floor. "I will save you, Lady Lily. I'll put this little nymph in her place."

I stiffened in his arms, and Nic froze, realizing what he'd said.

Of course it meant nothing to my family. My parents kept laughing. "Just carry her right on down the hall," Mom said. "I'll come back in a minute to help you settle in. Macy, Nic can sleep in your room, and you can take the other twin in Lily's room."

"Okay, Mom," I said, thoroughly relieved at their lack of shock or suspicion.

Nic actually did carry me all the way to my room. Once inside the door, he set me down and kissed me. When the kiss ended, I was breathless and filled with bubbles of delight.

"That was a little too early—carrying me over the threshold," I said.

He smiled against my lips. "I'd like to do other things out of order as well. If we weren't in your girlhood bedroom with your parents right downstairs, I might try my luck and see if you'd let me. I'm running out of patience." He pressed me tightly against him, one hand on my lower back and the other threading through my hair as he kissed my neck.

I giggled. "Well, you're going to have to find some extra, because you know we can't. We have to be careful... just in case."

Pulling back, he gave me a baffled look. "In case of... pregnancy?"

"No silly. In case... you know... in case we can't find the nymph sanctuary, and the healers really do need me to..."

I didn't finish the sentence because his expression had turned so harsh and forbidding. All flirtation and seduction attempts abruptly ceased. "That's *not* going to happen, Macy. We'll *find* your people."

"I know. But if we can't..."

"*If* we can't, then I will always be there for you and try my best to make up for the loss of the humans in your life. I'm not letting you sacrifice yourself, so you can put that idea out of your mind."

"You can't stop me, you know."

"The hell I can't," he growled.

I looked up at his angry-yet-frightened face, and my irritation over his bossiness faded. He loved me. I'm sure I would say the same thing to him if he was the one with the "miracle blood." And he had a huge stake in this whole thing as well. If something happened to me, he'd be mate-less for eternity. And he would never even have the experience of bonding with someone, even once. That alone was enough to drive a healthy nineteen-year-old male out of his mind.

Stretching up on my tiptoes, I planted a soft kiss on his mouth. "You're right. We *will* find them."

Dad walked into the room and stopped abruptly. "Oh. Didn't mean to interrupt. I brought your bags."

I smiled at him, stepping out of Nic's embrace. "Thank you. I was just showing Nic around my room."

Dad looked away, obviously embarrassed. "Yeah. Well, I hope you'll be comfortable in here tonight, son. Looking at that bed, I'm afraid your feet may hang off, but the couch wouldn't be any better."

"It'll be fine, sir. Thank you so much."

Dad nodded. "Macy, I'll uh… put your bag in Lily's room."

He darted away again, and I giggled. "I guess now I really *should* show you around." I padded to the door of the attached bath and opened it, flicking on the overhead light. "Bathroom's in here. Turn the shower tap all the way to the right for hot water. There's an extra blanket and pillow in my closet. And my diaries are all locked, so don't even try to peek."

He snapped his fingers and hung his head. "*Che due palle.* There go my reading plans for this evening."

I laughed. "*My* reading plans involve the contents of that envelope. Let's hope there's something helpful in there."

Stepping close to him again, I wrapped my arms around his neck and said, "Goodnight, sweet prince."

He grinned warmly, bending to kiss my neck and then my forehead and the tip of my nose. "That sounds like something from a faery tale."

"We're in one, aren't we? All we need now is a pair of sparkly shoes and a happy ending."

"And you shall have it, piccola—all of it. I'll do everything in my power to make you happy forever."

I left him with a kiss and went to Lily's bathroom to get ready for bed. In spite of Nic's vow, there was no way I could ever be happy if I failed to stop the Plague and allowed all the humans to be wiped out. Pulling my toothbrush from my backpack, I looked at the yellowed envelope sitting inside it, and my belly bottomed out. Those documents could literally be the difference between life and death for my family.

When I emerged from the bathroom, Lily was transferring from her chair to the bed.

"Need help?"

She rolled her eyes at me. "As if. I've done this, like, a *zillion* times. I don't even think about it anymore."

I wished she didn't *have* to think about it ever again.

Hopefully the transfusion would make that possible. Going to the twin bed parallel to hers, I pulled back the covers and slid under, leaving on the lamp so I could see her beautiful little face.

For a moment, I thought about ignoring the impulse to tell her what I was thinking—my impulsiveness had led to trouble in the past—but I decided in this case, it would do more good than harm.

"Lily, can you keep a secret?"

Her eyes sparked with instant delight. "Of course. What is it?"

"Well, I'm not exactly sure how to say this, but… I believe in magic. I didn't used to, but now I do."

Her grin was so big it wrinkled her nose and turned her eyes into straight lines of pure bliss. "Me, too. I always did, though. Did you find magic in Europe?"

Thinking of Nic, I smiled. "I did. And I think some magic is going to happen for you. I think you're going to walk again."

"You do? But Mom and Dad say it's impossible."

"I know. But magic makes anything possible. There's a new treatment you're going to have, and I put every bit of magic I could find into it. I believe it will work."

She nodded vigorously. "I believe it, too."

"Good. Now let's get some sleep."

I switched off the lamp on the night stand between our beds.

"Macy?" Lily's voice sounded younger in the dark, the way it had when she was very small and looking up to me as I read to her at bedtime—usually from Peter Pan, her favorite book.

"Yes?"

"I missed you a whole lot. I love you, Macy."

"I love you, too, Tiger Lily. See you in the morning."

When her breathing had slowed and evened, and I was sure my sister had fallen asleep, I switched the lamp back on and crawled to the end of the bed where I'd dropped my backpack. Retrieving the envelope, I opened it and withdrew the documents from inside.

I'd seen my birth certificate before, briefly, when I'd had to produce it for gymnastics meets, but I'd never paid much attention to it. Now I combed over it in detail. Because I was adopted, I had an amended birth certificate, with the name of my biological mother and father replaced by my adoptive parents' names. There was information about the date and place of my birth on it, but nothing about my birth mother.

Next, I read through my official adoption papers. Again, only my parents' names, and the one they'd given me, appeared in them. The date and place of my birth, etc. etc. There was a bit of information noting that I'd become a ward of the state briefly while a search was conducted for my birth mother. It said she had left the hospital without an official release and left a note behind, asking that I be given to a good family who would love and protect me. There was an asterisk beside two typed words— "Note attached."

Flipping the remaining pages so quickly I dropped the whole stack, I finally located the small rectangle of paper. On it were scrawled a few words.

Please take care of my daughter and find her a good family, one who will love her and protect her always. Someday when she is grown and asks about me, please tell her I love her and that I'm sorry. - F

There was no signature, only the letter "F" and a strange symbol. Was it a nymph marking? A letter from their language maybe?

I set the remarkable note aside and picked up the old hospital record detailing my birth and stay there afterward.

As Dad had mentioned, there were some handwritten notes at the bottom of the chart.

—Mother disappeared from hospital room four hours after delivery without being seen or notifying nurses' desk or physician. Very young and small of stature—teen? Nervous acting. May have given false name on intake papers. Different from name she gave during delivery while medicated—Fallon. Spoke with very heavy Irish or Scottish accent. Clothing bore foreign labels. Illegal immigrant possible. No phone or address. Unable to contact or locate. Abandoned newborn.

Abandoned. Abandoned. That word had always held a very negative connotation for me. You abandoned your chores in favor of going out to play. You abandoned a project when it got hopelessly complicated or too messy. Irresponsible pet owners abandoned a boxful of kittens on the roadside.

But this woman had left a note asking for a good family to take care of me, asking someone to tell me that she loved me and was sorry. And she walked out of a hospital four hours after giving birth. That didn't seem like abandonment. It seemed like an escape.

What would she have been escaping?

Elves.

Witches.

Both?

If she was from overseas, it was possible she'd come here nine months pregnant specifically so she could deliver me far away from those threats—or whomever else might have been hunting her and her kind.

I could visualize a young, small woman like myself, huge with child, flying across the ocean or maybe taking a boat, having her baby here in America—in the middle of the country nowhere near the Elven strongholds—and then hobbling away afterward, putting as much distance between herself and her infant as possible. So that her daughter would never be a target as she had been. So that she'd be safe.

So that *I'd* be safe.

Swallowing a lump in my throat, I carefully re-folded the papers and put them back in the envelope, planning to share them with Nic tomorrow when we boarded the plane. But where would it be going?

Heavy Irish or Scottish accent.

Turning off the lamp again and pulling up my covers, I tried to sleep. When I was on the verge of drifting off, my mind turned to our visit a few weeks ago with the young healer's grandfather and the odd remark he'd made about my appearance. My eyes flew open, and my heart began to race. He'd mentioned Scotland, where he grew up, said I had "the look" of a local. It was as good a place as any to start.

As I closed my eyes again and tried to relax, my mind's theater filled with visions of rolling Scottish hills and the people who might live under them. My people. The nymphs.

27

NIC

M acy woke me in the morning with a kiss. Not quite conscious enough to realize where we were, I pulled her down on top of me and returned the kiss with vigor.

She rolled off the bed and away from me, giggling. "Nic. Stop it. Breakfast is ready, and these walls are paper thin. Believe me, my parents busted me every time I tried to make a late-night phone call without permission."

"Okay," I sighed. "I suppose I can wait until we get on the plane to attack you. Where are we going, by the way?"

"Shhh." She drew close to me and whispered, "I'm not kidding about the thin walls. My mom and dad think we're going to Corsica to give your parents the news of our engagement—don't blow the cover story."

"Right. So where *are* we going?" I whispered close to her ear, and she shivered. I loved seeing her react to my nearness, so I added a kiss behind her ear for good measure.

"Stop that." She gave me a gentle shove, but there was a smile in her voice. "Scotland, I think. The hospital records indicate my birth mother might have been from there or Ireland."

I nodded. "The lore indicates Scotland used to be fertile, uh... hunting grounds. Before the nymph population was hunted to extinction, that is. It's a good starting place."

"I want to call Asher's grandfather and ask if he knows anything—he mentioned something when we were there. And you should call Estelle and see if she got the shipment of antidote Asher sent to her."

Sitting up, I swung my feet to the floor. "I will. I think we should leave a few doses here—for your family—in case the Plague makes it to America."

Her eyes widened. "Good idea. Hopefully, it'll never make it this far. I'll put them in my jewelry box, just in case."

Macy crossed the room to her dresser and opened the lid of a pink and white box with a ballerina on top. Music played in sporadic, tinkling notes. She looked back over her shoulder and shrugged.

"I used to like ballet before I got really into gymnastics and had to specialize. This jewelry box was my favorite thing, so I kept it for sentimental reasons. If it becomes necessary, I'll tell them where to find the cure."

Breakfast was a loud, cheerful affair, and there were many promises extracted and made about a return visit very soon.

"We have a wedding to plan," Macy's mother said.

"I know. But you and Lily may have to arm wrestle Nic's sister to get any of your opinions in there about the dress and the decor," Macy warned. "She is a fashion *queen*, and she's going to be in her glory when she hears her twin brother is getting married."

I chuckled. She was so right. I hadn't even had a chance to tell Estelle yet, and I wasn't certain my eardrums were ready for the squeal of delight that was sure to come through the phone.

"I can't believe I'm going to meet a *real* model," Lily said. "Your family is really cool, Nic."

I sauntered over to her and squatted so our faces were on an even level. "Well, I think your family is cool. I *never* get chocolate chip pancakes at *my* parents' house."

"Come back anytime, bro," she said, making everyone laugh.

Before Macy and I had left her bedroom, she'd asked me to sway her parents into consenting to a blood transfusion for Lily. Of course I'd agreed, and I girded myself for what would probably be the most important—and certainly the most noble—use I'd ever made of the Elven skill.

Gesturing to the two of them, I said, "Could I have a word with you in private before Macy and I take off?"

They looked at each other and smiled, obviously assuming I intended to make it official and ask for their daughter's hand in marriage. Which, now that I thought of it, was an excellent idea. There were so many steps to this process that my people skipped over in favor of arranged marriages.

I wouldn't use my Sway for *that* part of things—unless absolutely necessary. I didn't think it would be. They already seemed predisposed to say "yes." The greatest desire in each of their hearts was for their two daughters to have healthy, happy futures, and I wanted the very same thing.

They sat together on the sofa opposite the chair I took. Both dark haired, they looked like they could have been Macy's natural parents—apart from her diminutive size. They looked at me expectantly, and I realized with surprise that my hands were shaking. It was a big moment. Taking a deep breath, I began.

"Mr. and Mrs. Moreno, I love your daughter. I know you don't know me very well, but I promise you I will be a good husband to her—always. I won't ever desert her. I will love her and care for her until the sun no longer rises and sets."

From the kitchen behind me I could hear Lily's delighted giggle and Macy's admonishment. "Get away from the door. He said, 'in private' nosy bug."

I continued as if I hadn't heard *both* the girls eavesdropping. "She's already said yes to me and made me the happiest man on earth, but I would still like to have your blessing. I cannot promise you that our life together will be free of challenges, but I will always protect her with my own life and do everything in my power to make her happy."

Macy's mother lifted her hands to her mouth and burst into tears. "That's all a parent can ask for."

Her father rose from the sofa, extending one hand. "You have my blessing, Nic. Welcome to the family."

I stood, and we shook on it. Her mother composed herself and came to hug me. I found myself profoundly glad I'd asked. But now it was time for the other life-and-death issue. I checked over my shoulder to ensure that Lily was no longer in the doorway eavesdropping. And then I put the full measure of my Sway into my next words.

"I encourage you *strongly* to take Lily for the treatment Macy suggested. As soon as possible. She will come to no harm, and I believe it will result in the miracle I know both of you have been praying for."

When I broke eye contact with them, the husband and wife looked at each other. "It's worth one more try, isn't it hon?" Joel said.

His wife nodded, wiping a tear from her cheek. "I suppose you're right."

"Very good then. Macy and I will stop at the blood bank on our way to the airport and arrange for the transfusion procedure. Someone from the medical center will call you with the details."

I'd no doubt be applying my Sway a couple more times at least before departing Missouri, but hey, if you couldn't use it in a situation like this one, what good was it? Since meeting Macy I'd come to realize it *could* be used for good.

Both her parents promised their compliance, and I let out a long breath.

"Okay girls," Joel called out. "You can come in now."

Macy and Lily burst into the room, smiling and laughing.

"How did it go? Did they shoot you down?" Macy teased, sidling up to me with a sassy smirk.

I wrapped an arm around her shoulders and drew her close to my side. "Afraid not, piccola. Looks like you're going to be stuck with me for a lifetime."

As we made our good-byes, there were tears of the best sort. I was profoundly grateful I'd brought Macy here. Yes, we'd needed the information about her birth parents, but she'd also needed to reconnect with the family who'd raised her and obviously loved her deeply. They were just as much a part of her as her nymph heritage was, and I loved *them* for making my betrothed the amazing woman she was.

She wiped her wet cheeks as our car pulled away from the house, took a deep breath, and let it out.

"They loved you," she said. "*I* love you. Thank you for making me go home again."

Threading my fingers through the soft hair at the back of her head, I drew her face to mine for a kiss.

"I love you, too," I told her when it ended. "You have a lovely family. I only hope mine will be half as gracious about our betrothal. They've come around about some things, but they're still pretty steeped in royal tradition and the ancient ways of the Court."

"It's okay," she assured me. "As long as you love me, I can deal with a disapproving Elven mother-in-law, if necessary. And who knows? You may not be out of the woods yet when it comes to future in-laws. My nymph family might be a hotbed of family drama as well."

Before heading to the airport, we followed the pre-flight plan, stopping first at the blood bank for Macy's donation and then at the office of the Moreno family doctor to arrange for the transfusion. He was resistant at first, but a bit of Sway and he got with the program.

Now all we could do was wait, at least where Lily's cure was concerned. As far as the *next* health crisis—the Plague—we couldn't afford to wait. We had to find Macy's birth parents as soon as possible.

ONCE WE BOARDED the plane and reached proper altitude, I called Asher to work out the next steps in our battle plan. He confirmed he'd shipped the antidote overnight to Los Angeles and said Wickthorne had made good progress on a vaccine to prevent new infections, though it still needed tweaking.

Then I spoke to Estelle, who sounded like she was in a car on the highway. She told me she hadn't received Asher's package yet but would be on the lookout for it.

"I still haven't found out where the Plague was activated," she said. "My source in Italy knows nothing. It's terrible. It could be happening anywhere, and we won't find out until the media reports it. I wish Alessia had told you where it was before she... poofed."

I swore. "You and me both."

"I wish there was *something* I could do. I feel so useless, and it seems wrong to be in the back of a limo on the way to an awards ceremony. Anders feels awful, too."

"Anders? You're with him now?"

Macy leaned over from the seat next to me and yelled into the phone. "Hi Anders!"

From the other end there was a chorus of happy male voices.

"Yeah. With all the guys." Estelle's voice sounded funny, containing a forced nonchalance. "The Hidden is performing the theme song from a movie at the show tonight, and you may have been too busy to keep up with the news, but Anders is up for the Oscar for best movie score."

Okay, now I detected an unmistakable note of pride.

"Estelle... I know now is not a great time to talk, but when you get a moment alone, I'd like you to *call* me."

"Nothing's going on," she snapped back. "I'm just having a good time."

"Ooookay. I was saying that because there's something I need to tell *you*—but now I *really* want us to talk soon." When Estelle said nothing was going on, something was definitely going on.

"Okay, gotta go. Love you, *mio fratello.*"

Macy plucked the phone from me and held it to her ear.

"Estelle? You still there? Listen, don't feel guilty—Anders needs your support tonight. Tell him we're thinking of him. And you'll do your part to help the American girls when the antidote gets there. As far as I'm concerned, that's saving all my friends and family because they're in the line of fire on this side of the pond. You're right where you need to be. So thank you."

Macy smiled at whatever Estelle said in response and handed the phone back to me.

"*Ciao, mia sorrela,*" I said to my sister and ended the call.

"Can we watch it? I mean, can that thing pick up a live broadcast?" Macy nodded toward a big-screen TV mounted to one corner of the jet's passenger cabin.

"I'll find out." I went to the cockpit and spoke to the pilot, coming back with good news. "It has a satellite receiver. So yes, we can watch it. Want a glimpse of your old boyfriend, do you?"

She slapped my shoulder. "I want to see my *friend* realize his dream and win an Oscar. *And* see what my future sister-in-law is wearing."

I laughed, and we settled in to enjoy the pre-show broadcasts. Estelle did look rather resplendent on the red carpet, in the company of all the members of The Hidden. Even the snarky humans doing commentary for the red carpet coverage had nothing bad to say about her silver evening gown and upswept hair. When it came to Nox, Anders, Rolf, and Matteus, the hosts positively *gushed*. I was a little embarrassed for them.

Several hours later, the awards show itself was well underway. The Hidden had already rocked the house with their live performance, and the Best Original Score category was introduced.

As the nominees were announced, the camera focused on their faces. Anders looked nervous, smiling tightly and nodding his head.

The starlet in front of the microphone on stage opened the envelope. There was a dramatic pause before she read the name inside. "And the Oscar goes to... Anders Jensen for *Mirror Image Mirage.*"

Anders reappeared on the screen, displaying genuine shock this time. His mouth open, his eyes wide, he rose slowly from his chair. Beside him, Estelle jumped and clapped. Her smile was euphoric. She turned to him, spreading her arms to hug him.

Instead of returning the gesture, he took her face between his hands and planted a kiss—a very long, very deliberate kiss—on my sister's mouth. The audience around them went wild.

Grabbing my arm, Macy let out a little squeal and

drummed the soles of her shoes on the floor in a rapid pattern. "Oh my gosh, Nic—are you seeing this?"

How could I miss it? Everyone in the world could see the tall, blond musician declaring his *unmistakable* affection for the internationally known supermodel. The entertainment programs would love it. But how did my sister feel about it?

When they pulled apart again, Anders' bandmates slapped him on the back and pushed him toward the aisle, encouraging him to go up on stage and accept his prize. He gave them the come-along gesture, shaking his head to indicate he was going nowhere without them.

My eyes stayed on Estelle, who remained in place, holding one hand to her cheek and wearing a very dazed expression. That answered my question. She was either terrified or completely smitten. Probably both.

I laughed out loud and pointed at the screen. "*Te l'avevo detto, mia sorella*. I told you so."

Macy crawled into my lap and wrapped her arms around my shoulders. "You're feeling pretty good about that glamour of yours, aren't you?" she teased.

"At the moment? Yes. Very good, indeed."

My hands slid over her back and hips, all thoughts of Estelle and Anders instantly banished. As we shared a lengthy kiss of our own, Macy's clever fingers explored my shoulders, chest, and abdomen, running up beneath my sport coat.

Encountering something protruding from the inner pocket, she lifted her head and withdrew several sheets of paper folded together.

I captured her wrist, realizing what she'd found. I'd completely forgotten they were in there.

"What's this?" She was genuinely intrigued now that I'd tried to stop her from taking the love letters.

"Nothing." I tugged the papers from her hand and held

them out of her reach. "Just some thoughts I jotted down while I was looking for you."

"Thoughts? About me? Oh, now I *have* to read these. You've been able to read my thoughts since the day I met you—it's my turn now, buddy."

She wriggled her hand until I released her then stretched it up and made another grab for the papers.

"Not your thoughts," I corrected. "Only your deepest desires."

Her eyes rolled upward. "Right. That's *so* much better. Hand them over and give me some reading space."

My heart tapped a nervous rhythm in my chest as I surrendered and placed the letters in her waiting palm then watched as she read.

Her face showed nothing. Did she think my words were corny and stupid? I'd been in a terrible state when I'd written those letters, not knowing if I'd ever get the chance to share my thoughts with her in person.

Finally, she looked up. And pressed the letters to her chest, closing her eyes and tipping her head back on the headrest as tears ran from both eyes, leaving shiny tracks that reflected the light from the TV screen.

I ventured a guess. A hope. "So… you like what I wrote?"

Her eyelids opened, and she trained glistening eyes on me, giving me a watery smile. "And the award for best love letter ever goes to… Nicolo Buonoccorsi. Come and get your prize, mister."

I followed her instructions, leaning in for a kiss worthy of the big screen and thunderous applause. As she returned it with equal enthusiasm and my body heated, I was thankful we had no audience.

I SHOULD HAVE WON some sort of prize for self-restraint.

Somehow I managed to make it all the way to the airport in Inverness without picking Macy up and carrying her back to the jet's onboard bedroom.

It wasn't easy, but we still had a mission to complete. As the plane taxied, I watched Macy's face. She was looking out the window, lines of tension bracketing her mouth. I had a feeling I knew what was bothering her.

"My little hero ready to save the world?"

She laughed, but it wasn't a purely happy sound. "I wish I *was* a hero. Some Wonder Woman skills would come in pretty handy right now."

Turning to me, she revealed green eyes tainted with uncertainty.

"I'm scared, Nic... of what's going to happen— when we find them— or if we don't. The problem is so big. What if I'm not enough?"

"You *are* enough. You are exactly what you're supposed to be. None of us can be any more or any less than that."

I stroked the underside of her chin, lifting it so our gazes connected. "We *don't* know what the future holds, but we'll do the best we can and trust that good will triumph and life will go on. And we'll always be together, you and I... no matter what we find here in Scotland."

EPILOGUE

I *sle of Eigg, Scotland*

I AWOKE to the smell of ocean air, and hay, and what was that? Was that... animal dung? *Ugh.* The trace of revolting odor was not helping the queasiness that already rocked my stomach—or the splitting headache.

Sitting up, I looked around me. I was in a tiny room with bare wooden walls. The bed beneath me was small and not all that comfortable, but it was covered in clean sheets and several quilts. Other than the bed, the room contained a small dresser, an overstuffed upholstered chair, and an even more stuffed bookcase. A door stood open to reveal a tiny bathroom with a sink basin, toilet, and a smallish clawfoot bathtub. Though everything seemed fairly clean, it looked old. Shabby. Like the furnishings inside a poor person's home—not that I'd ever *been* in a poor person's home. Where *was* I?

To my right, a single small window punctuated the rough-hewn wall. I slid from the bed and went to it, holding the wall for balance. I felt strange, as if I'd slept very deeply after staying up way too late or overindulged at one of Babbo's opulent Court gatherings. Peering outside did nothing to help me ascertain my location. It was night, and high clouds covered the moon.

It appeared I was on the second floor of a building because my vantage point was high. In the muted light all I could make out was what appeared to be a large open field, and beyond it, the ocean.

But which one? I'd done so much traveling recently, I momentarily lost track of my point on the map from time to time. Considering my tacky accommodations, I got the distinct impression that this location *hadn't* been one of my choosing.

The last thing I could remember was staring into Nic's eyes. He'd offered to leave with me, go back to Italy, and marry me. My heart, which had frozen over long ago, shimmered with a spark of something—hope? Redemption? He seemed to understand I hadn't *meant* to activate the virus, and he seemed to have some sort of plan to stop it.

And then… pain. Blinding, deafening pain. An excruciating pressure in my ears that wiped every thought from my mind and dropped me to the ground, feeling like my head would explode.

The nymph. *She* must have done something to me. The lore on them was sparse—who knew what secret powers they might have? She'd made Nic fall in love with her, that was for sure.

Why had she stopped me from speaking with him? I was about to tell him where the Plague had been unleashed.

I went to the door and turned the handle—or tried to. It

was locked. Pounding on its sold surface with my fist, I called out. "Hello! Hello out there. I demand that you unlock the door this instant."

There was no sound at first, and then... a whinny. *What?* Yes, there it was again, the unmistakable sound of hooves stomping a wooden floor followed by another horsey cry. Was I in a *stable?*

What on earth would I be doing in a stable? As an avid rider and horse lover, I'd spent time in them my whole life, but this was definitely *not* the stable at my father's castle in Italy. Our horses lived in far more luxurious circumstances than this.

Turning to survey the sparse room again, I realized it must have been a stable boy's lodgings. It wasn't even nice enough to suit a stable master.

Beating on the heavy door again, I said, "If anyone's down there who speaks Italian instead of *equine*, I demand that you open this door and release me at once."

Then it occurred to me that whomever might be listening may *not* understand Italian. I tried the same words in French, and then in Spanish. Nothing.

Hmmm. The last place I'd visited was England. The village of Bristol where the young girl Macy had corresponded with lived. Yes. It made sense that I could still be in England.

Speaking in English now, I repeated my demands. "I want you to let me out of this room right now. If you have any idea who I am, you know my father will come looking for me with an entire *army*, so it would behoove you to obey me."

There was no answer save for a few additional whinnys. Wonderful. Either I was alone in here except for the horses, or whoever had locked me in this room heard me but had no interest in answering.

Stomping in frustration, I went back to the window and

attempted to push it open. It was the kind that cranked open to the side instead of sliding up. Furious, I rotated the crank as quickly as it would turn, but it opened only a few inches before stopping. There would be no jumping from this window—it was designed to admit fresh air, not to open fully.

Well, if it could admit air, it could also release sound. Putting my mouth to the opening, I screamed, "Help! Help me. I've been kidnapped. I'm being held here against my will —upstairs over the stable. Somebody help me."

I kept that up in every language I knew as long as my voice held out, about two hours as best I could determine. Finally, my throat dry and aching, I cranked the window closed again—the night air pouring into the room was cold— and went into the small bathroom to get a drink from the faucet.

On the back of the sink there was a porcelain cup and a toothbrush, along with a small tube of toothpaste and a bar of soap. A folded towel and washcloth lay draped over the side of the bathtub. I snorted.

Welcome to hell. Make yourself at home.

Grabbing the cup, I filled it and drank until it was empty, then filled it again, drained it again.

Okay then, what now?

I was exhausted—the mirror above the basin confirmed it, showing bleary eyes and sallow skin. I was also hungry. But seeing as my dinner choices were either a bar of soap or book pages, I decided to go to bed. I'd be better able to determine my escape chances in the daylight anyway.

Opening the toothbrush package, I took it out and used it then washed my face. I didn't exactly have a suitcase here in my jail cell, so I crawled under the covers wearing what I'd put on this morning and pulled the quilts up to my chin, a bit regretful I'd left the window open for so long. It was chilly.

Though my body was tired, my brain had a hard time settling into sleep. I had no idea where I was, how I'd gotten here, or what was going to happen to me. Someone could unlock that door and come in during the night, and there wasn't a thing I could do to stop them. Suddenly I felt like screaming again—not for rescue—simply out of fear.

There was a loud, creaking noise, and I did scream, bolting upright in the bed. The horses below me made no sounds of alarm. Whatever the noise was, they were used to it. Knowing the creatures as well as I did, that reassured me —they had an excellent sense of danger. If some kind of threat was around, they'd definitely react.

Don't panic, Alessia. Stay calm and rational. Keep your wits about you.

I still had my glamour. Dr. Schmitt had taught me to control it somewhat. He'd told me there was no way to tone it down or pull it back, but if I wanted to, I could turn it up, increase its intensity and take someone from healthy to gravely ill in an instant. My little captor was going to get a big surprise when I finally saw her face-to-face.

I was convinced it was Macy. Had to be. And then it hit me. Nic must have helped her—how else could she have transported me here... wherever *here* was. He had *tricked* me —*lied* to me to give her a chance to strike. Beneath the covers, my cold fingers clenched into fists. I *hated* him, hated them both. They were going to pay for this.

I had been ready to tell him the location of the fan pod girl who'd touched me, to give him a chance to try to stop what I'd inadvertently started and save the *precious* humans he cared so much for. *Ha.*

Now he could find out where she was the way the rest of the world did—by tracking the path of death and destruction. The thought gave me solace, and the fear for my own safety subsided.

Sometime during the night I must have drifted to sleep because rays of sunlight falling on my eyelids woke me the next morning. I opened them, looked around, and confirmed that no, the room above the stable was not a nightmare but my new reality. *Bellissimo.*

The temperature in my wooden cell was warm again. I threw off the covers and stalked to the door, intending to beat on it, but stopped before I reached it. I'd nearly stepped on a tray full of food. Ah, so it would be solitary confinement but not forced starvation.

I would've loved to spite my jailer and leave the tray untouched, mounting a hunger strike. But self-deprivation was not my style. I was ravenous. I lifted the tray and carried it to the bed, snagging the bread roll first and wolfing it down before picking up the spoon and tasting whatever grainy hot cereal filled the porcelain bowl. Cream of wheat. *Blech.* I'd always despised the stuff.

It didn't matter. I ate it anyway. I needed my energy if I was going to mount a full-power glamour attack against my captor… who'd apparently entered the room while I was sleeping to deliver this tray. That gave me pause.

I shivered at the thought of someone watching me while I slept, but then I smiled. If I was still in here tonight, I'd make sure to stay awake and be ready to strike.

I finished off the breakfast plate, which included several slices of bacon and a pear, then investigated the contents of the small, lidded pitcher on the tray. Coffee. Fine. I was more a tea drinker, but it was hot and contained caffeine. It would do. Filling the china cup I'd been provided, I left the bed and walked over to look through the window at the daytime view.

I'd been right about the open field and the ocean. In the light of day it was quite a lovely vista—or would be if you weren't viewing it from a prison. Rolling green hills sloped down to a wide-open seascape. Small whitecaps dotted the deep blue of the water.

Shifting to look in the other direction, I caught a glimpse of a structure farther up the hill. I could only see part of it—covered in weathered shingles, it had an octagonal tower at one end and seemed to be quite large. A house. Or maybe another barn?

Cranking the window open again, I prepared for this morning's shouting session. Perhaps in the daytime someone would be around to hear me and come to my rescue. Fresh salt-scented air rushed through the window. It was a windy day, apparently.

I inhaled deeply, opened my mouth... the loud creak came again. And again. It was coming from outside—not here in the stable. The creaking picked up speed then faded, replaced by a slow and regular whooshing noise. What *was* that?

Stretching to push my face through the narrow window opening, I craned to see more of the structure up the hill. Something large swooped through my field of vision then disappeared. Came back. Disappeared.

Oh, a windmill.

That's what the noise was. No wonder the horses weren't alarmed. They heard this every day. Okay, so there was a stable, and an ocean, and a windmill attached to a wood-shingled house. Where on earth was I?

"Hello?" I shouted through the window. "Can anyone hear me? I need help. I'm being held captive. Help me. Please."

I continued to call out as the sea breeze carried my voice up the hill where it was shredded and scattered by the windmill blades. I watched and waited. No one came. No one heard, or if they did, they didn't care.

Sometime in mid-morning I heard the sound of footsteps below and then a distinctive scraping noise. Someone was mucking the stalls. There was a person nearby! Or an Elf. Or a nymph. Whatever. At least there was someone who could hear and understand me—and soon, hopefully, no more manure smell.

"I know you're down there," I shouted through the door. "You *need* to let me out. This is kidnapping, and you are going to be in a *lot* of trouble."

It had gotten quiet down below. I took the opportunity to amp up my warnings. "Do you know who I am? I am a *princess*. My father is very rich and powerful, and you cannot even imagine what he'll do to you when he finds out what you've done."

There was no response, only the resumed sound of a shovel scraping on wood and noises of recognition and camaraderie from the horses. They knew what was coming next, either some fresh hay or turnout time. The person below was probably their regular caretaker, maybe a stable boy or someone else who wasn't actually party to the kidnapping but had been warned to ignore the crazy woman upstairs.

Hmmm. Maybe a different approach was in order. "You know… even if you're only working for them, you'll be held responsible. Do you hear me?"

The silence infuriated me. I was about to yell again and pound on the door, demanding to be set free, when I thought better of it. If the person down there *wasn't* actually in on my abduction, perhaps reasoning with them—or gaining their sympathy—instead of threatening them, was a better tack.

Calming myself, I leaned against the door and made my voice more pleading than dictatorial.

"Please—if you can hear me… please tell me what's going on. I'm frightened. I have no idea where I am and no idea how I got here."

The scraping below stopped.

Encouraged, I continued my appeal. "My head aches horribly from whatever they did to me, and..." I scrambled for another pity ploy. "And it's rather cold in this room. I was freezing last night."

At first there was nothing. But then I heard a new sound —footsteps mounting the stairs. My heart leapt and kicked into a rapid, optimistic rhythm.

My fingers wiggled in anticipation. The second the door opened, I would attach them to the bare skin of whomever was on the other side and give them the worst sickness of their lives. Then I would get the hell out of this crummy wooden box and send someone back to burn the place down —after the horses were removed, of course.

The footsteps stopped right outside the door. I renewed my efforts to sound pitiful and helpless. "Please let me out of here. Or at least tell me where I am. I'm confused and afraid. Also... I don't really care for cream of wheat."

There was a laugh. Low. Masculine. The sound shocked me. I moved back from the door, my heart pounding.

"Nic? Is that you? Nic, are you out there?"

The voice that answered was deep and resonant and sent chills down my spine. "Who's Nic?"

The accent was English. No one that I recognized. If he honestly didn't know who Nic was, then he really *was* just a stable boy—man—whatever—or I'd been *very* wrong about who had brought me here and locked me up.

Fighting a fresh surge of panic, I fired off several questions, unable to control myself. "Where am I? Why am I here? Who are you?"

There was a chuckle, but then the guy answered. "You are a guest at my home. You're here because apparently you got on the bad side of some pretty dangerous witches."

There was a pause.

"And my name is Wes. You might as well settle down and

relax, *princess*, because you're going to be here for a long, long time."

The Hidden Saga continues with HIDDEN HERO, coming soon! Keep reading for a message from the author and a sneak peek at the story…

AFTERWORD

Thank you so much for reading Hidden Magic, Book 2 of the Ancient Court Trilogy (Hidden Saga, book 8.) I really hope you enjoyed it. If you did, please consider leaving a review at the retailer where you purchased it, and if your fingers aren't too tired, at Goodreads, too. Just a few words is all it takes, and reviews help other readers find great books!

To learn about upcoming releases from the Hidden world and other Amy Patrick books, sign up for my newsletter. You will only receive notifications when new titles are available and when my books go on sale. You may also occasionally receive teasers, excerpts, and extras from upcoming books. I will never share your contact information with others.

I love to chat with my readers! Follow me on Twitter at @amypatrickauthor and visit my website at www.amypatrickbooks.com. I'm on Instagram and have lots of fun pics from the Hidden world on Pinterest. You can also connect with me on Facebook, where I hang out the most.

If you haven't yet read the earlier books in the Hidden

Saga, they give you the chance to delve into the Hidden world in America, from the backwoods of rural Mississippi to the glittering cities of Los Angeles and New York. I think you'll enjoy them! Book 3 of the Ancient Court Trilogy is coming soon! Here's a little about the story:

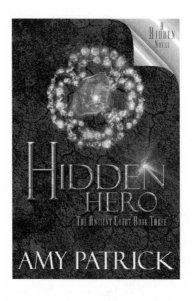

After a year-long separation and a search across continents, Macy and Nic have found each other again. Now they must find her family—the birth mother who abandoned her at the hospital and fled back to her people's secret sanctuary—if they are to beat the clock and save the human race from the onslaught of the coming Plague.

Alessia didn't intend to activate the deadly virus, but after determining that Nic betrayed her, she's almost glad she did. The only problem? She won't be around to enjoy the aftermath—she's being held captive on a remote, windswept island by a mysterious guy who's completely immune to her

Sway and won't let her get close enough to use her deadly glamour on him.

Give in to the Glamour once more as the end of the human world looms, an ancient secret is unearthed, and a hidden hero emerges.

ABOUT THE AUTHOR

Amy Patrick grew up in Mississippi (with a few years in Texas thrown in for spicy flavor) and has lived in six states, including Rhode Island, where she now lives with her husband and two sons.

She's been a professional singer, a DJ, a voiceover artist, and always a storyteller, whether it was directing her younger siblings during hours of "pretend" or inventing characters and dialogue while hot-rollering her hair before middle school every day. For many years she was a writer of true crime, medical anomalies, and mayhem, working as a news anchor and health reporter for six different television stations. Then she retired to make up her own stories. Hers have a lot more kissing.

I love to hear from my readers. Feel free to contact me on Instagram, Twitter and my Facebook page (where I hang out the most and respond to every comment.) And be sure to sign up for my newsletter here and be the first to hear the latest news from the Hidden world as well as other new books I have in the works!

ACKNOWLEDGMENTS

Living in the Hidden world is a joy for me, but that's only true because of all the people who have made it possible. First, love and thanks to my Hidden honeys, the best readers in the world. You make all the hours, weeks, and months of work worth it.

Huge thanks go to my lovely editor Judy Roth and to Cover Your Dreams for another beautiful cover.

Thank you to my husband John, who never doubts my abilities and always expects the best, has learned to love dust bunnies and even to weigh in on inspiration photos for hot Elven guys. Love to my precious Jack and Sean, who make me laugh every day and would be the ultimate book boyfriends if they were fictional teens.

To my lifelong best friend Chelle, who loves me no matter what, to Margie, for being a cheerleader and wonderful friend in every way, and to the Westmoreland Farmgirls, who are always ready to read and celebrate.

I would be nowhere without my brilliant and sweet-as-peach-pie critique partner, McCall Hoyle, whose heart is as big as her talent. Love and thanks to the rest of the fabulous

GH Dreamweavers fun and friendship, and special thanks to my Lucky 13 sisters for their continuing loyalty, good advice, and virtual Prosecco. Big hugs and forever love to my Savvy Seven sisters.

No acknowledgments could be complete without mentioning my first family. I've been blessed to have a mother who made me believe I could, a loving dad (who's quite a storyteller himself), a funny and loyal brother, and the best sister anyone's ever had. Thank you to Joanne and Larry, for all the love, encouragement, and puppy-sitting. And thank you to the rest of my friends and family for your support and for just making life good. I am blessed!

THE HIDDEN SAGA

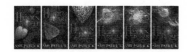

Hidden Deep
Hidden Heart
Hidden Hope
Hidden Darkness (Dark Court, 1)
Hidden Danger (Dark Court, 2)
Hidden Desire (Dark Court, 3)
Hidden Game (Ancient Court, 1)
Hidden Magic (Ancient Court, 2)
Hidden Hero (Ancient Court, 3) -- Fall 2017

Made in the USA
Columbia, SC
12 January 2018